DOGMA, A RED DOOR, AND A BIRTHDAY

Dogma, a Red Door, and a Birthday

A novel
by

ALBERTO AMBARD

BOOKS

Adelaide Books
New York / Lisbon
2020

DOGMA, A RED DOOR, AND A BIRTHDAY
A novel
By Alberto Ambard

Published by Adelaide Books, New York / Lisbon
adelaidebooks.org

Editor-in-Chief
Stevan V. Nikolic

For any information, please address Adelaide Books
at info@adelaidebooks.org
or write to:
Adelaide Books
244 Fifth Ave. Suite D27
New York, NY, 10001

ISBN: 978-1-952570-47-6

Printed in the United States of America

"No slave was ever so much the property of his master

as the child is of his parent."

–Maria Montessori

PART I

November 03, 2017
Between 10:20AM - 4:33PM
and
between Portland and Baker City

1) 10:20AM Adriel.

"If there was ever a good lie to tell a kid, it's the lie about Santa Claus. Don't you think?" said Adriel, looking wistful. "I mean, a father should only lie to a child about Santa, that's it. Unless of course, you are my father," she paused and raised her hands, palms up. "He's a lie. His life is a lie, and everything he ever told me is a lie—except, of course, for what he told us about Santa Claus. He had to tell us the truth about Santa." What kind of father does that?" She looked up, her mouth in a grim line. "I hate the motherfucker. I wish I could slice off his balls and shove them up his ass."

Adriel made a shoving gesture, wrinkling her nose and averting her face.

Monica laughed out loud, nearly spilling her coffee. Her large, expressive eyes narrowed. Ironically, the mimicry was something Adriel had copied from her. When she was excited, Monica talked with her hands, like an orchestra conductor waving off a fly.

"Don't you think that's a bit extreme?" she asked.

"Are you kidding me? If you only knew a quarter of what he's done to my mom. And who the fuck knows what else he's done since I left?"

The unwelcome specter of her father—Richard—erased Adriel's smile. In her mind, she saw the glint of his glasses, the shiny gold frame that barely fit his chubby face, the goatee, the cynical smile she loathed. And the image stayed with her until Monica, holding her hand and stroking it, blew it out the window.

"Man! Why are you making that face? Must be tonight's eclipse—because you're on fire! Kyle's right: you tell an upsetting story and get pissed again!" said Monica.

Adriel shrugged. For the tenth time that morning she checked the time on her phone. The fleeting image of Richard had given rise to a vortex of anxious thoughts. At the nucleus of the thoughts rushing through her mind was Leah: Mom. The long-waited reunion with Mother was everything.

Just as she'd figured it would be, the breakfast was a bad idea. She appreciated Monica's motives, but all she wanted was to get to Baker City. It would take over four hours to get there, and she still needed to pick up Kyle. Yet here they were—still in the restaurant. Where the fuck was Monica's order?

"Dude, we waited in line over an hour. Now what? Are they waiting for the hen to lay eggs? I already digested my food!" she said.

"Oh, come on, sweetie. I told you, this place is family style!" Monica said.

Adriel leaned back to look for their waiter, but her eyes met a toddler's. He was staring at her like a cat, devouring a huge waffle, his face covered in dark, sticky sauce—syrup maybe, or chocolate. She forced herself to smile at the little boy and was glad when he ignored her. The last thing she wanted was to have to interact with some random kid.

She looked around for the waiter but saw no sign of him. Frustrated, Adriel sighed and then inhaled the aroma of pancakes, bacon, and maple syrup that was floating around the restaurant.

How many pancakes would you like, Adi? Breathing in the delicious smells, Adriel was transported to early childhood—to the kitchen table, where she saw Leah caressing her long blond hair.

Two, Mamma! she answered before coming back to the restaurant.

She assumed her parents at least was still living in Baker City. When she googled his father's name, she found him working at the same insurance agency. *Men like him never change,* she thought. *They must be there.* But what could have happened to her mom and brother? Adriel pictured a thousand possibilities. Would they be there? Would Jacob even recognize her? Would they want to come to Portland with her? Would Richard let them? Would this be the best birthday she'd ever had or the worst? All the possibilities had lived in her head for months, like a visiting uncle who never seems to leave. That everything was happening on her birthday wasn't her choice. In a way, circumstances had forced her to wait that long, almost four years to be exact.

"Where the fuck is the waiter? This whole family-style bullshit is just an excuse for slow service!"

"Relax, we have time. Here, have more coffee," Monica said and handed Adriel her cup.

"I don't get it. Does this oblivious attitude toward time come from the Peruvian in you? Or is it the Portlander who only feels this way in restaurants?"

"The Portlander in me? What does that even mean?" Monica said, rolling her eyes and smiling.

She understood Adriel's uneasiness. She knew too well this could end up being the happiest day of Adriel's life, or the saddest, and "saddest" should be put into perspective: Adriel's life had been incredibly sorrowful.

"It means you love restaurants that don't take reservations and make you wait in long lines outside, rain or shine—like this one!" said Adriel.

"Everything's gonna be just fine, sweet pea. We have plenty of time. It's just twenty past ten," Monica added.

Her idea of a nice breakfast was simple. One way or the other, they had to eat breakfast before leaving. So why not come to Tasty N' Sons? Adriel had wanted to try it for months. A good breakfast would relax her some.

At first, Adriel rejected the idea, but when Kyle said he wouldn't be able to leave until ten thirty in the morning, the argument became a moot point. Adriel couldn't imagine going to Baker City without Kyle. Having him come along was like having a powerful, faithful dragon sleeping by your side, ready to jump at anything remotely menacing. Adriel wasn't willing to face her father on her own.

Monica sipped her coffee and stared into those deep blue eyes that matched the blond hair turned blue. The clear, bright light coming through the window that looked out on the street somehow made them look even bluer than she remembered. Behind them—Monica knew—melancholy and anger lay concealed. Monica had never seen Adriel cry, not once.

She stroked Adriel's short hair, then her slender neck, pulling her closer. They kissed tenderly, a long kiss. A young, plane-going-down kiss.

The inside of Tasty N' Sons was long, narrow, and dim. The only window—where Adriel and Monica were seated— was just wide enough for two small tables with chairs.

Maybe it was the retro way they dressed and the way they were kissing, but from outside the window they looked like a couple in a vintage tinted Doisneau photograph.

It had been a little over a year since they met at Dante's Sinferno Cabaret, a weekly burlesque show in downtown Portland, popular among the college crowd.

Dante's had a theater with bright red curtains along the wall of a large, dark room decorated with crimson red velvet. On a platform with human cages, topless goth dancers made their best moves. On the floor were small round tables like those one finds at jazz clubs. All the tables had a small, lighted, red candle in the center, setting the scene for what might be a satanic ceremony, where people already destined to the hot flames of hell could have a last drink and enjoy the show before receiving eternal punishment.

That night, Monica was sitting at one of those small tables, close to the stage. She'd already seen a contortion aerialist, a naked, roller-skating woman spitting fire, and a grotesque, mini Marilyn Manson, interpreted by a shameless little person. She'd downed three or four vodka tonics when Karaoke from Hell Night took place. It was like Dante's version of amateur strip karaoke.

Adriel was the third person to come on stage, and by far the best. Monica would never forget the skinny, pale, topless dancer moving like a butterfly across the small stage, hips swinging as if to keep an invisible hula hoop afloat, all accompanied by a scratchy, bluesy voice singing Patti Smith's classic without remorse:

"...make her mine, make her mine, G-L-O-R-I-A, Glooooria! G-L-O-R-I-A, Gloooria!!!"

In a month Adriel would be seventeen. How had she gotten into the club? A fake ID?

"Here it is! Baked eggs, runny yolk, no sausage!" said the server, appearing suddenly and leaving just as swiftly to take an order at another table, leaving only traces of gleaming light and a smoky smell, like The Flash.

Monica leapt on her food like a hungry mastiff. Cutting into an egg and realizing the yolk was fully cooked, she dropped her fork and pushed the plate away, finicky, like a miniature French poodle. She said,

"I told the guy I wanted a runny yolk, didn't I?"

"See! This place sucks!" Adriel said, but seeing Monica's disappointed face she rushed to add,

"Thank you for being here and thank you for this wonderful breakfast."

Sipping her coffee and hanging out with Monica was all Adriel could ask for. Monica was much more than her partner in love; she'd organized Adriel's life, she was her best therapy, her biggest fan, and at twenty-three, Monica was the guide Adriel needed.

They barely noticed their server approaching the table again. He was young, wearing tight black jeans, a T-shirt, and a mustache that would have been in fashion around seventeen fifty. He played with it, as if waiting for Adriel and Monica to settle down, and then said,

"How wonderful did everything taste?"

"Oh, hmm, it was good. Well, it would have been nice if the yolk was runny. I mean, I think I asked for it to be runny, but maybe I didn't," Monica said, waving her hand to signal the server she wasn't done, and added,

"But it was wonderful, the thing is…" She meant to keep talking, but Adriel interrupted abruptly.

"What she means is that it was wonderfully dried and delayed."

The waiter pulled his head back in surprise before responding.

"Oh, well, you know, family style isn't for everybody."

"Nor are dried eggs," Adriel said, enduring the frantic kicking at her shin from under the table.

"Everything was wonderful, thanks. Can we please have the check?" Monica said before rolling her eyes at Adriel, and then changed the subject.

"Dude, last night was amazing. Best Cyanide gig ever."

Adriel sipped the last of her coffee, introspective, looking nowhere. Her punk power trio had been together just for over four months and was already making noise at several bars around town. They sang punk classics—a Ramones and Sex Pistols type of thing, but they were starting to do their own songs as well. The exposure at the Alberta St. Pub was fantastic and the three hundred bucks a night they were going to get were welcome, given their tight finances.

Still lost in another world, she smiled with satisfaction that stayed with her even as she began singing with a low voice, a song they'd debuted during the concert.

"Oh my sweet Apple, you hold my dearly dirty secrets, you're the only bitch I loooove…"

Once again, Monica laughed out loud and said,

"A song about a man singing to his own computer. You're sick, sweet pea."

"Here's the check, whenever you're ready, no rush," said the waiter. Monica barely had time to hand him a credit card, just before he performed his disappearing act again.

"So singing that song, I mean the lyrics. Are you sure it doesn't bother you?" Monica asked.

Adriel thought about it. She remembered the source of the lyrics so vividly one would think it had happened hours ago, but she was just twelve when it all took place. She sang the line once more, jokingly.

"Not really, I mean, now I see it even with a bit of humor, you know? But yeah, it was hard to write it. Growing up and slowly discovering lie after lie. And then one day, you find yourself reflecting on it and you go: fuck! I didn't see that back then."

Monica held Adriel's hand and smiled at her, loving and supportive. Adriel felt the warmth and somehow that was enough for her. She smiled back without saying another word. Instead, after a brief pause, she turned to the counter, to see if Moustache was there so they could signal him to take the credit card.

Adriel's memories took over to a point she couldn't hear Willie Nelson playing in the background. She was no longer at Tasty N' Sons, but back at her parents' home, several years before.

She was helping her mom get the house ready. Some friends of her parents were coming for dinner. Richard was in his small home office, downstairs—as he always was, preparing an insurance policy for a client, while Jacob was engaged in a battle of imaginary dragons versus green plastic soldiers spread all over the floor of a narrow hallway that led to the downstairs where, in addition to the office, there was the laundry room.

"Careful, Jimmy! Another one coming behind you! Pufff! Auggg! Help me Captain! Hold on Jimmy, Hold on! Mayday, mayday! Aerial support on the way! Fhhhhhh!"

Adriel remembered Jacob immersed in his own world, swinging his arms around, assigning different voices to the many imaginary characters. Leah was fixing dinner, busy in the tiny, crammed kitchen. As always, she was wearing a brown towel hanging from her belt. And that yellow mid-length dress Leah wore often. When Adriel thought of her mother she always pictured her wearing that dress.

For Adriel, remembering the scene was like looking at a TV show one has seen a thousand times, where you recognize the tiniest details, almost as if you were a house spider—the type Adriel was secretly afraid of—sitting high in a corner watching it all.

Dinner was meatloaf, roasted potatoes with garlic, and a green bean salad. Sitting in the restaurant, Adriel could still smell the sweet fragrance of the potatoes wafting throughout the house. They were her favorite.

She remembered Leah leaving the kitchen for a moment, stepping carefully over the messy battlefield as though she was crossing a minefield and down the narrow hallway to the edge of the stairs where she called for Richard. Their guests—a family they'd met at a homeschooling group would arrive soon.

"Richard, the Stegemanns will be here any minute. Are you ready?"

"I'm running behind here. I'll come up when they ring the bell," Richard shouted from downstairs.

"Adriel, can you please help with your brother? This is a real mess. I'm so behind."

"Ahhg! Mother!?" Adriel said from the living room. She was putting a few things out on the coffee table: glasses, napkins, a small jar with tooth picks, and a large, round, black Costco cheese plate with red grapes in the center, surrounded by cubes of cheddar, swiss, pepper jack cheeses, and nuts.

The doorbell rang.

"Adriel, say hello first. You can pick up your brother's toys once we settle, okay?" Leah said.

She opened the door to let the Stegemann family in. Handing a German chocolate cake to Leah, smiling from ear to ear, they looked like people in a teeth-whitening commercial.

Just as they were sitting around the cheese plate and Richard was getting up from his desk downstairs, a dingo must have growled at Jacob because he screamed his lungs out. Everyone in the house, including the guests ran to him to see what had happened.

Adriel couldn't remember much more, other than through the chaos, words of concern and then of consolation, she was preoccupied with the gigantic mess she was going to have to clean, not with her brother's wellbeing.

Next, she remembered smiling at the guests and pretending she loved spending time sitting there, in silence in their cramped living room, just big enough for a sofa and two chairs separated by the coffee table where the cheese was. An old Persian rug lay over the carpet, and a couple of houseplants stood near a small fireplace they never used. The sofa was small, *certainly too small to sit on with three guests*, she thought, crammed together with the Stegemanns.

"Adriel's growing to be such a beautiful girl. God bless her!" Stefan Stegemann said in his loud voice. He was a very tall man with curly grey hair that made him look like a younger Einstein. His legs barely fit between the coffee table and the sofa.

Julia Stegemann came to Adriel's memory next. "The weather has been such a teaser this year," she said. Her hair was blond, almost white, and like Adriel's mother, Julia seemed much younger than her husband.

Adriel remembered the Stegemanns' son Christian most clearly. He had a severe case of acne and greasy skin Adriel remembered vividly because they asked her to sit next to him, the boy's arm touching hers.

She kept trying to move away from him. But with the armrest preventing her from moving further, she had no option but to adopt a weird tilting posture, leaning away from him, keeping her neck straight so nobody could tell what she was doing. Her back was beginning to hurt, when miraculously,

Leah reminded her to pick up the mess her brother'd left, a task she gladly accepted. Suddenly the mess didn't look as big.

Adriel was so disgusted by the memory of the boy that this was how she described him while telling Monica the story, to explain the origin of the song in question:

"There was this family, the Stegemanns—one of a group of families who, like us, homeschooled at Mrs. Fuiten's house. The Stegemanns were creepy and had this creepy giant pimple of a boy."

"Pimple?" Monica asked.

"Yes, a giant pimple with eyes, mouth, and probably a cock with acne of its own," Adriel answered emphatically. "Anyhow, they were sitting on the sofa while I was picking up the toy soldiers Jacob had left lying all over, all the way to the stairs that led to Asshole's office, and that's key. Because if it wasn't for the fact I was on my knees picking up the toys and Asshole had left the door of his office open, I'd never even have considered going down there. Going into his office was definitely a no-no."

Even now Adriel couldn't figure out how she'd dared go into Richard's office. Curiosity? Rebellion? She'd never know. But whatever it was, she walked downstairs, making sure not to make noise on the creaky stairs. Finally inside the forbidden room, she looked around like a panting, nervous dog allowed to go upstairs, into the cat's territory.

Two things surprised her: the room's size—it turned out to be much bigger than she thought it would be—and the twin-size bed in the corner.

The bed had an inviting bright red blanket that looked comfy. Adriel almost jumped on it, but realizing she'd mess it up and wouldn't be able to put it back exactly as it was, decided to move on.

From the corner of the bed, where she stood, she could see the whole room. She was surprised that, given the bed and all the time Father spent there, there was no bathroom. There was a plastic plant in the corner. She had no opinion about it then. Behind a desk with a laminated wood pattern hung a large poster of a football player she didn't recognize. He was celebrating a touchdown.

What attracted her the most was, of course, the bright computer screen.

"You know what really pisses me off?" Adriel said.

"What's that?" Monica leaned forward, still navigating the discovery phase in their relationship.

"He ruined porn for me."

Monica laughed so loud people turned to look. She was caught off guard.

"No, I mean it, Monica. And not because the images shocked me—and trust me, they did. I had no idea why two women would smile and shove some weird black thing into another woman's ass. I mean, remember, I was pulled out of school so early. I'd never even seen a *photo* of a penis."

"Yeah, I understand. When I was twelve I'd have been shocked too."

"No, no, you don't get it," Adriel said, waving her hands in the air like that same orchestra conductor fighting the fly.

"But, if it wasn't the shock, what was it, then?"

"It was the lies." She paused.

"I didn't know what he was looking at was called porn. But later, knowing what porn was, I always remembered that screen and the thousand times I heard him say the internet was bad for Jacob and me. Because of all the sinful people posing naked. I mean, he wouldn't call it 'porn.' Shit, I've been wanting to tell him to his face, like, you fucking sicko, I KNOW. You're a fucking fake!"

Monica opened her mouth to speak, but Adriel was on a roll, angry, roaring as if she was singing another punk song with her Cyanide Roses.

"You know the worst thing? On the computer screen, next to the porn there was an opened Stickies window with one of those typical poison BS messages he loved reading in his parallel world. I'll never forget it, ever."

Adriel went quiet, recalling the computer screen in her mind's eye. But Monica interrupted her.

"What did it say?"

"It said: *Our submission to male leadership at home and churches reenacts Christ's submission to God His Father.*"

"Fuck, that's convenient!"

"Yep," Adriel said.

Landing the processed check on the table, the waiter, cold as the Pacific waters of the Oregon coast, startled them. "Thank you again for coming today, and Happy Birthday!!" he said, and left without ceremony.

"If you weren't such a bitch, maybe Moustache would have sung Happy Birthday for you," Monica said, pointing at the waiter.

"We have to go. It's 10:30," Adriel said.

2) 3:14PM. Leah.

It was a surprisingly dry, sunny day in Baker City, at least for November. The house felt so silent without Jacob, and of course, without Adriel. Leah missed them both so much. Standing at the living room window, hidden behind the curtain, Leah scanned the outside; Nicole was about to call her. She was sure Richard was at work. *But who knows?* she thought. There was always a chance it was a slow day at the office.

Her hands were moist, even though it was cold. She'd been talking to Nicole almost every day for the last two weeks, but her fear of being caught hadn't faded.

That she finally connected with Nicole had to do with a renewed desire to leave Richard for good. A desire that Richard reawakened, scolding her because he wanted to wear a shirt that was still in the drier. There was no time to iron it. He had to go.

With Richard gone, Leah began taking the laundry out of the drier. And she was angry. She started imagining a life without Richard. As always, her fantasy fell short. She couldn't leave without Jacob, and she'd lost Adriel already. She'd been thinking about her daughter's return for months—and re-membered the last words she'd spoken to her:

Sweetie, under no circumstance come back until you're eigh-teen. Promise me!

Her expectation had cooled over the years until now it was a remote wish. But the idea of seeing Adriel again revived as her daughter's birthday came closer.

Putting the ironing board together, Leah daydreamed of seeing Adriel again, sitting with her on that bench in the park nearby where they'd played cards when she was little and they were still living together.

Happy birthday, Adi! she imagined saying. And in her dream, little Jacob came to help them blow out the candles.

With the thought, Leah went from angrily slamming the laundry into the basket to slowing down until she was still. She took a deep breath.

The hope of seeing Adriel again was what her spirit needed to pull out from who knows where yet another deeply buried memory—of the napkin she'd concealed over four years before with the email address and 800 number of the place where Nicole worked, an organization that helped victims of forced marriage.

Right away, forgetting the ironing board, she decided to call the number. She rushed to the kitchen to grab a chair, tiptoeing as if Richard was still home. Placing the chair in front of her closet, she climbed up and stretched to reach the highest shelf where she'd stored boxes filled with everything from family photos to cards, and even the children's artwork she'd saved. One by one she brought the boxes down and set them in order on the floor, making sure she'd be able to put them back where they'd been. She didn't want Richard to know she'd been looking up there.

The closet was stuffy and smelled of mildew, which made her sneeze. At last she uncovered a large shoebox filled with old birthday and Christmas cards. Inside the box was a small tin can decorated with a 1930s French motif, and inside the can was the crinkled shred of napkin she'd kept for years.

She fished out the paper and sat on the edge of the mattress that was set directly on a low frame. This made her look even taller than she was. Sitting with her knees raised above her belly, she was almost in a fetal position. Leah was taller than the average woman and, despite pregnancies, still quite slender. Everything about her was long: long, narrow nose, long earlobes, long face, long legs, long arms, and long fingers.

Looking at the napkin, Leah felt sadness swelling inside her like a water balloon, which exploded and flowed through her eyes. She only knew one person who wrote number eight like that—clumsy and fat. Brandi, the only adult friend she ever had, a person she couldn't see anymore, and who'd done so much for her.

She almost made the call, but it dawned on her that Richard would probably find out about her calls through the phone company. So instead, she googled the company and sent an email. A smart move, as she'd learn later.

Nicole responded. They arranged a time for Nicole to call her, from a number that couldn't be traced, and not without first emailing five minutes before the phone call, to confirm that it was safe to talk. As for the emails, Leah sent each to the trash, which she emptied immediately.

Two weeks later, the day had come—Adriel's birthday. Standing standing behind the living-room curtains, Leah looked outside again. Other than the few plants she'd planted in their modest front yard, there was no sign of life.

Nicole was a young, inexperienced social worker who took calls at the non-profit. Her job was to listen to and guide people in Leah's situation, but beyond all, her duty was to give them practical support, referring them to a local therapist, an attorney, or a hotline.

She was doing an externship at this particular non-profit only because she'd been assigned there by the school. She dreamed of going back to Chicago and changing the inner city, like Wonder Woman. But as the weeks went by, learning about the realities of those who called for help transformed her idealism into a real determination to help victims like Leah.

A minute had passed from the time Nicole said she'd call. Leah began pacing from one corner of the living room to the next, circling the room faster till finally, she heard the phone ring. Breathlessly she sat down and, after the brief mutual greeting, began to talk.

"Today's my daughter's birthday. I thought I was going to handle it better, but I'm a nervous wreck, Nicole. It doesn't help that my son isn't here either. He's in Little Rock, with my parents. I haven't seen him in weeks. He'd be so much help right now. I feel so lonely without him. And the thing is, I have this big expectation that Adriel will show up today. I told her not to come back until she was eighteen, but I didn't tell her to come, you know? I guess I really hope she'll come, but in the back of my mind I can't stop thinking that if she wanted to see me she'd have come already, no matter what I told her to do."

Leah let the last bit of air escape before inhaling again.

"Sooner or later, she'll come, Leah. She'll come," Nicole said. But realizing how irresponsible it was to say so, she quickly added,

"In any case, Leah, remember: whenever you feel ready I can refer you to a nearby therapist. A professional might be able to help you even better, although of course, I'm happy to talk to you anytime."

"I know, Nicole. But do you mind if we talk for a while, just now?"

"Of course, it's not a problem. I have about an hour. Is it safe for you to talk?"

"Yes, it's about three ten here in Oregon. Richard shouldn't be back for at least a couple of hours."

Speaking of the time reminded Leah that she was going to roast a chicken for dinner. She'd left it thawing on the counter. There was also the full basket of clean laundry that she had left on the sofa, so she could fold it and then put away at some point in the afternoon.

While she figured out the time there was a silence until Nicole spoke again.

"Have you tried doing the stress-releasing exercise we talked about yesterday? Before going to sleep?"

She had.

Before going to bed, Leah had wasted as much time as she could in the bathroom until Richard fell asleep, to avoid having to deal with his sexual overtures. Those days were long gone, but Leah didn't care to risk it. She washed her long hair, filed her nails, smoothed moisturizing cream all over her body, and brushed her teeth as if she was going to a dental appointment. And when he asked her if she was coming to bed, she said she wanted to smooth the calluses on her feet.

Later in bed, the darkness inside the room made her feel protected, like a bear cub inside its den. She could hear Richard snoring and feel the warmth emanating from his skin. That was the closest she could tolerate him.

Tucked under the covers, she took a hesitant breath. Feeling a feeble volume of air go through her pipes, she let go. She'd forgotten air existed until that moment.

She imagined running with Jacob and Adriel in a field of golden grass that led to a Hawaiian beach. Leah had never been to Hawaii, but this was how she imagined it: The sun, big and round like a tennis ball, burning the grass mercilessly. Laughing with the children as they made their way through the tall grass, until she suddenly realized little Jacob was falling behind.

"C'mon, Jacob! C'mon, sweetheart!" she called.

"I can't hear you Mama!" he yelled, laughing.

"Run faster, knucklehead!" Adriel yelled and once again he responded,

"I can't hear yooouuu."

The exchange turned into a little game, and they laughed louder and louder as they ran. Leah let go. Her blond hair danced free in the wind like birds playing in the air.

On the sofa, reliving the memory as she talked to Nicole, Leah could almost feel the cool breeze on her face. But as they were laughing, out of nowhere, the sound of a truck coming up the driveway brought her back to her living room.

"Hold on a second, Nicole!"

Begging God it wasn't Richard, she rushed to the window, wrapped in penetrating cold. But as soon as she saw the FedEx logo and a young man getting out of the truck with a small box, the icy sensation melted down to the carpet.

"Sorry, Nicole. Are you still there? I have a package being delivered," Leah said.

She opened the door just wide enough so she could reach through to grab the package the man had left on the ground in front of the door.

"That's okay. And a nice way to put yourself to sleep, Leah."

Nicole began elaborating on relaxation while Leah brought the package inside. It was a small cardboard box taped as if it held a nuclear bomb. Seeing it was addressed to her from Mother, she frowned. She wondered what Mother could have sent. Their relationship had deteriorated over time and now they barely spoke.

Leah sat back on the sofa, leaving the package on the coffee table. Nicole went on and on, and Leah sat very straight with her knees together. The effect of the box coming from her mother was undeniable. She wanted to return to her fantasy and tell Nicole how she and Jacob kept going down that grassy hill until they reached a narrow dirt road along a beautiful but dangerous cliff with a fence of negligible security value. From the cliff's edge she could see the deep blue sea, and at the bottom of the hill, a cute red car waiting for her. The car was an intruder in the fantasy—an emotional memory, no doubt. It was the same red car Maxwell Smart drove in the Get Smart

TV show she'd loved watching as a child, and then again as an adult, first holding Adriel next to her, and later Jacob. Instead, she opened the present with one hand, erratically and nervously.

Inside, she found a sealed card and a small ornamental wooden box protected with shredded paper. The box was clearly an antique, with a pink flower painted on the lid.

"You see, Leah. It's going to be important to learn to replace the images—" Nicole was saying, but Leah wasn't listening anymore. She'd read the card.

While Nicole talked, Leah got up and paced around the room, directionless, until she was confronted by characters trapped in photographs, framed and placed over the fireplace. She looked at each of them, but in the end, directed her cloudy eyes to a photo of her brothers and sisters as if pleading for help or a nice memory of them that never arrived to rescue her.

The card bore a black-and-white photo of a lake, with a bright orange sun hiding behind a cloudy, dark sky, which also was black and white. The sun rays filtered through the clouds, illuminating the greyish waters just a little. Hope, it said in white.

Leah opened the card once more and read it in silence for the second time:

It doesn't take a good man for a woman to have a good marriage, but a woman willing to honor God by being the kind of wife God intended. With Love, Mother.

The message in the card couldn't be any clearer, and it transported Leah back to her parents' kitchen. A child again, she entered that typical mental state where somebody is talking to you and you can hear the person speaking—Nicole in this case—but your mind is somewhere else. In this trance, Leah relived the first time she'd heard the quote from Mother.

She was sitting at her usual spot at the dinner table, playing Solitaire, when Father, standing right in front of her, began lecturing Mother, who was cooking. He stepped on a toy car and fell on his back. More embarrassed than hurt, he spit his fury while pointing at the carpet of toys Leah's youngest brother, Aaron, had left.

Knees together and hands pressed together between her legs, as if she was freezing, young Leah began rocking her faulty chair from side to side.

"And you, Leah!" He suddenly pointed at her, stabbing between her eyes. "Why in the world are you playing cards when you could be picking up this disaster!!"

Looking at the toys, Leah felt this was unjust. *Why can't Aaron learn to pick up after himself?* she thought.

"I need peace when I come home. I need harmony. I need order, not this headache-inducing mess!!!" Father yelled at his wife.

Mother kept calm—numb, if you asked Leah—and smiled hesitantly, making a futile attempt to get a break from her hostile husband.

"Darling, I'm sorry, time flew today bec—"

"This is *your* fault, young lady!!! It's your responsibility to keep toys organized! You're out of control. Out of control!!!" Father interrupted aggressively, facing Leah. Incredulous, she turned to her mom, looking for support. Yet all she got was the same look she'd seen so many times, begging her to keep quiet, to not upset Father, and the hands reinforcing the message, signaling discreetly—but desperately—to remain quiet.

Leah made a gesture, as if she had something to say about the accusation. But her father, who luckily for her didn't notice, stomped out of the house before she could make a terrible mistake.

"Mother, Father's being mean." Leah articulated her feelings the best she could at her young age.

Holding the card with one hand and the phone with the other, the now adult Leah remembered her mother's hands touching her cheeks, and her mother's words:

"Darling, this is my fault. Good man or bad man—and your father is the greatest man—*a woman honors God by being the kind of wife He intended.* I should have picked up that mess or told you to do it before Father got home from work."

Back in her living room, Leah heard Nicole finish her explanation. This brought her back to the present.

"You know, Nicole." She spoke, just to say something, but now the ocean of feeling that had welled up in her was a river coursing down her cheeks.

Nicole heard Leah's voice crack a little. She waited for her to finish the sentence.

"I'm sorry, Nicole. It's just, I got a card from Mother, and well, that card truly sums up my life."

Leah related the story behind the card to Nicole, looking at the card as if Mother was about to rise up out of it and blame her for it all.

"Mother erases any possible doubt about who's at fault here. I don't know that I want to leave Richard anymore, even if he lets me go."

Nicole took a few notes and thought a moment before saying anything else.

What do you mean if he lets you go? All you've got to do is file the papers! She wanted to yell at Leah but restrained the impulse. Encouraging clients to divorce wasn't ethical or even allowed by the non-profit.

In that moment of silence, Leah watched herself as a child, kneeling on the floor, picking up everything Aaron had left behind. One by one she picked up each of the toy cars. She must have picked up at least twenty when she found herself holding Aaron's favorite car, a replica of the Mach Five, a Speed Racer. She could hear the television was on; she knew some of her brothers were outside playing. Holding the car tightly, she clenched her teeth and thought about throwing it away. She imagined Aaron crying and Mother and Father consoling him, saying it was their fault, but ultimately, she let the car go.

"How old were you when this happened, Leah?" Nicole finally spoke.

"I'd just turned twelve. You know, Nicole, I pray every day that the Lord will forgive me for this. But sometimes I'm so angry. Father and Mother could have spared me so much."

3) 10:40AM. Adriel.

When they finished eating, Adriel and Monica left the restaurant and walked to the car, parked half a block from the entrance. It had rained all night long in Portland, but although it was cold and cloudy, the breeze felt dry on Adriel's lips.

"Shoot, I forgot my coffee. I'll be right back," Adriel said.

She jogged back to the restaurant and signaled thumbs up to Monica when, from the car, she told Adriel,

"Okay, I'm going to call my mom, before she calls me!"

Monica emphasized the last sentence, knowing her overprotective mom would indeed call her, as she did every morning. She was a lovely Peruvian from Cuzco who had retained the Incan appearance of her ancestors; a well-rounded face framing a wide, punched-flat nose below slightly hooded brown eyes that always looked straight at you. Monica's dimples, her own narrow dark eyes and her thick, luscious hair all came from her mother.

That she turned out to be gay didn't come as a surprise. An eternal tomboy, little Monica preferred playing with boys, demanded short haircuts and never wore anything but jeans.

The Christmas she was seven, she wrote a letter to Santa. "All I want this year is a penis," she wrote. "Love, Monica."

At nineteen, hesitant and fearful of rejection, she came out to her parents. They laughed at her for believing they wouldn't know by then.

"You're the son I never had!" said her father jovially. He was an eternal hippie and middle school teacher.

He met his wife while traveling the Peruvian Sacred Valley, looking for some spiritual Incan force he never found. His consolation—as he often joked—was the tour guide, a tiny young girl, so short he couldn't find her when the lights were out—another of his jokes. Their mutual attraction grew little by little as they made their way slowly through the Andean mountains. And it was consolidated through the purchase of an Incan sweater he wanted badly, but couldn't afford. She bargained with the seller and got him the sweater for a quarter of the price.

The relationship between Adriel and Monica began as a friendship—a crazy friendship, Adriel liked to say.

They hit it off right away after meeting at Dante's and went out the following days, feeding their infatuation with high amounts of endorphin, local beers, and coffee, until one night it finally happened. They were back at Monica's from Latin Tuesdays at Dig A Pony, where they drank and danced reggaeton all night to the music of DJ Blas, a nightlife Portland personality who was as successful as he was enigmatic. Nobody knew exactly how he looked like, mostly because DJ

Blas was so tiny that, when looking at him from the dancing area, all one could see was the top of his shiny bald head barely showing behind and above the computer monitor, moving up and down at the rhythm of the music, while reflecting light in all directions, like a discotheque ball.

Tired from the dancing and the effects of alcohol, they settled into Monica's big, soft, green sofa with some popcorn, but couldn't agree on what movie to watch. Adriel preferred a light comedy, but Monica insisted on watching *The Conjuring*. A playful struggle for the remote control led to a silly wrestling match that got out of hand. In the midst of it, Adriel moved to retrieve the remote, but her supporting hand slid and she hit her cheekbone against the edge of the sofa.

"OUCH!" she said playfully.

Monica's beloved dimples framed her lips and her eyes narrowed, and Adriel admired all of it as if she was seeing a Botticelli for the first time. Hypnotized, she didn't see Monica's hand extending toward her, but felt it a moment later, traveling her body and slipping over her skin like wet soap, prompting a series of body reactions Adriel didn't know existed.

In the soft light of the television, ignoring the random movie dialogue, Adriel felt Monica's full lips grabbing hers, and her whole body shaking and her hair standing on end, as if Monica's lips were electric. It was the first time she'd felt anything like this—the first time she'd been kissed. For Adriel, it was a huge sexual awakening. Free at last from all inhibition, her desire was a charging bull. She kissed Monica back, biting her in a playful, almost pained frenzy. There was no sin to stop her, no Hell waiting for her and no one preaching what was right and wrong; the days of believing in her parents' tales were long gone.

Back from the restaurant, Adriel approached the car with coffee in hand and a big smile, walking with her usual tiny steps and her feet pointing out, like a ballerina.

"C'mon little penguin, hurry up!" Monica yelled.

Adriel was wearing a white sweater with a black Siouxsie & The Banshees' print on the front, broken-down black jeans, possibly a little short —and tight—for her, and black punk-style boots.

She went to open the door, forgetting that it only opened from inside. This was one of the many "peculiarities" of the rusty old 1985 Honda Accord Hatchback. She finally got into the car and they looked at each other and laughed.

Like Adriel, Monica biked to her job, but needed a car to drive to Eugene, where her parents lived. She liked to visit them often. When she found the Craigslist ad, offering the car for four hundred dollars, she called right away—and bought it— but not without bringing the price down to three hundred. The ancient Incan dealing skills were too intact in her DNA.

That they only used the car occasionally was perhaps a good thing, considering the many "small details" they had to let go.

The upholstery was deeply decayed, the back passenger's seat belts didn't work at all, and the driver's window didn't completely go up using the handle. To fully close it, they had to stop the car, open the door and help the window up or down manually, one hand on the inside and one outside.

"Let's go and get Kyle," Adriel said.

"Hold on, my Bluetooth isn't connecting," Monica said.

Adriel rolled her eyes, knowing there was nothing she could say to get Monica to start driving without the music playing. To Monica, a car without good music and a good sound system was like an egg without salt. After she bought the car, she endured driving without music until she saved enough money to get a sound system connected, even before she purchased badly needed new tires.

The role of music in Monica's life was best exposed the day she almost killed a cat on her way home from visiting her parents. The cat appeared out of the dark like a ghost, and Monica, a fierce animal lover, reacted by swerving sharply to the right. The car struck a wide wooden light post with enough speed to cut her forehead open and give Adriel a boxer's nose for a few days.

Right after they hit the post, ignoring Adriel's condition and her own scratches as well as the damage to the car, Monica rushed to turn on the music.

"Shit, good thing the music still works!" she said, exhaling all her worries away.

Adriel thought of this episode as she patiently waited for the Bluetooth to connect. She shook her head and laughed.

"C'mon, Monica, let's go. You can get the music going once we get to Kyle's," she said.

Kyle was a Norwegian, six-foot-two, ex-professional rugby player with a body like a refrigerator who, after seeing his career fail because of knee injuries, rebranded himself as a highly reliable strip-club bouncer. He knew Monica from her days at the pole at Casa Diablo. where he took care of business for her—more than once. He even offered a shoulder for her to cry on, like that time in Casa Diablo's dressing room all her money was stolen from her bag along with a ticket to see Florence And The Machine at the Memorial Coliseum.

Adriel and Kyle met that night—the only night—Adriel worked at Casa Diablo. After seeing Adriel doing strip ka-raoke at Dante's Sinferno, Monica thought, erroneously, that

Adriel had a talent and appeal for the very lucrative business of stripping. As a dancer herself, she recommended her new friend to Casa Diablo's manager, Olga—a cranky, middle-aged, redheaded Russian who smelled like an ashtray. She wasn't the most popular figure among dancers. Her job was to keep them on a tight leash: on time, no drugs, no stealing.

Call it the street university, but when Adriel went to the club that morning to "try out," Olga fell for her fake ID like everybody else did—but not Kyle, who right away knew Adriel was a minor.

He confronted her later that night. She was standing in a narrow hall that communicated between the dressing room and the club's main floor, waiting her turn to go to the pole for the first time in her life.

Kyle watched her turning her head everywhere, nervously, like a little bird in an open field. She was wearing a shiny blue mask, several blue bead collars and old-fashioned, tight, blue French dancer attire, all matching her hair. The Mardi Gras motif had to do with her stage name—Blanc, given to her by a veteran dancer because of Adriel's strikingly pale skin.

Kyle approached her.

"So how old are you really? Sixteen?"

"Oh please! You saw my ID, I'm eighteen."

"Your skin's too good and you have no manipulative skills. Don't worry, I'll keep it in the vault," he said, winking at her and patting her shoulder as if she was a puppy.

She smiled, but the announcement that it was her turn to go on stage brought back all the anxiety she was beginning to overcome. It was like a punch.

"I'm kind of scared," she said.

"Don't worry. Just remember, no sobers, and no falling-down drunks. Go for the drunk enough—they're the easiest to deal with. Look at their eyes. You're looking for droopy eyes and dilated pupils, but they have to be able to talk," Kyle said.

What Monica didn't see from the get go was that Adriel's passion was singing, not getting naked for the pleasure of a stranger. Raw and inexperienced, she wasn't ready for sly, dirty hands rubbing her skin.

It only took a little over two hours before Adriel found herself at the club's back door, facing an angry Olga. It was rare for a strip club to believe the customer's version, but the blood trickling down the man's forehead seemed to be unequivocal proof of the aggressor's identity.

The man, a forty-something real-estate agent, was enraged, vehemently accusing Adriel of smashing a glass in his face, but omitting that he too had taken a piece of the same broken glass and gone straight for her face. He swung hard, but slowed down by alcohol, just barely slashed her eyebrow, which she ended up piercing to hide the small scar.

"I had to do it, Olga. I kept telling him he couldn't touch me. He wouldn't listen, and ultimately grabbed my pussy and told me to shut up, or else he'd wait for me in the parking lot all night!" This last part was Adriel's fabrication, she played as well as she could, trying to sound innocent, but Olga being Olga, looking alternately at her and at the man's bloody face, wasn't convinced.

It was Kyle who, in the middle of the commotion, took Olga by the shoulder and brought her aside for a discreet talk.

"Between you and me, Olga, the girl is right. I don't wanna give names, but a couple of dancers have complained about this customer before, and I have to say, I've seen him. Not to be trusted, mate, not to be trusted."

Lacking space in her spirit for dreams and hope, Olga recognized bullshit—as she called typical dancers' lies—a mile away. But Kyle's comment was masterfully vague, and coming from the best bouncer in town, a guy she related to and with whom she wouldn't have minded a wild night of fluid exchanges.

"Well sir, my bouncer says several girls have complained about you and that you were indeed forcing your hands between her legs. He saw you *twice*!"

Olga was no amateur in the art of bullshitting herself. She put her fingers in front of the man's face, thinking he'd back down and go home, but he didn't.

"You're a fucking liar, bitch. A fucking liar, bitch. You're a fucking liar—" The third time, before he could finish the sentence, Adriel, whose head was boiling like a hot, spicy Korean soup, approached him and spat in his face.

Everyone froze. Silence. Then she looked at her saliva running down the man's cheek, and at last she met his eyes, filled with red light.

She clenched her teeth and braced herself. He charged like an angry bull. She shrank and extended her arms as if a meteorite was about to fall on her, when all of a sudden, the man flew skyward and then landed flat on the ground. Kyle had stopped him and tossed him away as if he was a dummy.

By then, Kyle had achieved hero status in Adriel's world. But the large paper package he brought made her realize what kind of friend he was.

This part of the story begins with a hairy, gentle beast named Diesel:

Adriel was almost fifteen when she escaped from her home with the help of Brandi, Leah's friend. They lived in Olympia, Washington until Adriel turned sixteen. That year, Adriel moved on her own to Portland.

Brandi helped her rent a room in the northeast of the city in a house owned by Brad and Rebecca Johnson. The situation seemed to be ideal, except the Johnsons were on the verge of divorcing. Renting the room was the Johnson's attempt to fill its empty space, originally destined to be a baby's room. But the precious baby never arrived, despite the fortune they spent in medical treatment. There wasn't enough extra cash in the world to heal their broken relationship. Truthfully, no baby would have been able to repair it either, but that was something Rebecca in particular couldn't see.

When Adriel rang their doorbell for the first time, a gentle Bernese Mountain dog welcomed her to the house. Diesel wagged his tail when he saw Adriel, and excited, Adriel wagged her tail too. She'd never been allowed to have pets.

Shortly after Adriel's arrival, in crescendo, the Johnsons resumed the fights they'd avoided at first, out of embarrassment. Diesel, a sensitive dog that he was, went to sleep with Adriel every night.

The day Rebecca finally knocked on Adriel's door to tell her they were divorcing and selling the house, Adriel was lying in bed with Diesel.

She let Rebecca in and sat on the bed next to the dog. Listening, she hugged Diesel tighter with every word.

"Can I keep Diesel?" That was her only question. This was much more than bonding between a dog and a human. Diesel was Adriel's first friend in Portland. This was the third time she had to leave a loved one behind; first it was her mom, then Brandi, now Diesel. When Rebecca saw her dog licking Adriel's tears as they said goodbye to each other, she promised her she could visit her friend as much as she wanted. Rebecca was renting a place nearby.

Adriel moved in with her co-workers Alyssa and Donatella and together they formed Cyanide Roses. The change did Adriel good, although no matter how many times she went to visit Diesel, she missed having a pet of her own. None of her roommates wanted a dog, but Adriel persisted, until at last they came to a compromise: a cat would do well for all of them.

At the local human society, Adriel looked at several cats. And then she met a rambunctious grey and white kitty who jumped on her chest while she was sitting on the ground. Driving back home with Donatella, Adriel counted how many times she had to lie to get the kitty—eleven times in total if one included the use of her handy fake ID. She named the cat Pinocchio.

Adriel really hadn't thought through the expenses of having a pet. When bills accumulated, she convinced her manager at Taquería Por Que No, a tiny taco store overly decorated with a Mexican theme, to let her work double shifts.

Her finances improved a little, but only fully resolved after she moved in with Monica. As a scrub technician at a local hospital, Monica made much more than Adriel. At least until she had to cut hours to attend college—Monica wanted to be a nurse—she agreed Adriel didn't need to contribute to the rent, just help pay for groceries and bills.

One morning, Adriel found Pinocchio curled in a corner of their apartment, making a terrible crying noise. Drops of urine were sprinkled all over the carpet, which was alarming because Pinocchio never, ever urinated anywhere but inside his cat box. A urinary tract blockage. And this is how everything came together with Kyle coming to the rescue with his package.

Adriel had used the little money she had left to pay for the emergency visit, hospitalization, first flushing of the urethra, and medicines to resolve the problem, apparently common among male cats. What she didn't know was that once a cat suffered a blockage, it was common to have it a second and even a third time, and that the veterinarian protocol called for waiting until the third time before finally performing a more radical, but also more definitely effective penectomy. This is exactly what happened with Pinocchio.

By the time Adriel had to make a decision about whether to do the penectomy, she'd used all her money and had a balance of only eighteen hundred dollars that didn't include the additional eight hundred she needed to proceed with surgery.

"What an irony," she told Monica as they were discussing options in the vet's waiting room. "I want to cut off my father's dick. Instead, I'm forced to do it to my poor cat, or else put him to sleep."

"Sweetie, there's no irony here. I'm sorry, but we're going to have to put him to sleep. We can't afford this, and I think Pinocchio's suffering here. He hates this fucking place. And who knows if this will really work?" Monica said.

"Fuck you!" Adriel said without thinking. All she could see was Pinocchio as a kitten chasing that tiny red light as if it was his last meal, or as a young adult, lying on her legs while she was reading in bed.

"Here you are. Stop whining already and go pay the fucking vet," Kyle said later that night, hitting her chest softly with the paper package, the size of a shoebox.

She didn't understand right away. And then she tore open the paper bag that was sealed with tape. Inside, she found a disorganized pile of two dollar bills, fifteen hundred of them, to be exact. Knowing the source of the bills, she laughed from the bottom of her soul before jumping on this gentle giant who was always there for her.

4) 10:45AM. Richard.

"Shit, Richard. You really know how to fuck up a contract, don't you?" Mike sounded unruffled, calm, almost sinister.

He was short and balding with an underdeveloped jaw and a funny voice that had gained him his nickname among friends: Pesci, in honor of the famous actor.

Richard knew his boss would be upset, but didn't understand the extent of his anger until, through Mike's eyes, he saw the volcano that was about to explode.

Shrinking before those eyes, Richard looked down at his folio and pretended to be examining his notes.

"I'm sorry, Mike. I'm really sorry," he said.

He wanted to add that the loss had hurt him the most. He wanted to point out how much money he'd made for Mike over the years, and for his father before him, but the words wouldn't come.

Inside the small and humble conference room, the silence landed like a weight on Richard's shoulders. He hoped Larry or Charles would say something, but nobody said a thing.

Fuck!!! Richard scribbled in his folio, avoiding confronting Mike, who was going on about how much the loss meant.

Richard kept his head down. When he finally raised it to look in front of him, he encountered, inevitably, the large marker board that was hanging on the wall. *Get payment from Bilakanti and celebrate!* Mike had written during their morning huddle. Next to the board was one of those insurance agency calendars with a photo of Mount Hood, which they gave their clients every year. BILAKANTI was written and circled in red inside the square for Friday, November 03.

A glass wall separated the conference room from the waiting room. Looking from the receptionist's point of view, one could see four distressed men dealing with terrible news. Mike kept talking animatedly, his arms in the air. Sitting at a round table, they were drinking weak coffee while lamenting the loss of a big policy renewal with a nearby farm.

Richard was wearing a short-sleeved shirt and tie. A sport jacket slung over the back of his chair. This was Richard's perennial uniform for work, which he always wore with one of his three pairs of beige khakis, soft brown leather shoes, and a worn brown leather belt that seemed older than him.

He was in charge of retaining the contract. The farm's former owner had been his client, but sold the property to Mr. Bilakanti, an Intel engineer from India, who'd decided he was done with corporate life and wanted his children to grow up in a small town, surrounded by nature. Although the previous owner had endorsed Richard, ultimately, Mr. Bilakanti shopped for a lower price and went with a different agency.

"I'm sorry. I tell you, Mike, he assured me—"

He was locked with us, Richard wanted to say, but Mike, whose internal volcano had exploded, interrupted him abruptly, banging on the table.

"Being sorry doesn't bring the client back, Richard!"

Startled, Richard almost jumped out of his chair, but settled back right away.

You fucking spoiled little shit. I told you to lower the rate, Richard wanted to say, but something different came out of his mouth, in the most apologetic tone possible.

"But Mike, I gave him the rates you told me to give him, and I delivered them on time. You know, I tell you, the internet is killing us, Mike."

The thought that everything was Mike's fault for insisting on not giving that extra five percent discount floated into Richard's head, but he said nothing else. Sitting at the corner of the table, looking like a defeated boxer after the fifteenth round, Richard loosened his tie, hoping the tension in his neck would go away. But it didn't.

Mike listened to Richard, shaking his head repeatedly. Once again he spoke, sounding cold.

"No Richard. You see, the internet can't drink with clients, but, oh, wait: You don't drink! And you refuse to take clients for a round or two, don't you, Richard?"

"C'mon, Mike, don't be harsh. We didn't get beat on drinks. We got beat on pricing," said Larry in Richard's defense, pacing the room to release his own tension.

"Thanks, buddy," said Richard. He exchanged a look with Larry and somehow thought they were thinking the same thing. They'd talked about it many times: being the head of an insurance agency wasn't that hard. They could do it just as well as Mike, but didn't have a daddy to hand them a business, like Mike did.

"We'll get him next year. Just wait until he has a claim. He'll have to call an 800 number and they'll put him on hold for hours." Charles finally spoke, smoothing his moustache with his fingertips, as if he knew something nobody else did, even though he didn't.

"Bullshit. If you have a connection with the buyer, he'll tell you he's comparing prices early in the game, and he'll pay a little more if he connects with you. You fucked it up, Richard, you fucked it up," said Mike again before leaving the room.

Minutes later, angrily, Richard threw his jacket over the chair in his cubicle. *You fucked it up*, Mike had said. The words resonated in his mind. He could officially say goodbye to that bonus he was hoping for and with that, the new truck he wanted so badly, and to the several upgrades long due at home. He looked at his phone. 10:45AM, it said. *Thank God it's Friday*, he thought.

With no energy or desire to work on anything related to insurance, he reluctantly began looking at a quote that needed to be finished for a client by 2 PM. As an insurance agent, his territory covered La Grande—where the office was located— Baker City, Pendleton and some of the farms and wineries around Walla Walla, Washington. They sold everything from land, fire, property, farm, and ranch as well as liability insurance. This wasn't a job Richard enjoyed, although he'd been doing it for almost twenty years, the number of years he had been married to Leah.

Looking desperately for a source of distraction, Richard tapped at his desk with his fingers, his eyes wondering around the cubicle. Just then, he heard his computer ping: "You've got mail."

He switched to the email window and seeing that the new mail wasn't important, glimpsed at the list of read emails below until one caught his eyes. It was an email that had stayed with him since he received it four days before, on Monday.

From: Verizon FamilyBase 10/31/16
Weekly Update: Leah's top contacts this week were xxx-xxx-9193, See all their activity…
To: Richard Jackson
Verizon Shop Support MyVerizon
Leah's week
Monday, October 24 – Monday, October 31
Activity Highlights
5 phone calls
1 Unknown Contact
Top contacts
xxx-xxx-9193
View Activity

Richard clicked on "View Activity" and the system prompted him to sign in to his account. Then he navigated the page through Family Base to Leah's phone where he clicked "All Activity." His chest tightened when he saw that, every day of this week, just like last week, Leah had been calling or answering calls from an eight-hundred number.

He tried—for the third time in two weeks—to call the mysterious number, but every time, he got the same result: no tone. Staring at the screen like a neurosurgeon looking at his working field, he did a Google search for the number. But that didn't help either. One of his legs was going bananas with its involuntary up and down shaking, when he heard his boss walking into the room. Frustrated at his failure to find out where the calls were coming from, he quickly closed the browser and mail windows, and pretended to be looking at an Excel sheet.

"Are you gonna watch the eclipse somewhere special tonight, Mike?" Richard asked, putting on a false front. But Mike didn't answer. He had no desire to speak to Richard and the insistent urge to smoke a cigarette was pushing him out the door.

Richard thought about Leah's phone calls. He pictured her speaking with an imaginary attorney, and all of a sudden, the whole process of a terrible divorce emerged inside his cubicle like an asphyxiating cloud: court sessions, money getting flushed down the toilet, and of course, the blame and an impossibly negative outcome facing him.

"We're gonna go for a couple beers after work. Wanna join us?" Larry said from his cubicle and, with that, liberated Richard from his agony. Even though Richard didn't drink, he went out with his friends every now and then.

"No thanks, guys. I got a couple of things I really need to attend to at home."

His mind went straight to Leah and how he was going to confront her about the phone calls. He was sure she was going to play the victim, making up a story about the number, playing dumb. It wouldn't be the first time.

What went wrong? he asked himself.

Metallica's Master of Puppets sounded though a small radio Larry had playing all the time, just as Richard began reflecting on his own question. The song took him back to that day of the concert, during his honeymoon with Leah. They were visiting the Portland International Rose Garden.

The plan was to spend the weekend in Portland before heading to Baker City, where the moving company would meet them at their new house. They would never have left Little Rock if it wasn't for Richard's aunt dying tragically in a car accident almost a year before the wedding and leaving the small house to Richard's father. He allowed Richard and Leah to live there without paying rent as long as Richard took care of maintenance. The savings made it impossible for Richard to say no.

The Rose Garden had an impressive collection of over seven thousand rose bushes of all colors and shapes, distributed in rows aligned over four acres, and Leah, to Richard's dismay, somehow wanted to smell them all. As a fifteen-year-old girl who'd never been out of Little Rock, Leah, wanted to see as many tourist attractions as possible. Richard had no interest whatsoever in visiting a garden. But Leah begged him to take her to both the Rose Garden and the Japanese Garden. He thought it would be a good gesture to please her since she was going to put up with the true reason he'd picked Portland and not Boise as their honeymoon destination: Metallica was performing that night at the local basketball arena.

It was one of those sunny days that hurt your eyes in Portland, dry and breezy, with a sky like a picture in a coloring book. The air was clean and perfumed by the thousand roses, although Richard couldn't smell them: he was holding a hot dog he'd bought from a cart at the garden entrance, which made the visit more bearable for him.

"Show her things she's never seen, son. That's how you'll win her heart," Richard's mother said a few weeks before the wedding. *She was so right*, he thought, when Leah, after smelling a flower, ran toward him and held his hand without him asking her to.

Already in his twenties, he felt a little silly for feeling a sudden tingling in his belly. He smiled, feeling laughter well inside. He released his hand and quickly looked around, to be sure nobody was watching them. "Be careful in public, son," his mother had told him before saying goodbye. "Some people just don't understand."

Not wanting to lose the golden opportunity, relieved that there wasn't anybody around at the moment, he rushed to caress her back in circles, his hand traveling down her spine, before Leah ran on, excited to smell the next flower. His smile vanished.

"You know Leah, consider this a landmark day: your pre and post I-love-Metallica," he said.

"I don't know, Richard. That music sounds evil. What do you like about it?" she asked, and his face lit up. He rushed to hold her again, and with his arms around her shoulders he said,

"I can play some of their songs on my bass. I'll tell you which ones during the concert." She smiled at him before leaning down to smell a flower that had caught her attention.

"Come and smell this one, Richard. It's amazing!"

The rose was pink and in full bloom, its petals fanned out in a circle and folded down, a bed for the remaining petals, folded upward and inward. This was certainly unique, but this flower's secret weapon was its fragrance, so intense and sweet it seemed artificial to Richard at first.

"Richard, this is so great. I'm so thankful you brought me. So grateful for this whole trip, really," Leah said and held Richard's hand again.

She smiled at him. He looked into her sweet, blue eyes, staring at him, and a fantasy about what would happen later that night flashed through his mind. Their first night together as husband and wife:

Leah coming out of the hotel bathroom in her robe with her hair still wet and smelling just like that fancy flower; him pulling the belt and slipping her robe off; her letting him explore her body and do whatever he wanted to her, in total surrender. Aroused, Richard felt a million cold ants run through his belly. At that moment, everything vanished around him but her. *She's in love with me*, he thought.

The song was no longer playing on the radio. A loud commercial about switching to Dish Network went on and on, but sitting at his desk, Richard was immersed in that state of mind of being able to perform a task automatically while thinking of something else, fully engaged in the image of Leah looking at him admiringly. The image stayed with him, but gradually it transformed. First, everything dissolved but her blue eyes, except that this time, they were as evasive as their new owner, who appeared slowly, the older Leah.

There was no robe, no wet hair. Leah was supposed to be sitting in front of him attentively, as she always had in the early days. She should have recognized the song he was playing for her: Master of Puppets, of course. He'd been practicing for months.

Although he was no virtuoso, he'd been playing along with some of his favorite songs for years. Most of his basic learning happened back in Little Rock when, as a teenager, his parents enrolled him at the local music school.

He loved the instrument, and while he never had the time or the talent to improve his skills, he kept practicing and learning through countless YouTube videos and as many as five-method books he could complete.

Usually he practiced down at his office, connecting the sound to his headphones, so he wouldn't bother anybody, neighbors included. This is why Leah wouldn't know he'd been practicing that particular song, which, at the same time, was the reason he thought it would be nice to surprise her with it. In his mind—but not hers—this was their song; they'd seen it played live the first night of their honeymoon. If not this song, what else could be symbolic of their union? Deep down, it wasn't just about impressing her with his skills. He wanted to serenade her.

It was a Saturday afternoon. He had waited patiently until Jacob—by then a baby—took his nap. Adriel was playing in her room. He'd set a chair where he was going to sit. His bass was ready to go, connected to an amplifier he'd bought a year earlier and rarely used.

He motioned to Leah to sit in a dining chair. He was about to press "PLAY" so his laptop would began playing the music, but then, he noticed Leah had connected the baby monitor right next to her. He could hear the electronic lullaby playing in Jacob's room.

A small argument exploded, but surprisingly, he let her have it her way. He wanted to turn it off but Leah insisted she wanted to be sure Jacob wasn't going to wake up with the music, which she'd made Richard promise wouldn't be too loud.

"Don't worry Richard. You won't be able to hear a thing once you start playing. This is just in case he wakes up," she said.

He began playing enthusiastically, even singing along with the chorus:

"Master of Puppets I'm pulling your strings, twisting your mind and smashing your dreams." But in the middle of the song, she got up to put the clean cups away in a cabinet near the kitchen door. She could see and hear him from there, and annoyed, he too could watch her ignore him. Despite this, and the disruptive, metallic clatter of the cups touching the plates, he managed to play the song flawlessly. He'd been working on that song for weeks.

"I don't know, Richard. I can't say I have an opinion. It's great I guess. But you know, I haven't been sleeping well, and with this headache I can barely tolerate that type of music," Leah said once he finished.

He opened his mouth to say something, but just then Jacob awoke. She ran away like a firefighter in response to the fire alarm.

Richard clenched his teeth tightly then and again now, returning to his cubicle from his memories. He opened a browser and began another futile attempt to find out who owned that eight-hundred number.

5) 3:25PM. Leah.

Leah looked at her mother's card one last time before putting it back into the box, as though it was dangerous and best kept caged.

"That day in the kitchen, what I don't understand is what your father meant by the idea that you were out of control. Clearly you were a well-behaved child with very little freedom," Nicole said.

Leah, still sitting on the sofa, remained rigid, her posture almost forced. Her face, and particularly her thin lips, seemed as stiff as her back. A black-and-white photo of the scene could have fooled anyone into thinking that Leah, with her blond hair knotted into a bun, was a lower middle class Victorian character, following a rudimentary version of finishing school.

"He didn't always mean that. You see, Father says you're out of control whenever you do anything against his will."

"Well, my point is that when you look back, Leah, it's important to keep things in perspective, to balance what truly happened against your parents' judgment. They may be very different realities. In the end, if your relationship with them isn't the best, that isn't your fault," Nicole said.

Leah had reflected on this. She wasn't the type to judge her parents. Dealing with two babies and the responsibilities in the house had helped her imagine what her mother had gone through. She had vivid memories of Mother about to explode in the middle of the day, like that particular day when Adam dropped a glass full of water on the kitchen floor. Mother was helping Bethany in the bathroom and Mary cut her foot on a piece of broken glass. She'd screamed so loud that Mother left Bethany on the toilet to rush to the kitchen and see what had happened. Seeing the shard of glass in her daughter's foot almost made her faint. She struggled to decide whether to call 9-1-1 or remove the glass herself, which is what she did, tortured by Mary's even louder crying.

The wound wasn't as bad as she originally thought, but there was blood on the floor and clearly Mary, just eight then, was scared to death. And to make it worse, in the midst of the chaos, Bethany began crying too, while Adam decided to torment his little sister by improvising a song alluding to her losing the foot forever.

"What happened, Mamma?" David arrived and began asking Mother to stop.

"Adam, be quiet or I swear you'll be sorry!!!" Mother yelled, but her voice was barely audible, drowned out by the singing, Mary's crying in pain, Bethany's hysterical screams, David's questions and Adam's song. Leah just watched quietly from the corner of the kitchen. She remembered how Mother threw the towel—literally threw the kitchen towel she always had tied on her waist right where the broken glass was, and then went to her room and closed the door. Leah had followed her. She needed help with a drawing she was working on. When she opened the door, she found Mother crying in bed.

Their house was chaotic from early in the morning until about nine at night, every day. There were kids' fights, accidents, and toys all over. That Mother was able to keep it relatively clean and organized was something Leah couldn't discount.

"Well, my childhood was pretty normal. They weren't hard on me, at least at the beginning. Father worked a lot, and Mother stayed home, taking care of all of us. There were seven of us, so they had their hands full."

"Hmm, Leah," said Nicole, sounding jovial. "Having seven kids isn't so common anymore."

"It isn't? Well, it was normal to us, you know?" Leah said.

"Sure, of course. And I can see how stressful it could be for a father, so much responsibility," Nicole said.

"Father worked as a trucker for a big shipping company. But after a few years he got promoted to manager of the distribution center. He had a decent salary, but with a wife and seven children to feed, he struggled financially. And then, well, he got fired."

Father's transformation after losing his job was plain for all to see, even in the eyes of a little girl like her, perhaps because Father was vocal about it. He blamed his ex-boss, but more than anything, reprimanded everybody in the house for being so wasteful, all the time.

"Deep inside, Father's a loving man. He loved me very much. And who knows? Maybe he still does. But our relationship went downhill right about the time he lost his job, and from that point on, we never seemed to do anything fun. I remember we used to go to Denny's for breakfast, you know? Just like we went to Dairy Queen on Sunday nights. But all that stopped, and Father suddenly got quite irritable. I mean, he yelled at Mother a lot, and at me too."

Leah could understand a lot about her parents' behavior, but to a point. It was one thing to yell at her for not helping to clean, or for ruining a brand new pair of shoes, but there were other things she couldn't forgive.

"Looking back, I can see he was stressed out, having all those mouths to feed and no job. But it wasn't just him. Mother changed too, especially after what happened when they took me out of swimming."

Curled up on the sofa, Leah glanced cautiously at the mailbox where the card was trapped, as if it concealed a microphone set up by her mother. Suddenly chilled, she moved the laundry basket to the floor so she could stretch her legs, unfolded the old blanket that had been in a corner of the sofa and pulled it over her. Ironically, her mother'd made the blanket for her when she was expecting Adriel.

"What do you mean?" Nicole asked.

Leah waited a moment before answering. With the blanket around her shoulders, she went to the kitchen to pour herself a cup of tea. Then, walking back, holding the cup steady, she began to talk.

"You see, Nicole, my parents caught me kissing a boy one day after swimming lessons. And because of that they took me out of swimming," she said. "His name was Daniel."

Nicole imagined the incident: An innocent girl infatuated with a classmate, sitting on the pool's edge, whispering to her girlfriend and pointing at the boy she likes. Then, she sends a small note to the boy through the girlfriend, or maybe the girlfriend tells the boy she likes him. The next day, the girl's caught wearing her mom's lipstick. That alone causes a bit of a commotion in the car where Mom forces her to wipe it off, and then, at the swimming lesson, the boy and girl kiss behind a big tree. An innocent peck, really. The instructor catches them and tells Mom, thinking the whole thing's no big deal, but it is: two years before that, they took her out of a "sinful" public school.

That afternoon when they got home, after telling Leah she'd never go to swimming class again, they sent her to her room. The decision had been made, but that wasn't enough. Father's rule was not just that you had to comply with his decisions, you had to agree with them. Leah wasn't ready to agree.

The boy—Daniel—didn't even matter. To young Leah, swimming was the last fun thing she was able to do, the pool the one place she had a friend who wasn't forced on her. She loved the underwater silence, the markings on the bottom of the pool swimming back as she swam forward. She loved feeling the cold water when she jumped into the pool, and how the water warmed up with her, stroke after stroke. And she loved the bubbles coming out of her mouth on each breath out, and the cold breeze hitting her cheek when she lifted her head to take a breath. Leah loved swimming more than anything.

She stomped into her room yelling at the top of her lungs, slamming the door behind her. On her bed, she jumped as though she was leaping off a cliff, landing head down. Using a pillow, she covered her head and yelled at the poor mattress even louder, wetting the sheets with her tears.

When she heard her father's steps, she thought she was going to have to endure endless lecturing, or worse. She froze like a bug playing dead when it's touched.

"Don't you dare leave your room until you're ready to accept the family decision, Leah. If you do, I swear you I'll beat you till your hide's raw," her father said.

It was a relief when he walked away, and hearing his steps recede was like turning a switch to relax her muscles. The only thing she wanted more than to be alone was to be alone underwater, swimming.

"She was just a weirdo!" Leah imagined the other children at swimming lessons gossiping about her absence. She knew that's what they thought of her. She could see it in their eyes when, sitting on the edge of the pool waiting for their turn, they asked her why she didn't go to school anymore, looking at her as if she was a strange Amazonian native they'd never seen before.

Shame made her angrier, and the angrier she got, the blurrier her reasoning became. She grew in confidence, believing she was so right and her parents so wrong that they'd eventually come and apologize to her.

Hours went by. She calmed down and out of boredom began drawing. She drew a valley, and then drew a beach with people on it, filling in the details until, tired of the pencil, she switched to trimming her nails before starting to reorganize her closet. As time went by, Leah's position grew stronger.

At around eight o'clock, Leah's younger sister Mary came to the door. She protested that the room was hers too, and that her parents were going to make her sleep in the babies' room if Leah didn't change her mind.

"Would you just cut it out? Would you, Leah? You know Father will have it his way," Leah heard her sister say.

"Mind your business," Leah said coldly, staring at the door as if it was her sister. But all she could see was a Saved By The Bell poster she'd taped to the door. She loved that TV show.

Mary kept insisting, and Leah, realizing she needed to use the bathroom added in a low voice,

"Mary, are Father and Mother around? I need to use the bathroom."

"They are!" Mary said.

When Leah's mother heard them talking, she stood by the kitchen door where she could listen to her daughters without Mary seeing her. When she heard Leah needed to use the bathroom, she approached them to take advantage of the golden opportunity for Leah to reconsider her position. But to her disappointment, Leah didn't.

"Leah, this is your last chance. Are you sure?" Mother said one more time.

Leah thought about it. Her head was resting on the door.

"It's not fair, Mother. It's not fair."

"Don't you dare leave that room, Leah. I'll hold you during the beating if you do!" Mother yelled.

There was a brief moment of silence. Leah was once more staring at the Save By The Bell poster. She sensed her mother was still there.

"Mother, please, I need to pee."

Leah waited for an answer, but her mother didn't speak.

A couple of hours later, all her feelings of pride and power were gone. Blurry memories of the last beating kept Leah from defying her parents. Sitting on the floor, resting her back against her bed, she stared at the Save By The Bell characters, all happy, smiling at her.

She was dressed in the loose, grey sweatpants she always wore as pajamas and a red sweater, two sizes too big, that said

Arkansas Razorbacks. Her face and hands felt sticky from wiping away tears.

She pulled her sweater up, to clean herself a little, but another round of inconsolable, body-shaking sobs began, without her own consent.

"Mother! Mother!" Leah called, but there was no answer.

Next to her there was her diary, a small, hard-cover notebook with Hello Kitty on the front and a pink page marker. She tried to write to console herself, but the urge to pee and the humiliation were such that she couldn't think straight.

She called her mother again, and staring at the poster, stood up and began banging at the door in desperation.

After a few moments Leah sensed her mother's presence. She felt the first drops of piss moisten her underwear and had to make an effort to hold it in.

"Mother, please help me. I can't hold it. Please help me, Mother," she said, but no words came from behind the door.

"Mother, I agree with Father's decision! Please, Mother, I swear, I accept it, let me out, please! I'm about to pee myself!!!" Leah was yelling by then.

Just then the door opened. Leah was hoping to meet the eyes of the person who, in the past, had protected her from Father's anger—who'd helped her win at Scrabble and fed her hot Ovaltine and cookies in winter. Instead, she met her mother's unrecognizable, icy gaze. The penetrating glare was like a dagger between her ribs. She froze in shock. Her mother acted first, seizing her forcefully by the hair and pulling her toward the bathroom. In silence, she waited for Leah to finish, and without giving her any privacy. As Leah was about to get off the toilet, she jerked her back down...

"Do what you need to do, but stay there. I'm going to get your father so you can tell him what you just told me. He's working in the garage," Mother said before slamming the door.

Leah finished telling Nicole the story. But the image of the bathroom door closing stayed with her as if her parents were there, wanting to prolong the punishment.

She tried to remember the feeling she had when the boy kissed her. That was the closest she ever got to making true love. The aberration that came later suppressed the memory forever; the boy's wet hands holding hers, his dreamy brown eyes admiring her, and the uncontrollable shaking that was going on inside her belly; it was the birth of a million butterflies taking place in the form of a swirl. She just didn't know this. She felt the cold grass underneath her naked feet and his hands on hers getting warmer and warmer by the second. His lips felt so warm, so soft, like a vacuum, they gently sucked her inside, the swirl of butterflies exploded and butterflies flew to her feet and her arms and her mouth before dissolving.

Leah wished she could remember it, but all she remembered was jumping off the ground when she heard their instructor asking what was going on. She remembered him smiling and patting her on the shoulder. "C'mon kids. You shouldn't be here," he said. The sudden paralyzing tightness in her neck dissipated. *He won't tell Mother*, she thought.

Sadness made it hard to breathe. It took a moment before Nicole spoke.

"Did your mother ever apologize for that, Leah?"

Leah was silent. The idea of an apology had never occurred to her. She thought about it and naturally, the first image that came to her was of Mother slamming the door on her with such unrecognizable wrath, without even minimal compassion. It was hurtful. The memory looped a few times, but again, the Saved By the bell poster was gone. She said,

"You know, Nicole, that door closing on me wakes me up often, even now. For some reason, in my dream, the door's bright red."

6) 10:53AM. Adriel.

Monica parked the car in front of Kyle's apartment at the corner of Killingsworth Street and Albina Avenue. Like many neighborhoods in northeast Portland, Kyle's had both modern and old northwest architecture where small streets with restaurants lay between residential blocks.

With the car door still closed, Adriel squeezed her body through the window and sat on top of the car facing the modern, three-story building. Resting her arms on the roof, she took out her phone and texted Kyle.

"We're here."

"Coming. Gimme five," Kyle responded immediately.

Adriel began drumming her fingers on the roof to the music Monica was playing on the radio, watching an old Mexican woman selling tamales next to their car. The steam coming out of her pot made Adriel want to buy a couple, even though she wasn't hungry. The Portland sky was ready for its nap, covering itself from the cold air in a cloudy grey blanket.

Chilly as she was, Adriel enjoyed the crisp air in her face, at least for a minute or two, until the song ended and rushing anxiety took over her mind. She looked at her phone to check on the time. It was 10:53AM.

"Hurry!" she typed.

"Can you wait, fuck face? Getting your bloody present together!"

Reading Kyle's text she could almost hear his Norwegian accent. She laughed.

A minute later, the building's front door opened and the tall young man came out. Kyle had short black hair and his chest was tattooed up to his neck. His small, brown eyes made his nose seem more prominent, which wasn't a good thing; it had seen better days before getting fractured in rugby games. Kyle approached the vehicle carrying a decent-sized box, with a sweet smile that belied his mean, scary features.

"What did you get me?" Adriel asked, excited.

She withdrew back into the car and then opened the door to get out, rushing to see what her present was.

"You're gonna love this," Kyle said.

"Hold on," Monica said from inside, surprised by the size of the box.

"The trunk has a trick."

She got out of the car and, after struggling with the lock for a little while, finally opened the trunk.

Kyle rested the box inside it to greet Monica with a hug, then went ahead and opened the present.

"Shouldn't I be the one opening *my* present?" Adriel asked, sounding quirky, but Kyle ignored her. The gift was a Sony turntable and a Tacocat album.

"My God! A turntable?! This is too much, Kyle. How much was it?"

"Nah, relax, and don't ask questions. It was a lot less thank you think, trust me. And I have to confess, I listened to this garbage last night. It's unbearable," Kyle said.

"What's important isn't your ignorance of music, but your big heart," Adriel said and hugged him enthusiastically.

"Happy birthday, Adriel. I guess that ID of yours is getting to be obsolete, huh?" he said.

The fake ID had been crucial in Adriel's life. Without it, in chronological order, there'd be no high school in Olympia, no moving to Portland, no Dante, no Monica, no Casa Diablo, no Kyle, no playing at bars with Cyanide Roses, no job, no IPAs, no Pinocchio the cat, and no so many things. It was a story both Kyle and Monica knew well; Adriel had told them about it in excruciating detail. Talking about the fake ID really meant talking about one of Adriel's favorite subjects: Brandi.

When Adriel first met her, Brandi was in her late thirties and heartbroken. She was a relatively short woman, slightly overweight. Her hair was quite thick and wild, burnt by the persistent use of cheap, bright yellow coloring, which, despite how often Brandi applied it, could never completely hide the dark brown of her natural hair that grew like a bad weed. She wore her hair loose and blow dried, eighties style.

A free spirit, she'd learned to get used to the monotony, harsh hours, and low pay of jobs for high school dropouts. Her financial struggles and disappointments with men promising a better future had left her with nothing, but the realization that in life, she only had herself.

A guy named Jerry was responsible for her broken heart. He'd moved in with her about a year before she met Adriel. It was love at first sight, a soulmate encounter of the first kind, as he liked to say. He was a true nerd, fascinated with everything sci-fi.

Prior to meeting him, the fact that she'd never been pregnant made Brandi doubt her atheism. It was a miracle of a kind. "Nobody's ever fucked as much as I have," she often said, reflecting on her past with a strange mix of pride, humor, and shame. Ready to settle down, she wished she could have given Jerry the children he wanted so badly, but after a whole year of trying, she discovered that she wasn't fertile.

They were given several options to get around the problem, but with no insurance and little money, there was nothing else to do. Infatuation faded and Jerry melted away like many others had before him.

Wanting to get as far away as possible from Jerry and the memories surrounding him—and that meant leaving Baker

City—Brandi had planned to move out months before she offered Leah help with Adriel. Little did she know she'd still become a mother, but to the tormented child she'd agreed to take on.

The same day she arrived in Olympia with Adriel, Brandi rented a tiny apartment in a dubious neighborhood in the southern part of the city. She'd chosen Olympia because a cousin who lived there had convinced her to, promising a warm reunion and help settling in, a promise never fulfilled.

A cheap motel was their home for the first two nights while they found a place to rent. They drove around endlessly, looking at apartment complex after apartment complex, but one after the other, they were either rejected because of Brandi's poor credit history or decided to pass because the rent was too high.

"Check this place out. I know they have a lot of vacancies right now and they'll take you for sure," said the last landlord they visited, an old black man with a gentle voice and sleepy eyes.

Twenty minutes later, they drove into the apartment complex that became their home for the next year and a half. Outside, a group of shirtless Hispanic men were playing small soccer in the abandoned ruins of a basketball court. To Adriel, the scene was like something out of a movie where dangerous prisoners interact in a remote, arid prison yard.

Seeing Adriel's worried expression, Brandi said,

"I think we took the wrong turn. We're in Tijuana!"

"Are we safe here, Brandi?" Adriel said, sounding worried.

"Of course we're safe! What are you talking about? I know these people. I like 'em chimichangas. I mean, we buy them some tacos and we'll be fine!"

The apartment had one bedroom and a bathroom, a living room slash dining room, slash office, slash whatever else, and a small kitchen with no windows or ventilation. Everything but the kitchen and the bathroom had been carpeted back in the eighties, when the place was built. There were so many stains on the carpet, one might think they were actually a decorative pattern.

"C'mon. Let's get things inside. You'll see, once we fill this place with furniture and decorate it, it'll look like new. I have a magic touch—a plant here, a poster there, and next thing you know this'll feel like home. Stack the boxes in the corner so we can organize things a little easier, okay? If we do it quickly enough, maybe I'll have time to go to Goodwill to pick up some furniture."

Adriel obeyed, in silence. She helped bring everything inside, until the front of the apartment was filled with boxes. It wasn't the number of boxes, but the size of the apartment.

The Red Hot Chili Peppers were playing loud through a CD player Brandi had brought with her. Brandi always had music on, a habit she later passed on to Adriel.

"Do you like this band?" Brandi asked.

Adriel shrugged. Emotionless like a tree, she kept herself miles away from Brandi.

"C'mon! You gotta like them or not like them!" Brandi insisted. She smiled, unashamed of the gaps on both sides of her mouth, the product of having just her front teeth remaining.

She wants to be my friend, Adriel thought, but evaded Brandi by pretending to reorganize the boxes, which they began opening.

All of them were Brandi's, except for one: a medium-size box Leah had given Brandi before saying goodbye. Inside, there were school documents of all kinds—transcripts, enrollment forms, and a few certificates. There were also a manual about homeschooling, copies of standardized tests, and a few samples of Adriel's work.

Brandi, nosy as she was, browsed the papers, curious about homeschooling. She tried to imagine a school without other children, how boring it would be, but she had a feeling she was being watched.

She turned to Adriel who, looking straight at her, finally opened up to say,

"I don't want to do homeschooling, Brandi. I want to go to an actual school, or not study at all."

This time it was Brandi's turn to be evasive. She kept emptying the boxes, thinking about what to say, until the answer came to her. Turning her head to Adriel, she said,

"Listen, honey, I hear you, you don't want that bullshit, brainwashing garbage they were feeding you no more, but this will be real homeschooling, I mean, the useful stuff, like knowing your math and knowing about health and places in the world and stuff like that—stuff you can use in real life, you know?"

Adriel shook her head quickly, like the wings of a hummingbird.

"No, Brandi, you don't get it. I want to be normal and have friends. Homeschooling is so boring," she said.

An imaginary version of homeschooling finally developed in Brandi's mind, but she couldn't see reality as it had been; Adriel receiving lessons at her own home, or at Mrs. Fuiten's, along with Mrs. Fuiten's daughter Hannah, and Julia Malmquist. The basic math, reading, and writing didn't bother Adriel any more than it bothers most teenagers. What killed her was the endless hours of biblical instruction, being told what to do and not to do, and having to hang out with two girls she didn't even like.

"Look, it's just the beginning of summer. Let's figure things out, get settled and go from there, okay? Can't promise, but we'll see what we can do, okay?"

"Yes, ma'am."

"Yes, ma'am?! Don't you 'yes ma'am' me. I'm not that old, young lady! Don't you ever, ever 'yes ma'am' me again!"

Adriel smiled at last, and seeing her reaction Brandi gave her a hug, unsure about how she was going to manage to get her to accept homeschooling, because public school didn't seem to be an option at all.

A week or so later, Brandi began working at a Walmart as a cashier, a job that was a piece of cake for her, considering her many years working at supermarkets. The salary was barely enough, but resourceful as ever, she knew she'd manage.

At Walmart, Brandi brought her own lock for her locker, and walked through the halls behind the store like a new boy at a juvenile detention center. Soon she realized that the "iffy" Mexicans from the neighborhood weren't the criminals she thought they were.

Her paranoia didn't completely vanish until she met Hilario. They always ran into each other in the small, smelly break room, down the hall from the store bathrooms. Every day, by lunchtime, Hilario was finishing his break, reading the local Hispanic newspaper. He ate elsewhere, but came to the room to drink the free coffee after his meal.

Initially—and this lasted several days—they didn't speak to each other. Hilario was a short man of sweet nature but few words, and Brandi didn't think he could speak any English.

One day, Hilario finally broke the ice and asked Brandi a question. Little did he know he'd turned on a radio that would never, ever turn off again. Brandi would talk through her lunch, telling Hilario details of her life he probably didn't want to know, tormenting him with stories that made no sense to him, told in excruciating detail. He spoke every now and then, but mostly limited himself to saying "hmmm" and "yes."

One day, Brandi sat with a microwaved frozen vegetable lasagna steaming in front of her. She sat right next to him and began eating it with pleasure.

"You got to stop eating like that, Brandi. It's not healthy, too many chemicals," Hilario said.

"What? This is healthy, Hilario. What are you talking about? It's all vegetables."

"I don't know about that, microwaves have a lot of chemicals, you shouldn't heat your food there."

"Really? I mean, what do you want me to do, bring fucking chalupas from home?"

"How many times do I need to tell you chalupas are a Taco Bell invention?"

"Whatever, tell me what do you want me to do, Hilario."

"First, for the hundredth time, it's not Heelario. You don't pronounce the h in Spanish. Say: eeelario." He said his name slowly and loud.

"Whatever, A-ELARIO!" Brandi said, doing her best to pronounce it right, but in a joking voice.

"Don't bring lunch tomorrow. Let's meet here. Just switch breaks with Angela so you can be earlier. I'll show you real food tomorrow," he said.

She lifted her head to look at him and shrugged, her mouth full.

The next day, Hilario came for her and took her to the storage area behind the store, where he worked. Right pass the trucks and all there was an empty, grassy lot where the Hispanic employees improvised a daily grilling of cheap meat—chicken thighs, pork shoulder, or beef short ribs for soup—along with homemade tortillas and the salsa of the day.

"Welcome, gringa, ven a comer, ven!" said an older man they called Don José.

Brandi recognized him because of that Mexican cowboy hat, the Ranchero he always wore. He helped at the cashiers bagging groceries.

These earliest interactions slowly reshaped Brandi's prejudiced and distorted image of Latinos. At first, she was prompted by curiosity, then fascination, infatuation, seduction, sexual desire, and ultimately love. Hilario was the lost soul Brandi had look for, for so many years.

The relationship didn't develop that quickly, but Brandi's attraction to all things Latino did. The more often she got invited to spend an afternoon eating posole, drinking beer and tequila, or just coffee, the more she realized she'd gotten it all wrong. *Shit, I've been living to work all my life. These people work to live*, she often thought.

She even began organizing her own gatherings, making hot dogs or burgers on a small grill, and Adriel absolutely loved it. There were a lot of Latino kids in the complex and as far as she was concerned, she was one of them.

By the end of summer, everybody in that small Hispanic neighborhood knew all about Brandi and Adriel; they were part of it. This is how it came to be that one afternoon, as they were all watching Cruz Azul Vs. Morelia, a woman named María called Brandi to the balcony.

"Listen, Brandi, I want to tell you about Adriel going to school. What we talked about the other day, about school and papers."

Brandi opened her mouth and inhaled deeply and was about to say something, but María stopped her, first signing with her hand and then placing it on Brandi's shoulder. She said,

"I know, I know, I talked to Graciela. She talked to Fernando, and I know Hilario tells Fernando everything. It's okay, Brandi. Tell her, Raul, tell her."

Raul, a scary-looking young man, was standing on the balcony, waiting for María to finish the introduction. Years before, he'd done jail time for dealing cocaine in Tacoma. From jail, he was taken to an immigration jail, and back to Mexico, but just a year later, he managed to come back. Regenerated, he looked back at the year he'd joined the gang with deep regret. His father had died in a job-related accident. Nobody seemed to care about that, and his mom, a cook at a local Red Robin, couldn't support her five children. The gang was the wrong exit to dilute Raul's anger and bring money home.

"I can get you papers for Adriel tomorrow if you want me to," he said with a barely detectable accent, to Brandi's surprise.

"What do you mean?" she asked.

"I got a past—stuff you don't need to know about. It's past, and well, because of that past I got connections too. I can help you and Adriel."

"How?" Brandi asked.

"What you need to do is cut Adriel's hair very short, color it dark—maybe get her some frames even if she doesn't need glasses—and take a photo at Costco. I'll get you a forged social and a driver's license."

Brandi hesitated. She stayed muted and still, like a tree.

"Look, Brandi, no offense, but there's no way you can homeschool Adriel. You work ten to twelve hours a day and you aren't the professor type. She needs to go to school," said María.

"But you guys don't understand—if she gets caught."

"Shh," María said, interrupting her.

"Trust me, a missing child who isn't reported ain't missing, you understand?" Raul paused, then added,

"Look, nobody will know. Her name sounds Latino anyways. All we have to do is come up with a last name. This is the most neglected school in the state. Nobody gives a fuck, you know?

And what are the kids gonna know? As far as they know there's nothing wrong. She is Adriel, isn't she? I mean, that's her name."

"They are going to know. What about transcripts? I have the transcript and they're under her name," Brandi insisted.

"If my friends can forge a driver's license, don't you think they can switch a name in some bullshit transcript?"

"Cuida esa lengua!!!" Maria slapped Raul on the head and scolded him. "Watch your language."

He kept going.

"Look, leave it up to me. Just do what I say. Get me a photo, and don't worry about anything else."

"*Everybody* knows about this?" Brandi asked.

María and Raul assented, smiling at her. Adriel leaned forward to avoid Raul's body and see the living room where Hilario was watching the game, as if he was clueless about the situation.

"Does Hilario know you're talking to me about this right now?" she asked, leaning back and forth.

"Of course he knows. You think he is pendejo? We just agreed it would be best for me to talk directly with you, you know?" said María.

Feeling goosebumps all over, Brandi kept looking at Hilario. She wanted to hit him and hug him and kiss him all at the same time. She said,

"I don't think I can afford to pay you for this right away, Raul."

"María was right," he said. He laughed and continued.

"You're so gringa, Brandi. Don't be silly. You're family."

7) 3:31PM. Leah.

Leah thought about the red door. It always came at her from behind, jumping at her shoulders like a cougar attacks its prey.

It had started about four months earlier, precisely the time her memory was able to take her back to. Her recollection of the time between that and Adriel's escape, about three years, was like seeing through quivering gelatin. She knew her memory wasn't the same, and she accepted this. She had no clue, though, how much hell she'd been through for over three years. In fact she couldn't remember anything of those three years. Not only had her mind blocked those memories forever, but it had created made-up answers to the questions she asked herself.

What do you mean with the red door coming at you? "Do you mean, like a recurrent nightmare?" Nicole asked.

"Well, yes, but it also comes to me during the day, when I'm in the middle of something—cooking or walking or whatever. I might be thinking about something random when suddenly the red door interrupts whatever is in my mind."

Nicole took note of this. While Leah talked, she looked at her database to find a volunteer therapist close to Leah. She was hoping she'd be able to refer her before the end of the call.

"Do you have good memories of your father before the relationship deteriorated?" Nicole asked.

Leah's memories of her dad were stored in her subconscious on two different hard drives, one labeled Father the Tyrant and the other simply called White Oak Lake. As she considered the question, one of her many memories of family time at the national park surfaced and she bloomed, blushing like the flowers on her dress. She was once again that shy blonde girl with dark, round blue eyes and that distinctive gap between her front teeth, although by now, one tooth was fractured as a result of that awful fall when she argued with Richard, the day of Adriel's escape.

"You know, when we were little, we used to go to this park an hour or two from Little Rock. We went every year. Father was all about tradition and that was ours. I loved going there so much!

I remember the last time we went there. In fact, that was the last time Father and I got along, the same year they took me out of swimming.

The night before we went to the park, I was in the garage with Father, organizing everything like we always did. We had this routine that I loved. He had a list that he put together, year after year. I mean, if there was anything we needed but didn't have, he'd add it to the list so we would bring it the following year. Anyway, he'd give me the list and with Mother's help, I'd find every item on it and lay them all on the garage floor, and once everything was ready, I'd call him. It was like a game: he'd go through the list, so we could check if I had everything ready to go."

Leah's mood fluctuated up and down according to the story she was telling. Relating this episode of her life to Nicole lifted her up, at least for the time being.

"I was super excited because that year I was sure everything was gonna be just right, which, you know, it was gonna be the first time.

'Matches?' I remember him asking. That was the last item on the list. I had butterflies because I knew I had them and that Father'd smile at me. You know, Nicole, he just didn't interact with us that much and having him there just for me was something else.

At the park, the boys and Father were in charge of pitching the tents. Father and Adam, my oldest brother, did the most, but they all helped. Now, here's the thing: in Father's mind, the most important job of all was choosing just the right spot to pitch them. That year, because I got the list ready just right, he granted me the honor."

Leah paused as if she'd just dropped a punch line.

This was by far Leah's biggest victory. In her house, women were in charge of doing everything. As a child, she could have seen these dynamics as normal. At the end, Mother did absolutely everything for Father. She cooked for him, made snacks for him, washed his clothing, picked up his plate from the dining table, brought him snacks when he was watching TV, found everything he'd lost, even ran to find a band aid to cover a boo boo he'd got working in the garage with his wood. This was what Leah the child perceived. It was okay because she'd learned, from hearing it often repeated, that father was a great breadwinner, that he worked harder than anyone in the house. But then he lost his job, and while he wandered around the house, it was still Mother who did it all.

Leah wouldn't have questioned this if it wasn't that it was hard to swallow the idea that the same culture of servitude extended to children, and that the next in line was always the oldest daughter.

She'd seen Mother doing everything not just for Father but for all of them, including her. She loved *that* Mother. But one day, when she was about eleven, the rules changed. Mother began being exhausted, having migraines. When this happened, Mother always chose Leah to do it all. Even worse, all of a sudden, it seemed Mother was doing everything for everyone but her.

And then there were the many things that were just for boys, always the fun stuff, as Leah liked to complain to Mary. Hunting and fishing was just for boys, playing ball was just for boys, eating and not picking up after yourself was just for boys, working with Father in the garage was just for boys.

Leah waited a moment for Nicole to say something, moving to wake her leg that had gone to sleep, and since Nicole didn't say anything, she resumed her story, emphasizing that last sentence.

"You have to remember, in our home, women had little say. So it was unusual that Father granted the decision to me. But that's how it was, even though my brothers protested. I knew that where we pitched the tents was the most important step in getting a good sleep, so I liked to believe that the outcome of the trip was on my shoulders.

'Are you sure this is the best spot, Peanut?' he asked. Did I mention he called me 'Peanut'? Well, he did."

Nicole finally spoke.

"Peanut's a nice nickname. Does he still call you that?"

"Nooo," Leah said firmly.

"As a matter of fact, by that time, I was pretty embarrassed when he called me Peanut in front of people. I think it was the day after we arrived at the camp, the same summer he embarrassed me in front of these girls I'd just met."

Leah was playing on the beach with her sisters and brothers. It was the afternoon after they arrived, that last summer camping trip. They all loved this particular game: Leah chased them around until they ran into the water. There, she'd turn into a shark ready to eat them, and they'd have to escape to the sand. And on land, the shark chasing them would turn into a hungry cheetah again.

"Run, guys, run!!!" Little David, pretending to be a safari explorer, was shouting at the top of his lungs, kicking up sand with each step as he ran toward the water. Mary and Bethany, the youngest girls, were running next to him. Leah was chasing them slowly, but fast enough so they'd think she was trying.

Running barefoot toward the lake water chasing the younger kids, Leah felt the hot sand getting cold and wet. She'd run faster at this point, leaving her siblings behind. Cold drops of water splashed all over her when she ran into the shallows.

She smelled the slightly sweet water just before submerging into the underwater silence she loved, but just for a brief moment before she came up for air, to the loud screaming of excited children.

David was her favorite brother. A daydreamer mixed with Tasmanian Devil, he followed her everywhere she went. He slept next to her during these camping trips, and at home, often moved to her bed in the middle of the night.

It was a sunny, hot day, and the water felt just right. Leah stayed underwater with only her head above the surface, looking toward David and Mary, who were coming her way.

"C'mon sharky, you can't get me!" David yelled, bouncing on his toes like a flea on cocaine.

"Hold on, David, hold on," Leah said, noticing from the corner of her eye two girls about her age watching her.

"*Dong ding dong ding dong doing...*" Leah began to sing the Jaws theme before putting a hand on the back of her neck and submerging her head.

Squatting under the shallow water, she could still hear her siblings, and knew they wouldn't go far. She lifted her head to breathe and to see where they were. Once she got close to David, she stretched her hands forward until she could feel his jumping body.

"Gotcha!"

"You were cheating, Leah. You opened your eyes!"

"No, no, I didn't," she said.

"I'm just too hungry of a shark."

"Let's do it again!" Mary said, wanting to be caught too. Adriel agreed and once again noticed the girls watching her. Their eyes met Leah's once, then a second and third time. A classic game began: You're watching me. No, you're watching *me*. *You* say hi. No, *you* say hi first.

Leah played with Mary and David until the other girls gave up and waved at her. Leah had won out of shyness, not stubbornness.

For a homeschooled girl, only one thing was better than running around freely at a park, swimming in a lake and getting all the attention from her father, and that was socializing and playing with other girls her age. So as much as Leah loved David, it was time to get rid of him.

"All right, Davie, I'm going to say hi to those girls over there, okay? So go play with Mary, okay?"

She stood up, the water now a little above her hips. She was about to walk toward the three girls, but David immediately held her hand.

"Not now, David, I'm busy. Go and build a sand castle. I packed all the tools for you. When you're done I'll join you and we can play battle castle, okay?"

"But you said you were going to play with me," he whined.

"I know, I know. And I promise I will," she said, pushing him away gently.

David insisted for a little bit, until Leah changed her tone, hormones taking over.

"C'mon, David, let's you and me build the castle. And let's invite that boy over there," Mary said, and walked out to the water with her little brother.

Leah approached the girls and introduced herself.

"Wow, it's gotta be annoying being followed around by your little brother all day long," said one of the girls, not in a malicious way, but looking to connect with Leah in her own way.

"He's okay. I actually don't mind most of the time," Leah said.

"Ugh, my little brother drives me nuts," said the other girl.

After they'd been chatting awhile, the tallest girl, who seemed to be the leader of the pack, asked Leah if she wanted to join them. "Hey, we were going to go hang out at the Welcome Center. Want to come?"

Leah had that empty stomach feeling, not wanting to say no, wanting to belong, hoping her parents wouldn't care. She started walking with the girls, fearing the inevitable would happen at any second. She knew it would wreck the prospect of being accepted by the other girls.

"Peanut! Time to make the burgers!" Father called. Making the burgers was the other father-daughter tradition they kept. Leah loved it too, but burger-making couldn't compete with three new friends.

"Peanut? Your dad calls you *peanut*? How old are you, eight?" asked the tall girl.

Father called her again. "Peanut, where are you going?" He was sitting next to their picnic table, about fifty yards away.

"Ughh, he's so annoying," Leah said, pretending to be the teenager she wasn't.

"It doesn't matter how many times I tell him to stop calling me that. He just won't!"

The girls laughed and the shortest even confessed her parents still called her "princess." They all laughed, but Father's third call interrupted them.

"Leah, come back please. You aren't allowed to wander around on your own."

"On your own? Is he blind?" said the tall girl. Leah wanted to keep the facade up, but she knew she'd already gone as far as she would ever go.

Isolation wasn't new to young Leah. It hadn't even started with her removal from swimming, but much earlier. Leah didn't know or even remember the circumstances of her removal from school. She only came to understand what happened as a mother herself, when Richard and her parents told her that

Adriel was better off studying with Mrs. Fuiten. This second time she was given the same explanation: homeschooling was better because it was one-to-one education with a stronger curriculum that avoided the "liberal agenda." But none of this mattered to Leah as a child. She only cared for all her friends at school, but especially for Shirley, a girl she'd known since pre-school who'd remained her friend. From one day to the next, it all changed: she was never going to see her again.

Young as she was, she forgot about Shirley, and slowly came to understand, through her experiences in public places, that when Father or Mother told her it was best to leave, it was because there was something wrong with those girls or boys she was playing with, something she couldn't see but needed to trust was the case. Father and Mother knew better.

"Sorry, guys, I have to go now. I'll catch up with you later, okay?" she said.

8) 11:20AM. Adriel.

IN THREE HUNDRED FEET, KEEP RIGHT TO MERGE INTO I-84 EAST, US-30 EAST TOWARD THE DALLES. Siri's voice sounded through the speakers. Adriel, Monica, and Kyle had departed for Baker City.

"Get in the right lane, sweet pea," Adriel said.

"I got it. Don't start bossing me around like Siri," said Monica. She sounded like she was joking, but she meant it.

"Okay, just don't drive like a Latina. We need to get there alive. If you're planning on driving like a lunatic, hand me a joint," Adriel said. She too meant it.

"Now we're talking!" said Kyle. "You got any, Monica? And sorry to tell you, but yes, you do drive like a lunatic. *And—*,"

Kyle said emphatically, "it would've been nice to keep the tradition alive from last year. That was a great birthday, wasn't it?"

Adriel rolled her eyes. She had a love-hate relationship with that birthday.

"Except for how embarrassing it was when we played Mimic," Adriel said, shaking her head.

"Don't be ridiculous. Nobody gave a fuck," Monica said.

On Adriel's seventeenth birthday a group of friends had organized a trip to Cannon Beach. Because it was November, the magnificent beach was deserted. The tide was high, but still, the vast extent of sand was such that from afar, sitting around a fire pit as red as the sky, they looked like a tiny, isolated star in the night sky.

They were a group of about ten people—Adriel, Monica, and Kyle included, along with some friends. Tired from playing touch football, they were eating sandwiches and drinking beer, and someone was playing tunes on an acoustic guitar. Somebody who worked at a beer bar had secured a keg of Pliny The Elder. They all drank the revered beer to the last drop—even Adriel, who secretly didn't like IPAs.

This wasn't her only secret. As they passed vegetable after vegetable around, eating without ever feeling satisfied, Leah's meatloaf suddenly tasted better than ever.

"Anybody want more beer?" asked Paul. "I brought a couple of six packs of Sticky Hands, if anybody wants any." They all worked in the restaurant business. But Paul was the only one who was a cook—at Navarre, to be specific.

He'd been responsible for getting Monica and Adriel to do the Portland Naked Ride, a tradition where everyone rides bicycles naked to protest oil dependence.

"YAYYYYYYY!!!!!" Adriel screamed, riding her bike down the first block, next to Paul, knowing inside that it was the last place she wanted to be. It was one thing to bike everywhere. That was necessary. But to bike without clothing!?

"No more beer for me," said Veronica, a bartender from Mississippi Pizza.

She took her backpack from behind her and removed a small plastic container with pot inside. Methodically, she began rolling joints, which she began passing along.

Adriel felt great. Things were happening for her. *To think I could have been married by now*, she thought. Olympia had been an amazing time. She loved Brandi and Hilario, but at seventeen, being on a beach with friends, smoking pot, drinking beer, and belonging was a dream birthday party. This was the best day of her life.

Two hours later, the fire in the sky had dissipated. Other than the fire pit, the full moon, so bright it looked like a desk lamp shining on Haystack Rock, was their only source of light. That, and the tiny lights traveling around the circle turning on and off like ships spotted on sonar—the burning tips of the joints they passed from hand to hand, while they sang Decemberists songs.

"Let's play some mimics before we head back to the house," Paul said with a smile stamped on his face that made him look like The Mask.

An irreverent, marijuana-induced game of laughing men versus laughing women began, and it lasted a long while. The rules were simple: A team assigned a movie or a famous character to one of the players from the opposite team, who had a minute and a half to get the rest of their team to guess the movie's name, by either acting out a scene or using signs, but without using words or signaling letters with fingers.

Adriel grimaced, remembering the game. "I'm not being ridiculous. Do you know how embarrassing that night was for me?" she insisted from the back seat.

"Monica's right, mate. Everybody understood," Kyle said, but Adriel wasn't so sure.

That night on the beach, as the marijuana's effects faded, somebody suggested they should all return to the house they'd rented. Before going up to the house, though, they decided to play the last round. It was Adriel's turn to perform. The men whispered together until they agreed on their assignment.

"We want to be nice to you, ladies. C'mon Adriel," said Peter, a tall, carrot-head guy with thick glasses. Adriel leaned in close, her ear next to his mouth, smiling.

"James Bond, Casino Royale," he whispered.

Adriel's expression changed. It was clear she was clueless. Adriel hadn't seen the movies all the other kids had.

"So you didn't know who James Bond was? So what?" Monica said looking at the rear-view mirror. "Look on the bright side: Didn't we have fun doing the James Bond marathon at home that next weekend?" she added.

None of them understood. Everybody wants to belong, but when you've been an outcast, belonging is more than crucial. For Adriel, belonging was perhaps the most important of her social needs, or at least she thought so.

In a subconscious impulse to repair the damage, she took her sweater off, and then the black T-shirt underneath, telling Kyle,

"You gotta see what Monica got me for my birthday, Kyle."

She wasn't wearing a bra. Kyle turned, and boy that he was, didn't notice the new tattoo at first. His eyes went straight to Adriel's breasts.

"Look down, you pig," Adriel said.

"What? I've seen those before, or you forgot Casa Diablo? I don't know, I thought you were getting new boobs."

He looked at the tattoo on the side of her belly, amused and slightly shocked.

"Well, that's nice, but tell him how you really feel about it," he said.

The tattoo was an elaborate, gothic blue heart that seem to be coming through an opening in her skin, drawn in red. Underneath, it said in black: *Fuck religion. Love is all that matters.*

They talked about the tattoo, where she got it, how much it cost, the artist, and many other details Kyle really had no interest in knowing. He wanted to know the story behind the tattoo, the same story Adriel told Monica at Tasty N'Sons.

She told him about going to Richard's office, what she saw on the computer monitor, her shock, how hard it was to keep a straight face when she went back upstairs, and how, day by day, she grew to realize the world her parents were building around her was a lie. Leaning between the front car seats, she went on.

"I'd be lying if I said I had an awakening that day. The truth is, the whole thing happened really slowly, you know? A lot went on and I guess I grew and you know, in the end, it was my mom who sealed the deal for me. Once I saw she'd give it all up for me and Jacob and after what she said that night in the kitchen—well, that was an awakening for me."

Adriel swallowed, an image of Leah giving her a slice of chocolate cake passing through her mind. She paused for a moment before resuming.

"On one hand there she was, pretending she was on board with everything. At times she was all smiles, especially when it was about Jacob or me. But she was always sick, like a zombie. I should have seen she was miserable. Now I see it, but when you're living in a shithole, you get used to the smell, and all you see is your mom and your dad. It all seems normal. Your dad yelling all the time, normal. Your mom doing every little thing around the house, normal. Agreeing with everything that comes out of that fucking idiot's mouth, normal!" Adriel's voice rose.

"And then, when I started to understand the whole thing was bullshit, I came to the conclusion that, fuck it, my mom was part of the lie. Until one day this shit happened and I saw it clear cut: my mom had her doubts. I could see she didn't believe all that bullshit anymore. She just didn't know anything else. And even better, I realized that to her, my brother and I were far more important than anything else, God and Asshole included."

Sitting in the back seat, Adriel looked back at her childhood once more, reliving the experience she related to Monica and Kyle.

"Adriel, your mom isn't feeling well. Can you please be sure to make a sandwich or something for my lunch tomorrow?" Richard had said.

"Guys, I'll never forget it. I was in bed, tucked in, listening to music and reading, I can't remember what. Oh, and the music part was a bitch because Asshole was the only one who could add songs. But of course, he didn't know how, so he wanted my mom to do it. He was more useless than a computer keyboard without the enter key. So all the music in my iPod was there because of this bureaucratic process where he had to approve it first, and then had my mom add it."

Adriel rolled her eyes and grinned. This gave Kyle a chance to intervene.

"Dude, so you were a pain in the ass with music that early?" Kyle said.

"Let me finish. So, he asks me to make the sandwich, and I go, like, can you make your own fucking sandwich for once?! You know? It pissed me off how he'd get my mom to clean his ass if he could. I'm not ready for him to make me his second maid so I pretend I don't hear him.

He asks me to take my earbuds off, but I just brush my hair and pull my blanket all the way up to my chin. So he sighs and says it again, louder.

Without even looking at him I say, 'I heard you.' And then I just keep reading, and of course that really pisses him off, so a big argument explodes. He wants to take the iPod from me. I mean, the guy's yelling like a maniac. His glasses are about to jump off his fat, fucking face. He's yelling at me, shaking his fist in the air like a dictator, but it's a tiny fist. His hands are tiny, so I laugh."

Kyle and Monica giggled a little. Empowered, Adriel swallowed again and took a deep breath, filling her lungs.

"So I keep asking 'Why?!' still under the covers, and frankly, enjoying the game a little. Then I realize I've gone too far. Asshole's as mad as a gorilla. I'm just there trying not to laugh at his tiny glasses falling off his red face. His eyes are popping when my mother comes into the room and asks, 'What's going on?' If our family was normal she'd be able to calm things down. But just her presence irritates Asshole even more. So he says something about regretting agreeing to the iPod and that it's useless garbage."

"Of course," said Monica.

"My mom tries to defend me, saying she only adds music he approves. She's clueless, though. She thinks it's all about the music. Then she asks me what's going on and I tell her, the usual—Asshole can't even make a sandwich by himself."

"You said that!?"

"Well, I didn't call him Asshole, of course, but yeah, I told her. And that's when the shit hits the fan. He takes his belt off and tells me to get off my bed and take my pajamas off. And

I'm in my panties and at fourteen, I'm not gonna let him see me like that."

Adriel didn't tell Monica and Kyle that what she saw in Richard's eyes made her tremble. That expression was why she wouldn't go to Baker City without Kyle there to protect her.

"I pull the blanket up to my chin and hold it as tightly as I can, but he's really angry. So he takes the end of the blanket and pulls really hard, and then gives me the typical bullshit, you know, the stuff he makes up and lives by 'cos it justifies him."

"What do you mean?" Kyle asked.

"A Christian life without fear is a life without God."

Remembering the scene made Adriel's whole body tense. She swallowed again, but her mouth was dry from talking so much. She resumed the story in the same entertaining way but the memory clearly bothered her.

Richard whipped his belt around the same way his father had before beating him, although he couldn't pinpoint that memory. Seeing the fear on his daughter's face gave him a perverse pleasure, not because he was a sadist but because he felt powerful. Adriel had shrunk like a human bonsai—the first time in ages he'd seen her afraid of him, respecting him.

"'A Christian life without fear is a life without God.' That's what Asshole said. Can you believe that shit?" But neither Monica nor Kyle were laughing now. They glanced at each other without speaking.

"So he tells me to get out of bed. But I just hold the blanket even tighter and hug my legs around my knees, as hard as I can. I don't even know if I said anything else. I was paralyzed. My mom's standing in the corner, like a mummy. If it wasn't for her crying and the desperate look on her face, I'd swear she was dead. But that was my mom ninety percent of the time.

So he goes, 'I said get the fuck out of the bed,' but I still don't move a hair.

That infuriates him even more. He swings for the first time, as hard as he can, but misses. Too useless even to beat his daughter. I remember I screamed as loud as I could and next thing I know, I feel this bony fucking bomb land on me.

It was my mom, dude. She jumped and landed on top of me with her body between my body and Asshole's belt, and said: *May the Lord forgive me for disobeying you, but you'll have to kill me before you hit her.* She was alive, dude, she was alive."

There was another longer moment of silence in the car. Monica and Kyle didn't know what to say, and Adriel was introspective. Familiar flashes began passing through her mind, until Monica interrupted them.

"Wow. I'm so sorry, baby," Monica said, wiping away a small tear.

"I'm not finished. Hold on—the best is coming," Adriel said.

"What do you mean?" Monica said.

"The motherfucker was setting me up to marry some guy behind my mom's back, right about that same time."

9) 3:37PM. Leah.

Leah saw herself saying goodbye to the girls at the lake, and then turning to her father, sensing their derision. She wondered what Nicole thought of her. She didn't dare ask. She wanted to believe Nicole didn't think she was weird.

All these childhood insecurities followed Leah to adulthood.

"Do you stay in touch with your sisters and brothers?" Nicole asked.

Still worrying about what Nicole would or wouldn't think, Leah didn't get the question at first. Nicole had to repeat it.

"Not really," Leah responded, glad that the subject had nothing to do with her.

"Joseph was killed in a car accident few years back, and Adam, Bethany, and Aaron got married. They have their life in Little Rock.

Don't forget: I married at fifteen, so I never got to be close to them. Especially not to Bethany and Aaron. They were just little kids when I left. I guess I was close to Mary because we shared a room for so long, but she got married four years after I did and moved somewhere near Atlanta. She had five children and as far as I can tell, she's happy. But I don't know."

"And David?" Nicole asked.

The question opened a can of worms. Suddenly, the only thing that kept Leah tethered to the present was the smell of coffee in the kitchen. The image of her childhood room surfaced, of being awake in bed in the middle of the night. It was a cold night and she was making room for her little brother to come and sleep next to her, his back against her belly. She covered him with the blanket and put her arm around his tiny body.

"Are you there, Leah?" said Nicole

"It was different with David," she said, sounding melancholic.

"David's long gone from my life, but, yes, he's in my thoughts all the time. I miss him so much, so much." Leah paused again.

"I have to tell you about my wedding, because when it comes to David, it's all about what he told me that day. You have to remember that in those days I was overwhelmed... David and I were inseparable, and I failed him."

Leah took a sip of coffee to wash down a big pill of guilt she suddenly felt in her throat. The coffee was too cool for her liking, but she drank the whole thing at once anyway. To add to her displeasure, it tasted burnt.

"The day before the wedding, all of us kids were outside, as we usually were on nice summer days. Our home was small, but we had a big back yard. I was sitting with Mary at one of those cast iron tables we had. We were playing cards next to the smoker and could smell the venison Father was smoking. I think he'd hunted the deer with the boys a few days before. I can't remember, but I loved the sweet, smoky smell.

So Joseph, Adam, and David are playing baseball, and the babies are jumping around under a sprinkler. And I'm watching them. It's really funny to see them jump, so clumsy. Just then, Adam calls me. They need an extra player. As always, I'm delighted when my big brother includes me in the game, even if it's to be the catcher, the one thing nobody else ever wants to be. So I jump off the chair to join them.

The ball hits me every time the hitter misses it. Let's be real: I don't know how to catch, but it's okay, it's just a tennis ball. I keep looking toward the kitchen, knowing that as soon as Mother realizes I'm with the boys, she'll call me away to keep me apart from them.

I can still hear her saying, *There's no reason for you to play with boys, Leah. They're disgusting. And unless you're married, boys and girls shouldn't be together.*

Sure enough, I haven't even been out there five minutes and Mother opens the door and tells me to come inside to make lemonade for everybody.

So I'm yelling, "Pleaaaase, Mother, ask Mary to do it!" But she ignores me. Her silence always means there's nothing else to discuss. She just turns around and tells me she's gonna lie down—that she has a migraine."

Defeated, Leah walked toward the kitchen. She didn't look at Mary, but somehow she was sure her sister was making fun of her, just like the girls at camp and so many others did.

In two days you'll be the one making lemonade, she thought. Strangely, part of her was excited about the wedding.

"I even started thinking about the honeymoon. So exciting—I'd only been in Little Rock all my life! We were gonna spend a few days in Portland before moving here to Baker City, and you know? Richard asked me to look at things I wanted to do in Portland, so I did, with Mother. We looked at the internet and I picked the places I wanted to visit, the Rose and the Japanese Gardens.

So I got the lemons from the basket on the kitchen counter and went to make lemonade, fantasizing about walking the aisle wearing the dress. I was so excited about the dress."

The white wedding dress that Mother rented to convince Leah about the wedding had a long, wide skirt decorated with small glass beads. The torso was fully covered, but to Leah's surprise, it was tight on her. For Leah, the highlight that absolutely sealed the deal was a really nice tiara.

"It's weird, Nicole, but I was excited and terrified at the same time. I had these exciting fantasies, but I also had this really negative feeling about the whole thing—of not wanting to get married. A real rollercoaster of feelings."

In the kitchen, making lemonade, Leah smiled triumphantly, picturing herself as the boss of her own house, lying on the sofa watching movies and eating Oreos with milk. And now Mary was making the lemonade and picking up their brothers' messes, something she didn't have to do anymore. She saw herself walking around a poor imaginary version of the Portland Japanese Garden, and then the Rose Garden.

She picked up a flower and raised it to her nose, but all she could smell was lemon. A new wave of thoughts arose, beginning with Richard as a younger version of her father.

She didn't like what she was seeing, but the reality was, she knew nothing about Richard. One consolation was that he'd taken her to the movies, to see shows she wouldn't otherwise see. She stayed with that thought for as long as she could until, exhausted of material, her mind drifted to an older version of herself, running around the kitchen with a T-shirt splashed with tomato sauce, hurrying to get the house ready before Richard's arrival. She saw herself putting her hands over her temples. A migraine, of course. What else? In seeing herself as Mother, she had to have a migraine.

Leah's thoughts grew darker with each lemon she sliced. Outside, David and Bethany were getting louder, bringing her sharply back to reality. More than ever, she didn't want to get married.

Feeling the urge to talk to her father and to plead with him to stop the wedding, she rushed to finish cutting the lemons. Her fingers were tiring and the lemons getting more slippery. She knew what the outcome would be, but she had to try talking to him.

"Ouch!" Leah screamed. A small cut, but the lemon juice made it sting. She rinsed her hand and found a Band-Aid in the first-aid kit and wound it around her finger. Then she went back to the kitchen to finish making the lemonade, but even with the Band-Aid her finger hurt. She could hear the little ones fighting now and, of course, Mother wasn't around. She was sleeping.

Telling the story made Leah thirsty. She reached for a glass of water and then sat back at the kitchen table.

"I called Mary to help me carry the plastic cups. We went outside and organized everything on the table where we'd been playing cards. We called everybody to come and get lemonade, although only the little kids came and they started fighting right away.

And David teased Bethany, saying 'You're not getting any lemonade, Bethany. Cheaters don't get lemonade.'

'I wasn't cheating! I was inside the water world. You just couldn't get me,' she said.

'No you weren't! You went too far so the water couldn't get you.'

'No, I didn't.'

'Yes you did.'

'No, I didn't.'"

"Nicole, they're yelling at each other, my finger hurts. All I can think is that I don't want to get married. But my head's spinning because I know I have to stop the kids from arguing. So finally I ask David if he cheated. He doesn't answer, but he's got this sneaky smile, you know? So I tell him straight out that he needs to say sorry to Bethany. He wants to say no. But I go out to the garage to talk to Father.

Maybe it sounds stupid, but you'll see, it'll make sense. Leaving David there without giving him a chance to speak might not sound important. But because of what happened later, well, this has stayed with me forever."

"So you didn't convince your father, right? Because you're married to Richard," Nicole said.

"That's right," Leah said looking introspective. Sitting at the kitchen table, frozen, she felt the same lightness as she had that day walking toward the garage.

It was one thing to go into the garage. But it was another to interrupt Father while he was working. Leah went through the laundry room and down two steps to the garage. Father didn't see her. The hand drill was too noisy.

Hesitating, she stood on the bottom step and read the words on a poster she'd seen a thousand times before.

I'll give up my guns when you pry them from my cold, dead hands, the poster said.

Her father loved woodworking. He was building a chair. Leah waited patiently until he stopped drilling, almost a minute.

"Father, I'm sorry to bother you, but I really need to talk. Is that okay?" she said.

There must have been something about the tone of her voice because he didn't react the way he usually did when someone interrupted him. Turning around still holding the drill in his hand, he asked,

"What is it, Leah?"

"Father, I'm not sure I want to get married. Could we wait another year?"

"It's already decided, Leah. But tell me, why are you having second thoughts?"

"I worry that I'm not going to like it."

"But Leah, it's not a matter of you liking it or not, although you'll learn to like it. As I said before, there's so much about married life to enjoy."

His eyes stayed focused on the wood he was treating with such patience and care. He didn't see her eyes growing red and watery, until tears began flowing down her face. Trembling a little, she finally broke down and coughed out the words she'd held back.

"Father, I'm not going to get married. I'm sorry. I know this disappoints you, but I can't do it."

At last, he stopped and set the drill on the worktable. Sighing, he looked down for a moment. She waited for his response, paralyzed except for her fingers, which moved rapidly as her hands approached each other below her belly. He turned his head and look at her, his eyes cold.

"Do you remember the time we took you out of swimming lessons, Leah? Do you remember what you made us do? Do you think that was fair to your Mother? That hurt us much worse more than it hurt you. You're getting married. Is that clear?"

She stayed where she was and lowered her head. She burst into tears, heaving with sobs, trying to wash away the doubts that haunted her.

"Yes, I understand," she said. And just then, he walked over and hugged her, kissing her forehead and stroking her hair.

"Listen, peanut, you know you're my big helper and that I'm proud of you. You're my favorite. You know that. Look, remember how excited you were yesterday trying that dress and all? And how you told me you really liked Richard and how much fun you had at the movies? It's going to be okay, trust me. It's going to be okay."

Nicole got up to reach for the bottle of water in her purse, but kept listening. Disturbed, she wanted to stop Leah and tell her what she really thought of it all. At the same time, the more she learned about the sickly world Leah was describing, the more fascinated she became.

"Once he said that, I knew there was nothing else for me to say. I guess I liked Richard. Like father said, he'd taken me to the movies. But I was fifteen, a very innocent fifteen."

"How did you get introduced to him?" Nicole asked.

Leah met Richard at a picnic their parents organized. She didn't remember much about this encounter, or the few other times she met him before the wedding, or even the exact moment they told her she'd marry him.

That afternoon at the picnic, Leah was sitting by herself on a bench, eating a hot dog. Her bright yellow hair contrasted sharply with her dark blue dress, which had a nice pattern of tiny red flowers.

She sat straight, with her knees together, a paper plate in her lap with the hot dog and chips. Her attention drifted between her meal and Mary, who didn't ask her if she could play with her volleyball. Leah was afraid Mary would lose it the same way she'd lost so many things.

At some point, from the corner of her eye, she noticed the guy she'd been introduced to earlier was approaching. He and his family had been sitting with Father and Mother all afternoon. Wondering why he was coming her way, she turned around to look behind her.

"Do you prefer ketchup or mustard, Leah?" Richard said with a smile.

Richard stood between her and the sun, seeming taller than he really was. She up at him, squinting a little.

"I don't know. Ketchup I guess," she said, looking down again. With a teenager's indifference to an unfamiliar adult, she leaned back to check on Mary before taking another bite of her hot dog.

"Would you like me to bring you something to drink?" he asked. She nodded.

Moments later, Richard came back with his own hot dog and two cans of Mountain Dew. He sat and turned to face her.

"I don't know why, but I hate mustard. Never liked it. Is that weird?" he asked.

She didn't answer. He tried again.

"Do you enjoy these picnics? They're boring, don't you think?"

"Yeah, I guess so. I like swimming better, but my parents won't let me. Mary! What are you doing? Don't leave my ball there!"

He watched her take the last bite of her hot dog. She raised her arm to wipe the ketchup off her mouth and then wiped her arm with the hem of her dress. He frowned in a funny way, staring at her spoiled dress. She thought that was funny, and smiled.

The rays of sunlight reflected in her hair as if a crystal goblet had crashed on it and the particles were trapped in the strands. It was such a shiny day and the sun lit her pale freckles.

He too smiled and looked at the gap between her front teeth. He'd never seen a smile like that. It was different.

"Does the space between your teeth bother you, Leah?" he said.

"Not really. Mary! My ball!"

Leah stopped to drink a little water before continuing her story, but the image of David snuggling beside her was vivid in her mind.

"I left the garage and switched off the light. I think it was a way to protect myself. I *hate* confrontation," she said to Nicole, emphatically.

"I didn't want to get into another nasty situation with my parents. So I got busy getting ready for the wedding, and here's the thing: I forgot about David. I forgot to tell him I was sorry about what happened earlier that day.

The day of the wedding, Richard came to our house. I could hear him talking to Father. I knew it was time to go, and I was just scared to death. I don't know why, but my reaction was to go to David. I guess I wanted to tell him I was sorry for not backing him up and truly, he was the only person I felt close to. Isn't that weird? He was a little guy, but I felt the safest around him.

So I went to his room and told him he could come over to mine. I could tell he was hurt. I made a lame excuse—I don't remember what—but he bought it. And I remember we got into bed with a few Lego pieces.

So we built this Lego house. And that's when, out of the blue, David asked me if I was going to visit him a lot after I got married."

David was sitting on the bed with his legs crossed. His hair was blond, cut like Moe's in the Three Stooges. He had his father's eyes and he was gazing at her with a child's directness. Leah wasn't afraid of that gaze. She loved him to death.

"Of course, Davie! I'll come often, I promise."

He lifted himself up, oblivious of the Lego masterpiece in front of him and hugged her tight, and then looking into her eyes, he said,

"Don't get married, Leah. Please, don't."

"Why?" I said.

"I don't like Richard."

In the kitchen, Leah sighed and slumped, hiding her face under her hands, like a turtle disappears under its shell.

"I'll never forget that moment. He'd been looking at the Lego the whole time. But when it came time to say that, he looked me straight in the eye the way only David could, you know?"

"And just as he says that and I try to tell him everything's gonna be okay, Mother comes in and says it's time to go to the wedding. I'll never forget it. As soon as she said it I felt a chill, but by then I had surrendered—mute, in shock and unable to argue anymore. It was David who protested and said we needed to finish the Lego house first."

Leah waited for Nicole to speak, but she didn't know what to say.

"She said to dress in normal clothes first—that I couldn't wear the wedding dress just yet. Funny enough, I wasn't excited about the wedding dress anymore. All I could think about was what David had just said. In fact, when I saw that nobody else was coming, I asked Mother if at least David could come. I really wanted to be with him, but she said there was no need. That there would be at a little gathering afterwards, at home."

Leah entered the tasteless monotony of the courtroom. It was warm, although she wouldn't have noticed if it wasn't for the court reporter, an overweight woman who typed incredibly fast, stopping only to mop her sweaty brow. Besides the typist, the court clerk, and the judge, few people were sitting on the benches: spectators, family members, people waiting their turn.

This is a little like church, Leah thought.

She sat with her parents. Richard joined them a minute later. His mother was with him.

At first, she was interested in watching the speedy typist. *Wow, so fast!* she thought. The ongoing case also fascinated her—a fight between a mother and her ex-husband, who wanted more parental time with his seven-year-old twins. But after ten minutes of listening, she spaced out.

When they called Leah's name, Mother tapped her shoulder and she got up, her anxiety awakened. She looked around but the room had emptied out, and only the court workers were there. Numbed by routine, they didn't look up at her. Clasping her hands together and looking down, she walked slowly to the witness table, carrying her anxiety with her.

"Imagine, I was expecting to walk down the aisle and instead, there I am in this completely foreign place, a courthouse with all these random people and this judge. I remember he was an old man with a soft voice. I was nervous, but his voice was soothing and frankly, even though I was trying to pay attention, I couldn't understand a thing he was saying and it got boring pretty quickly. In a way, what calmed me down was how boring the whole thing was and how little I understood. It was all over very quickly.

Then we came home. I was forced to stay in the living room with the adults. There were two other couples, too. Mother let me wear the dress for a while, but only indoors. The neighbors wouldn't understand why I had a wedding dress and all, she said. I felt trapped. I really wanted to go outside with David. Instead, I had to sit there with Richard and my parents and the other people. I remember their daughter. She was my age and had the reddest hair I've ever seen in my life, and she was getting married the week after. She was so excited she wouldn't leave me alone. Then everybody left and the next day Richard came to pick me up to go to Portland."

Leah paused at last. Near the end of the story she was getting more and more agitated. Nicole only interrupted her when she heard stifled crying coming over the phone. She wanted to comfort her.

"Well, maybe he knew, or maybe he was jealous, you know? You did a lot for your brothers and sisters, didn't you? You were like their second mother. And Leah, he was just a little boy."

"I know, I know." Leah said, still crying.

"But here's the thing, Nicole: David became the black sheep of the family. He left the house at seventeen and never spoke with my parents again. The funny thing is, he stayed in touch with me for a while, always telling me to go and live with him. But of course, he had no children. He couldn't understand. I mean, he'd have supported any decisions I made to leave Richard and all, but I never even told him I was unhappy. He just knew. I pretended everything was fine because of my children, and when finally needed support and help he wasn't around any longer and now, I've lost him. I lost him."

10) 11:45AM. Adriel.

When Adriel was thirteen, Richard started scouting for a suitable husband for her, knowing that it would take a while—a year at least, or two, he figured—to find the right person. Fifteen—almost the same age Leah was when he married her—seemed like a good age.

He loved his daughter; he didn't want just anybody to marry her. He wanted her to be happy—and as far as he was concerned, it was his duty to find her a good man so she wouldn't end up in an unhappy marriage, like he had. But he hadn't foreseen that it would take two years to finally find the right young man. And when he did, he orchestrated every step in architectural fashion. *I can't let this opportunity pass us by*, he thought. He knew the first step was the most important one: getting Adriel on his side.

He told her of his plans when they were coming back from Kentucky Fried Chicken. He'd waited a little over a week for the right moment. Until now, the opportunity to be alone with his daughter had eluded him. It wasn't just that his chances were limited to evenings and weekends, but that, most of the time, Adriel was doing things with her mother.

Usually, by the time Richard got home every evening, Adriel was helping Leah with dinner, or playing with Jacob in the kitchen or the living room, near Leah. After dinner, when they'd cleaned up, Leah and Adriel's routine was to play cards while Jacob watched The Crocodile Hunter. Only when Leah was putting Jacob to sleep did he have a little time to talk to Adriel.

Originally, he planned to talk to Adriel while Leah was occupied with Jacob. He knew that after the boy went to sleep, she'd be watching TV with Leah, and that once more, he'd miss the chance to be alone with her. As it turned out, he'd miscalculated how often Jacob wanted Daddy to read instead. Richard loved reading to him. It was the golden moment of the day.

Finally his chance arrived. Adriel bought a pair of shoes without noticing that one was torn, and she wanted to take them back to the store. It was one of those rare, busy Saturdays when they'd been out most of the day. There was little to eat at home, and anyway, even if the refrigerator had been packed with groceries, they had no time to cook.

They were all gathered in the kitchen, debating whether to go out for Chinese, get Kentucky Fried Chicken, or head out to the supermarket.

"Why don't we get Kentucky? I mean, the kids like it and so do you, Richard. It's the easiest. I'm not sure I have the energy to sit at a restaurant and deal with Jacob after all we did today," Leah said.

She sat at the kitchen table and bit into a pear she'd waited to ripen.

"My God, Leah. I guess we should decide soon before you eat one of the kids!" Richard said, seeing her devour the fruit like a dog.

Adriel looked to see what Richard was talking about. Leah was wiping away the pear juice that had dribbled down her chin. That made her laugh even more.

"Eat Jacob. He's even juicier, I'm sure!" she said.

Leah grinned with the stem between her teeth.

"Hey, Adriel, why don't you come with me? We can stop at Target to exchange your shoes on the way," Richard said.

"Don't forget to get corn on the cob too," Leah said.

Adriel never went anywhere with Richard and would rather have gone another time. But Richard cleverly insisted she should go along before it was too late. Target had a deadline for returns.

On the way to Target they didn't talk much. But once they got there, Richard got chatty, even encouraging Adriel to exchange the shoes for a more expensive pair that she liked. Then, on their way to KFC, he told her bad jokes and asked if she wanted to go to Baskin Robbins for ice cream too.

Strangely, and despite how much their relationship had deteriorated already, Adriel enjoyed her time with Richard. She laughed at his jokes when they reached KFC, she felt free to order more than she normally would. Somehow she knew she wasn't going to hear the usual sermon about overspending and eating with one's eyes, a talk she found ironic given her father's obesity.

On the way home, Adriel sat in the front seat holding the tub of fried chicken between her legs and the side dishes and ice cream between her feet. She would have preferred to hold her shoes, to look at them again; that thin red line traveling along the white welt was so cool—she loved them.

The warmth of the chicken against her thighs was comforting. She made a little game of pressing the warm container against one leg and then the other, automatically, because her mind was stuck on her new shoes. At least until Richard dropped the bomb.

The mushroom cloud formed. Adriel listening to Richard talking, making his case, trying to convince her of the many pros of marrying. She no longer felt the warmth of the chicken in her lap. Her excitement about the Very Berry Strawberry ice cream melted away. Her shoes were forgotten. Though she'd feared this would happen one day, all she could think was that it didn't seem real. How was she was going to walk away from this?

Without knowing exactly what Richard was saying, she finally interrupted him, pleading.

"But Father, I'm fourteen. I don't want to get married. Especially to somebody I don't even know!"

Richard kept his gaze on the road, driving calmly. The truck reached an intersection with a red light. He stopped and turned his head to Adriel, saying,

"You actually kind of know him. The Stegemanns are—"

"You're setting me up with Acne?!" Adriel interrupted him, startled, seeing in her imagination the greasy boy they'd pushed toward her on the sofa so many times. The container of chicken slid down her legs to the floor under the passenger seat.

Her eyes grew wide and she rushed to pick it up, lifting the plastic container and examining the carpet with anguish.

"It's clean, Father," she said, seeing the alarm in his eyes, and to draw his attention away from the floor she added,

"It's clean, I promise. Not a drop fell on the carpet."

They both sighed with relief.

"It isn't Christian Stegemann, it's his cousin from Kansas."

Adriel stared ahead, to nowhere, really. The warning signs she'd ignored over the years suddenly began playing in her mind. One memory surfaced in high resolution: Richard struggling with the chopsticks, digging into the chow mein at the Chinese restaurant and telling her all about the virtues of early, sacred marriage.

It didn't matter how many times she heard him talk about it, she never truly processed it. It had nothing to do with her, until now—this vague notion of an impending marriage.

"I know we've been having problems, Adriel." Hearing this, Adriel looked away, rolling her eyes. "I wanted to make it up to you in a big way. I thought you'd be excited about this. You know I love you very much and I only want the best for you. Think about it: You'll run your own house. You'll be the boss, eat when you want, listen to music that you want to hear whenever you want to. You won't have me bossing you around. You'll be free!" Richard spoke these last words as cheerfully as he could, but to Adriel, he sounded like a mattress salesman.

She thought of Leah, always sleeping on the sofa, tired. Not tired of physical demand, but tired of life, taking care of everything in the house, doing her best to keep her husband happy, or at least prevent his angry outbursts. She thought of Leah's air of contentment. She thought of her solitude, and her constant headaches. And she concluded that her mother was a miserable, tortured soul who, like a caged calf awaiting slaughter, was content with her existence because she simply knew nothing better.

She turned toward him, expressionless, and looking him straight in the eye, said,

"Do you mean like Mother?"

The light turned green. He evaded her eyes and the question. Sounding less like a salesman and more like the person Adriel was familiar with, he said,

"This young man is fully devoted to God, Adriel. This is a once-in-a-lifetime opportunity. Frankly, you wouldn't be rejecting this young man or me. You'd be rejecting God."

Doubt swept over Adriel. Richard noticed, and before she gave him an answer, he said,

"I can't say for sure, but I think your mother will be disappointed big time if you don't accept."

Could mom be involved in this? she wondered. She searched her memory of recent events but found no answer before Richard interrupted her thoughts one more time.

"Adriel, this is a secret between you and me, okay? I want this to be a surprise for your mother. We'll let her know soon. Okay?" This time he looked at her and then back to the road. He was waiting for her answer.

Adriel was only fourteen, but a perceptive fourteen. There was something about his sudden demeanor. She looked into his eyes and knew right then what she needed to say.

"Okay, Father, I trust your opinion. I'll wait to surprise Mother when you tell me to." She forced a smile.

That night, she took her journal from its hiding place under the mattress and began drawing. The journal wasn't a diary in the old-fashioned sense of the word. It contained no "Dear Diary" this or "Dear Diary" that. It was a plain notebook filled with more drawings and scribbles than words. But every now and then, before she went to bed, Adriel wrote down whatever was in her heart. This was a habit Leah had passed to her.

She drew a small tree with a big cat on one of the branches. The cat was disproportionally bigger than the tree and its tail hung below the branch and formed part of the letter "f" to begin a sentence that said: Father has finally asked me what I knew he would ask one day. I'll kill myself before I become my Mother, and I love Mother with all my heart.

"Wait! He set you up to be married? How old were you?" Kyle asked, surprised to hear what Adriel had just told him and Monica in the car.

"Almost fifteen," Adriel said.

"Is that legal?!" Kyle asked.

"Don't be silly, Kyle. It doesn't matter," Adriel said.

They drove over a stretch of road pocked by the passage of many snow tires. The little Honda hatchback began vibrating like a washer in spinning mode.

All was silent except for the rumbling of tires bouncing over the asphalt and the orchestra of sounds produced by the shaking of loose car parts.

Adriel was done telling her story, at least for now. She waited for Monica or Kyle to say something, but since they didn't—at least not right away—she leaned back to rest a little.

Monica knew about Richard setting Adriel up, although Adriel had kept the details to herself. That Monica had never asked about those details had to do with the natural discretion she'd learned from her mother.

Kyle, on the other hand, had no problem digging into a past that had dragged him on this long trip to Baker City. But shocked by the idea of a father setting his daughter up like that, he shuffled scenarios in his head, trying to make sense of it all.

"So you know, Kyle, I didn't say anything, for, um, three days. I'm not sure. I was so scared and so confused. It's funny because I didn't see the pattern until then. I mean, Asshole was so crafty." She hesitated, then said,

"He *is*, I mean." She took a deep breath and leaned back. "Honestly? I hope the motherfucker is a 'was.' But he's much older than my mom and my grandparents do the same shit. So you know? I figured it all out."

"I get it. I get it. So you escaped, what, the next day?" Kyle asked.

Adriel evaded this question and kept going with whatever her memory prompted her to say.

"I'm eating a bowl of cereal in the kitchen and Mom shows up. Asshole's already left for work. So I'm sitting there and she just sits next to me and puts the diary on the table."

Adriel continued, her voice cracking. Neither Monica nor Kyle interrupted her. After several false starts, she said,

"I figure she's coming to reprimand me because I kicked Jacob out of the kitchen for chewing with his mouth open. But it's not that. She looks at my face and maybe I look pissed at her for getting into my things, or maybe I look surprised. And she says something like, you know, Adi—" Adriel paused to explain.

"She called me Adi because that's what my little brother called me."

A moment of silence—the memory of little Jacob was always with her. He was so sweet and wanted so badly to please her, to be accepted. She wished she hadn't been so bitchy back then, so hard on him—far beyond the usual sibling rivalry.

She'd divided their room using craft paper tape into two sections and prohibited his "stinky, moronic ass" from crossing over to her side. She held his beloved toy cars perenially hostage, and swore to him they'd disappear if he ever told their parents that the tape wasn't a cool highway where he could play with his cars, like she'd made them believe.

As a backup, there was always Mona:

"Jacob, clean up the room right now or I'll call Mona!" she'd say.

"No, I won't!" he'd answer back. And she'd start turning in clockwise circles. First turn: barely frowning. Second turn: grimacing. Third turn: raising her claws like she'd seen a vampire do in an old, black-and-white Dracula movie.

"Stop! Stop, Adriel! Please stop!!!" he'd beg, knowing that after turn four there was no way back. She'd be Mona, the horrible witch he'd never seen who lived inside her and who'd eaten other children in the neighborhood.

"Fuck! I miss my brother. I miss my mom. That piece of shit forced me to leave them behind!" she yelled, then exhaled sharply, blowing out whatever was left of her anger.

"You want some water?" Kyle asked awkwardly, and that made Adriel laugh and go back to storytelling.

"Anyway, she goes and says, you know, Adi, don't get upset with me. I'm your mother. You know, mothers know it all. I'm gonna get to the point—plain and simple: Don't get married sweetheart. Just don't."

As she told the story, Adriel began sobbing softly.

"Adriel, you don't have to tell us more if you don't want to," Monica said, and Adriel ignored her.

"So fuck, I see her face and she's like fucking desperate, you know? I can see it. I can feel it. I mean, I hold her hand and she's shaking so hard I can't stop her, and so I start crying and saying I really don't want to get married, but that I can't kill myself either. So I'm gonna try to escape." Adriel talked without pausing to breathe, trying to stop her voice from trembling and holding back tears.

"'Mother, is it truly a sin? Will I go to hell if I disobey him?' I ask her. And man, I'll never forget the look on her face. And this is what I was trying to tell you. I mean, you were asking me about religion and the tattoo and all, and well," Adriel mumbled.

"She tells me that whatever she is, she is, and whatever she's done, she's done, but that I'm me and that I need to be happy."

Adriel stopped then, her tears dried, her voice coming in dry sobs.

"So it happened. You left?" Kyle asked, but for the second time Adriel didn't answer.

Monica, her sleeve drenched with tears, almost missed her turn. She took a sharp right to get off the road, cutting off the car behind them. The driver swerved to avoid them, leaning heavily on the horn.

The traffic light turned red before Monica reached the intersection. The woman honked again and rolled her window down to yell at Monica, but Monica rolled hers down to interrupt.

"Leave me alone, lady. Just leave me alone."

The woman didn't notice the tears at first and kept yelling, but a moment later Adriel pushed Monica's seat forward and leaned all the way out the window to scream:

"FUCK OFF, BITCH. FUCK OFF!!!"

"Adriel, what are you doing? Relax, relax. She was right, okay?"

Leaning back in her seat and with her voice cracking, Adriel said,

"Mark my words, guys: I'll never, ever cry in front of that miserable piece of shit. He'll never, ever see me cry. Never."

11) 3:47PM. Leah.

Weary of his father's demands and the absurdity of the whole situation—of his family's religious beliefs—David left home for good at seventeen. He wanted to go to Chicago. But when he realized he wouldn't be able to afford to live in the city, he settled for Houston, where he got a job as a dishwasher at a popular breakfast spot.

He wouldn't contact his parents or siblings again. But a year or so after his departure, he began calling Leah. The first time he called her, Adriel was just seven and Jacob was two. Leah and Richard were already having marital problems, although Leah didn't tell him what they were.

A solitary man with a passion for running competitively, David grew up to be quite the athlete, although this wasn't how Nicole imagined him while Leah vented about her brother. She could have added detailed features to the overweight young man she was picturing in her mind if it wasn't for a stomach ache that exploded all of the sudden, something she believed was due to stress. Nicole was one of those people who connect illness with emotions and spiritual being. Needing a break, she got up to get water from the office water dispenser.

Holding the phone in one hand she tried to get a paper cup out of the tower over the water bottle—mission impossible. The tower collapsed, leaving her with five cups all stuck together. She watched the rest tumble to the floor. Ignoring the accident, she kept listening to Leah, filled a cup and drank the water, and returned to her desk.

And Leah? Leah was completely immersed in the conversation. The only thought in her mind was the sound of David's voice.

"I don't like Richard," David had said.

A memory within a memory; this is what happened to Leah just then. She remembered being curled at the edge of the bed at the hotel in Portland, thinking about what had happened with David the previous day. She knew he was right, and knew that it didn't matter because there was nothing she could have done to escape the marriage. The hotel room was ice cold. She clutched the blanket the way a rock climber holds the edge of a precipice. Though her feet were sweating, she was cold. The smell of old carpet that had bothered her at first was still there, but she no longer noticed it. Between her legs where she felt sticky there was a burning sensation. Deep in her belly, a pain she couldn't explain tormented her, a reminder of what had happened just an hour before.

She never thought about calling home. She didn't think about running back to her mother's arms. For a moment, she wondered where all those butterflies were—the ones she felt the day Daniel kissed her at the pool. But it all seemed so long ago. She let the thought go. The profound desire to be with her little brother held her mind hostage. And now, back in the kitchen, talking to Nicole in a similar state of mind, she put a hand on her abdomen where she felt the same indescribable pain she'd tried, hopelessly, to describe to her mother in an email, weeks after the first night of her honeymoon.

Clarice Jackson
Re: Something urgent to tell you
To: Leah Jackson

Don't talk to me about pain. I gave birth to seven children. Do you think your body's special and has special needs? God created you and He expects you to please your husband.

----Original Message----
From: helloleahjackson1@yahoo.com
To: jacksoncla5239@comcast.net
Cc:
Sent: 1997-06-30 9:24:01 AM
Subject: Re: Something urgent to tell you

But Mother, it's SO PAINFUL. I'm afraid I'm getting hurt for real down there.

On Jun 30, at 9:22 AM, jacksoncla5239@comcast.net wrote:
Dear Leah,

I understand. I had the same pain. But you'll see. In no time you'll get used to it and start liking it too. Trust me. I'll call later this weekend and we can chat about it. There are ways to prepare better for the occasion. You don't need to feel ashamed.

If I didn't tell you about it before it's because you were too young. It's not a subject for children. This is between married women.

Don't forget, it's your duty to fulfill his sexual needs, a woman has no power over her own body: her man does.

Father is doing well, but the doctor told him he needs to lose weight. He's not happy about that, but he's certainly looking forward to our first grandchild.

Kisses,
Mother.

From: "Leah Jackson" <helloleahjackson1@yahoo.com>
To: "Clarice Jackson" <jacksoncla5239@comcast.net>
Sent: Monday, June 29, 1997 10:37:57 PM
Subject: Something urgent to tell you

Dear Mother,

I hope you and Father are okay. I miss you both.

I didn't write about this before because I was ashamed. I'm not sure if what's happening is right or not, but I can definitely tell something's wrong, and I don't know what to do.

The first night of the honeymoon, Richard told me how we needed to have sex to procreate.

He makes me do weird things, like kissing him everywhere, and I mean it. It's gross, but I play along. When he goes inside me it hurts a lot. I didn't know it was going to be like this.

It really hurts down there. Is it normal to have so much pain?

Mother, is there a way I can stop this for a while?

Love,

Leah.

Time went on. The phone calls between David and Leah became farther and farther apart. He'd climbed the ladder in the restaurant business, from washing plates at a breakfast spot to waiting on tables by the time he was twenty-two. He'd achieved a certain stability and wanted Leah to move in with him. Leah didn't have to tell him how miserable she was; he knew it.

"Once, I almost told David everything but I changed my mind. He wanted me to move in with him. He didn't like Richard. Of course, he also rejected God and religion, so we always argued a little about that. Anyhow, he did it again: he said he didn't like how things were going for me and urged me to move. Of course, what did he know about having kids?"

Leah sounded frustrated. More than anything, she needed somebody to tell her that he did know, that David would probably grow to understand her situation.

"I'll never forget it because it was just a few days after Richard's birthday. If you ask me, it was the day I finally accepted my marriage was over. David was so right! And then I never heard from him again. The whole thing is a bit blurry. I was sick for some time. I think I told you this, right? He never called me again and I lost his phone number on my phone. Nobody knows where he is. But he was always so right."

The tragic memory of Richard's birthday replayed inside Leah's head. She clenched her fist in anger as she related the story to Nicole.

"We were celebrating his birthday with Charles McCracken and his wife Eleanor. Charles has been working with Richard forever, but back then, we were getting to know him and his wife. We rarely did much together, but Richard and Charles had gotten a hefty commission after insuring this hazelnut farm and we went bowling at Elk Horns Lanes to celebrate. Then it turned out Charles had some porterhouses at home, and we agreed to have them over and grill the steaks here. It was supposed to be a treat. We left the kids with Mrs. Fuiten, something we never did over a weekend, so we had the house to ourselves."

Leah paused.

Their back yard was square and quite small. Well-trimmed weeds did a decent job pretending to be grass, except for certain patches where grass refused to grow. A small, religious garden statue, whose identity was difficult to discern, was set in one corner of the garden, next to a nice rosebush. In the other corner, the steaks were cooking on a small gas grill, while in the center of the garden, one of those plastic baby pools remained as proof that small children had lived in that house.

"We were in our garden playing monopoly. I was winning big time and Richard was losing big time too! He landed on my properties over and over and over. I remember I was wearing this short dress…"

Leah seldom wore dresses above her knees, but it looked quite nice on her, something Eleanor McCracken made sure to voice the moment Leah and Richard opened the door. She was a tall, loud woman with heavy brown hair, who refused to ever wear make up. "A smile's better than any make up," she always said.

"So Richard landed on one of my properties again and was forced to give up hotels and all. In fact, when it was my turn, I wanted to buy more hotels because I knew he'd land there again. But Richard wasn't gonna let me buy them. So Charles, who was the bank, intervened and said I could do it and complimented me, saying my dress gave me luck."

Leah had noticed Charles's eyes slyly checking her out all evening, passing over her chest as if it was the Monopoly GO. Richard couldn't see his friend because he was sitting next to him, but he certainly caught his wife's blushing and the way she smiled at Charles.

They were sitting at a picnic table. Richard was proud to have got it for nearly nothing at a garage sale. The wood wasn't in great shape because of the constant exposure to rain, but both Richard and Leah liked the National Park character the table gave their humble backyard.

Leah rolled the dice and made her move. Nothing exciting happened. She handed them to Richard; his token was eight steps from Park Place—and that belonged to Leah. He rolled a double four. His eyes turned as red as Leah's dress.

"So he landed on my most expensive property. I was so excited, I was yelling and celebrating. Richard was out, so

Eleanor, who was getting another diet Pepsi from the cooler, told him to go ahead and take care of the steaks. He was the one grilling them. I reminded him I didn't want mine bloody, and Charles made fun of Richard, saying his blood was all over the monopoly board."

Everyone laughed at Richard's expense. He faked a smile before walking to the grill to take out the corn. Leah watched him walking away in silence. She tensed her facial muscles and reactively drank the full glass of Dr. Pepper at her side.

"Give me your glass, Leah. I'll refill it. I guess I have to be nice to you in case I land on your real estate empire!" Eleanor said and winked, brushing away Leah's tension.

"Leah, let's quit playing. I need you to go get the plates and potato salad. Actually, just bring everything," Richard said.

He turned his back on the group, moving the steaks randomly and without purpose.

"But Richard, you just put the steaks on, and everybody wants them well done. It'll be a while," Leah said.

"C'mon Leah, bring it all out here, please," He turned toward her, forcing the "please" for the McCrackens. She understood and began to get up.

"Don't be silly, Leah, sit down. You're right, it'll be a while. We can help you bring it all out a bit later," said Charles.

Leah hesitated.

"I want to go and check on the potatoes anyway. It's okay," she said, looking at Richard. *I want to do what you're asking me to,* said her eyes.

"Baked potatoes take a while. They're fine! C'mon Richard, you're just mad because Leah's kicking butt!" Eleanor said.

Richard forced another laugh; his eyes still on Leah. But his smile changed to surprise and then to undiscerning anger when Leah, trapped by Eleanor's energy, said,

"Don't worry Richard. I'll win before you even turn those steaks. Just make sure there's no blood on mine."

"The McCrackens left around ten. I went into the kitchen to clean up while Richard was cleaning the grill. I could see him from the kitchen window. I sensed something was wrong even before Eleanor and Charles left. But when I saw the way he closed the grill and put the cover down, I knew he was really mad."

In the kitchen, Leah could feel the tension building like a balloon—the thin air in the room, the silence, and Richard's deep breathing, which she could hear a mile away. She heard him locking the back door and then heard his footsteps coming closer.

The hardest thing for Leah was not knowing who she'd have to deal with the next time around. She certainly preferred Dr. Jekyll—the man who'd brought her flowers that same morning as a token of appreciation for making bread and a chocolate cake for his friends. The same man who, every now and then, took her out to her favorite Italian restaurant. And certainly the same guy who so many times insisted on her seeing a physician.

"Leah, please, order the banana split if that's what you want. Don't be silly. You deserve it!" Richard had said the afternoon he took her and the children to spend the day in Hood River, a picturesque town by the Columbia River Gorge.

She looked at him and gestured, as if to say, "It's too much." But his eyes hushed her anxiety. He extended a hand to touch her shoulder, again urging her to choose what she liked.

Dr. Jekyll always came to her unpredictably, in fleeting glimpses, but often enough that sometimes it was hard to predict which of Richard's personas she would face. Living with this tension wasn't pleasant. It would have been so much easier if Jekyll were around more often. *Gosh!* she thought. *In a way, it would even be easier to know Hyde was here all the time. At least I'd know what to expect.* And this was exactly who she was worried was about to show up.

Nervously, she started moving things around with no particular order or reason.

"Richard, what would you like me to make for dinner tomorrow? I was going to make pasta, but I could take these pork chops out too," she said.

He didn't respond. She felt him coming toward her.

"Richard, what do p—" She turned in his direction but before she could finish he slapped her so hard that she fell sideways on the floor.

She heard a loud ringing in her ear and her whole body was suddenly cold and sweaty. Confused, she raised herself on her hands and knees. Her sight was slightly blurry, but she took a deep breath and it cleared—all but the ringing ear. She looked at Richard. He was standing over her looking down as if he'd just killed a cockroach.

"Don't you *ever* challenge my authority—especially in front of my friends. If I tell you to go get something, you go and get it, bitch."

"I thought they were *our* friends, Richard," she said, swallowing her tears.

"Shut up! And next time you ridicule me, I swear to God I'll make you pay for it."

Curled up in the corner of the kitchen, hiding her face between her legs, Leah began sobbing, and then her sobs turned to wails.

"It was just a game, Richard. I was happy, we were having fun like a real couple."

Richard didn't answer. This encouraged Leah to look up and meet his eyes.

"Why did you hit me, Richard? Why?"

He saw the redness in her face; he knew he'd gone too far. To liberate the tension that had suddenly invaded him, he began pacing nervously. Then he stopped to pour himself a glass of water and drank it in one gulp. Slowly, he approached her.

"I'm so sorry, Leah. Oh my Lord, I'm so sorry, you know I didn't mean this."

As soon as he touched her shoulder, she moved away in terror, making a strange sound.

"C'mon Leah, it wasn't that bad. You fell way harder than you should have; I barely touched you. Please forgive me, I didn't mean it, please!" Richard stuttered, pressing his hands together in front of his chest, as if he was praying.

She let him see her. Her cheek was as red as an apple. Her face, wet with tears, remained still. She didn't talk.

"I'm so sorry, Leah. You know I didn't mean it, but what you did wasn't right and I lost control. Look, let's go to the movies tomorrow, okay? So we can forget all this, but please, don't do what you did again. If you hadn't done it, we wouldn't be here, would we?" Richard said, looking at her in anguish.

"I'm sorry," she said.

He forged a smile.

"No, I am sorry, Leah. I am."

"Are you serious about the movies? That would be nice," Leah said.

"Of course, of course."

He helped her get up and sat her in a kitchen chair, then brought one of those gel bags to ice injuries and held it against her cheekbone.

"Ouch!" she said and moved away from the ice quickly.

"C'mon, let me do this, you need this ice. Here, hold it yourself," he said.

Once more he put the ice over the injured area and held her hand, placing it over the gel bag so she could hold it.

"I love you, Leah, you know that. I'd never hurt you," he said.

They hugged.

Nicole had stayed silent through the whole, long story, but knowing her legal duty, she asked,

"Is he still hitting you, Leah?"

"Oh, no, no, no, Nicole, it was just this one time. In fact, it was so upsetting, that, well, I wanted to call David. I dialed his number, but hung up because I realized I was being an idiot."

Nicole wasn't interested in David any longer; she had in fact forgotten the connection between the story and him.

"Are you sure he never hit you again, Leah?"

"Yeah, no, Richard isn't that type, Nicole. And, you know, in a way, I felt sorry for him. He grew up with very strict parents who beat him with a vacuum hose for just about anything. And he hated his job. The truth is, by then he wasn't even happy at home. I couldn't give him what he wanted, no matter how much we tried."

"What do you mean? What is it you couldn't give him?" Nicole asked.

Leah was quiet for a long moment. She still didn't feel ready to discuss sex with Nicole.

"C'mon Leah, I'm waiting. You can do all that later." Richard said later that same night, after they'd made peace. He lay in bed reading a copy of Guns & Ammo Magazine.

She knew what was coming next and wasn't looking forward to it. But instead of focusing on that, she began to make a mental list of what she needed to do the next day and how she was going to prepare the pork chops she'd left out. *I'll use Old Bay Salt and thyme. That would be nice. And maybe some mashed potatoes and gravy,* she thought, when she heard Richard again.

"Leah, darling, c'mon. I'm waiting for you."

She wanted to please him. After going to the bathroom, she did as she had learned over the years. She lay in silence and relaxed her muscles as much as she could. Knowing what was coming, she had put lubricant inside her, as the doctor once suggested. She closed her eyes. He kissed her. It wasn't a tender kiss, or a reconciliatory kiss. This was a suffocating invasion of her airway. Yet this was all she knew, all she'd ever experienced. His breathing in her ear, his sweaty belly on hers, and the tearing inside her, all of it she had accepted as good.

Later in the middle of the night, a pulsating, cramping pain aroused her. She was lying in a pool of blood. In the midst of her panic, she woke Richard, who, confused and half asleep, wasn't of much help other than to call the doctor's office to leave a message and to give her a painkiller.

"I really can't, Nicole, I can't do it. I can't have sex with him." Leah finally broke the silence.

"Of course not. You aren't emotionally prepared to have sex with that man, Leah." Nicole said.

"It's not that. I mean, physically, I can't do it."

As Leah said this, she recalled how many times Richard had suggested that she see a doctor. Ashamed, she wouldn't agree. There was the incontinence, the recurrent uterine bleeding and the partially prolapsed uterus. She knew a doctor could help, but the same feeling of being different she had experienced so many times, especially around other women, was stronger than her symptoms, and her symptoms kept Richard away from her.

"What do you mean, Leah?"

"After all the miscarriages, how do I say it? I have a lot of injuries inside, you understand? The first time I was just fifteen. I didn't even know I was pregnant until it was too late. Adam was born when I was sixteen and he was a huge baby, so I never recovered from that. I suffered from serious incontinence for a while. It's embarrassing, but the truth is I still have some trouble with that. Then I had more miscarriages. Oh Lord, just talking about it brings that image."

"Leah, we don't have to talk about this if you don't feel like it."

Leah ignored Nicole.

"I probably should be used to miscarriages by now, but a stillborn was too much to handle. Afterward, all I could see for a long time was that frozen, bluish, cold little body with my eyes, the same dark blue eyes staring at me." She began sobbing, but kept going,

"When Jacob was born, I almost bled to death during the delivery, or at least I thought so. It was a C-section. The doctors said they couldn't do it otherwise, and I was glad because I was terrified the baby would be stillborn. But the baby was fine. My precious Jacob!"

Nicole listened, processing what she was hearing. As she typed a note, she thought about what to say next, but Leah interrupted her thoughts.

"After Jacob was born, the doctor said we needed to stop. He wanted to do surgery or give me killing pills, you know?"

"Killing pills?"

"You know, those pills that make it so you can't have babies. Of course, I wasn't going to take those, and Richard— Richard really wanted more children and so did my parents. They all still do." Her voice was trembling and getting louder.

Her voice rose to a high-pitched wail and she coughed as though her feelings were unwelcome, like a virus.

Embarrassed, she quieted down and rushed to excuse herself.

"I'm so sorry, Nicole. I got a little excited. As I said, I'm not feeling well today. I haven't been sleeping well, you know? Here I am hoping Adi's gonna show up and she isn't, but I'm so thankful I can talk to you. It does me good, Nicole. I just need to sleep better. Dreaming of that red door closing on me, it's just too much, every night, all night. It's hard on weekends with Richard here. I'm glad it's Monday."

It was the second time Leah mentioned dreaming of the red door, but Leah's lack of awareness of time was what drew Nicole's attention.

"But Leah, today's Friday, not Monday."

"Friday? Are you sure?" Leah looked at the clock on the microwave to see if it showed the day of the week. It didn't, but it showed the time: 3:47PM. *Time to put the chicken in,* Leah thought.

"Yes, I'm sure," Nicole said.

Leah got up and turned the oven on at four hundred and twenty degrees.

12) 12:20PM. Adriel.

Other than Kyle's humming along to the music of Arcade Fire, there was complete silence inside the car. Moments before, they'd entered highway 84E, a long and boring stretch of road that goes straight from Portland to Baker City.

It was cloudy and grey. Earlier, at sunrise, the rain had finally stopped after coming down for five days straight in the form of a gentle drizzle that Portlanders grow oblivious to. In the streets, the use of umbrellas separates long-term residents from tourists and those new to the city.

Monica broke the silence. "If we don't stop we should be there at three thirty or so." But neither Kyle nor Adriel said a thing.

Adriel was resting in the corner of the back seat, looking out the window, although her mind was on Brandi. *She hasn't called. How strange*, she kept thinking. The silence in the car felt even more isolating without the squeaky, drunken-macaw voice of Brandi. There was something strange about her not being there, but Adriel preferred it that way.

What's that they say? That we don't know what we have till it's gone? This is what happened to Adriel. During the last year they lived together, Adriel couldn't have imagined ever missing their endless arguments. But it took Brandi's departure for Mexico for her to realize what Brandi truly meant to her.

Beginning the day after that rainy morning Brandi said goodbye in Portland, they'd spoken every evening, and what's more, on Adriel's seventeenth birthday, Brandi had called four times. No wonder, now it was past noon with no news from Brandi, Adriel had begun to feel that little apple of melancholy caught in her throat, painful at every swallow, reminding her of the guilt she felt. She knew she could have been so much nicer to Brandi.

Looking intermittently out the window and at her phone—checking WhatsApp for a message from Brandi— Adriel began to revisit that night when Hilario showed up with the big news about the move.

Shortly after Hilario and Brandi married in the winter of 2014, almost six months after meeting at work, he became an American citizen and began seeing new opportunities coming from Walmart. As the most experienced worker in his department, he knew the complexities of the storage unit in and out.

"You're not gonna believe the news!!!" he told Brandi one day in the parking lot at work.

The company had offered him a managerial position at their central storage department in Mexico City. The salary wasn't great by American standards, but it was nearly double the misery he was making in Olympia. Knowing how much lower the standard of living was in Mexico, Hilario hurried to accept, not without negotiating a position for Brandi in the same store he was going to be at, working in the ordering merchandise department where they needed an English-speaking person.

Brandi got really excited. From the moment she was introduced to it in Olympia, her love for Mexican culture had grown week by week, and was sealed right when she knew Hilario was the man she'd been looking for since her days in Pendleton and Baker City.

With an idealized vision of moving abroad and leaving behind a hard life, she agreed to the proposal instantaneously, without much forethought, until in the middle of the exciting conversation, a certain face popped up in her mind, putting the brakes on her enthusiasm.

"What about Adriel?" she said to Hilario.

They went back and forth, trying to find a solution, the conversation extending to dinner, where, together with Adriel, they looked at ways to make it all work.

Brandi was reheating some amazing shrimp a la diabla Hilario had prepared over the weekend. The wall behind the stove had an opening that communicated to the small dining room where Adriel and Hilario were sitting.

The warm steam coming from the pot was rising into Brandi's face. Dozing for a moment, she was lost in thought. Her biggest concern was Adriel. Every scenario she ran through her mind involved Adriel coming to Mexico because the memory of her promise to Leah kept returning to her.

"I promise you, Leah, I'll take care of your kiddo like she's mine, girl. Don't you worry about that," she had said.

Brandi only broke one promise to Leah; she'd tried to contact her. They had agreed it was too dangerous to connect, but Brandi thought she could probably reach her friend at work. Yet, when she called, they told her that one day, Leah just never returned to work—precisely the day of the escape—and that later they received a call saying she wasn't coming back.

Stirring the shrimp, she listened to Hilario talk. It wasn't clear to her that he intended to include Adriel. *Actually*, she thought, it looks like *he's giving her the option to stay on her own*!

"One thing is for sure: we aren't going without you, Adriel. That's not optional, honey. You have to come," she said, looking at Adriel and Hilario through the wall opening.

They looked at each other. An uncomfortable silence filled the room.

"What do you think, Adriel? This could be great, don't you agree?" she insisted.

My God, is she serious? Adriel is a woman, for God's sake! Hilario thought, but smiled at his wife and at Adriel.

He'd taken for granted they would leave on their own. For a man who'd had a very short childhood, who at fourteen had crossed the border by foot with strangers and seen death coming at them in many forms, leaving a sixteen-year-old on her own wasn't the end of the world.

"That's gonna be difficult, mi amor. Adriel doesn't have a passport," he said.

Walking toward them to bring the hot pot, which she held with a towel in each hand, gave her time to think over her answer. She hadn't thought about the passport.

"So what, Alejandro can find one. He said he could produce any document, remember?"

Hilario got up to bring a soda for Adriel and a couple of beers. He shook his head and wagged his index finger. *You got to be kidding me!* he thought.

"It's one thing to fool a school principal with a fake I.D. It's another to go through airport security," he said, coming back with the beverages.

"But we don't have to fly! We can drive there, can't we?" Brandi kept trying.

She too had gone back to the kitchen to bring the tortillas.

They kept arguing, Brandi throwing out absurdity after absurdity, while Hilario, at the edge of exasperation, beat each of her attempts with the stick of brutal reality.

Meanwhile, Adriel was contemplating the idea in silence. Like Brandi, she was excited at first.

Mexico!—It sounded fun, but the more she listened to Hilario, and the more she thought about turning eighteen and wanting to reunite with Leah and Jacob, the more she realized there was no way she would leave. It could have been the realization, or Hilario looking at the ceiling as though it was the sky, pleading for patience from God and angels, but at last, Adriel reached a decision. Knowing she was going to disappoint Brandi, she still said firmly,

"I don't wanna be away, Brandi. When I turn eighteen I got to go to Baker City."

Brandi, who by now was serving the shrimp, almost dropped the spatula full of spicy tomato sauce over herself. She recovered clumsily and looked at Adriel with begging eyes.

"I can't leave without you, Adriel," she said, and then turned her head toward Hilario, adding,

"You understand that, don't you?"

She served the shrimp and the tortillas, and opened the two bottles of Pacifico beer and poured the beer into glasses. At no point did she say a word, although her face said it all.

Adriel noticed Brandi's rare silence and demeanor, the erratic way she was serving the food, going back and forth from plate to plate, without order.

"What if I stay with Juanita?" Adriel said without thinking, holding Brandi's arm and smiling at her.

Hilario immediately threw a folded tortilla with shrimp on his plate and swallowed whatever was left in his mouth so he could speak.

"What a great idea, Mija. That would work perfectly, don't you think, mi reina?" he said.

At first, Brandi said nothing. In her own simplicity, she didn't understand right away that the child was giving her permission to go for her own dreams, that she'd done more than enough for her.

Juanita was a gentle woman from Michoacan whose daughter was one of Adriel's friends. As a schoolteacher, she often helped struggling Adriel with school matters.

All of a sudden, Adriel began picturing living with a friend. Secretly excited, she argued to Brandi that Juanita would be delighted having her at home to fill an empty house. Her husband was a pipe feeder who travelled often to Alaska to do projects because the pay was much better there. Hilario seconded the idea, teaming up with Adriel to convince Brandi.

The responsibility of a promise versus the idea of following a dream drove Brandi to a breaking point. In the end, a third element helped Adriel prevail: Brandi was human, and Brandi was tired. Deep inside, she was feeling burned out with the many parental responsibilities she'd taken on over the past year and a half in Olympia, and very specially so, she was tired of battling Adriel over school.

"Okay, let me talk to Juanita and see what she says, but I'm telling you right now, missy, if you stay I'll call you every day. *Every* day, you get that?" Brandi said.

In the car, Adriel recalled Brandi saying this while pointing at her, smiling. She checked her phone again and seeing no news from Brandi, sent another WhatsApp message. Still holding on to the memory of that night at her apartment in Olympia, she opened her window to get some fresh air.

"Isn't it cold enough for you?" Monica said sarcastically.

Memories kept flowing one after the other. Looking through the car window, Adriel could see the buildings of downtown Portland running away from her. She checked on her phone, to be sure the ringer was on. It was, and Brandi, who called her twice every day hadn't called yet.

She probably would have let go her thoughts about Brandi if it wasn't for the Oregon Health Science University cable car appearing in her view, coming down from the old hospital on the hill to the waterfront, where the new hospital was built. Instead, the cable car brought back the memory of the day she said goodbye to Brandi and had seen it coming down the same hills and wondered if she'd ride it one day.

Reclining in the back seat, but with her eyes still on the cable car, she began recollecting that day, from the moment she dropped the bomb to Brandi and Hilario, just a few weeks prior to their departure to Mexico.

The days following Adriel's decision to stay with Juanita were hectic as one might expect, but in general harmonious, at least until Adriel's change of mind created true pandemonium. She made the announcement in the middle of a TV show they were all watching.

"I've decided I don't want to stay here. I think it's time for me to take care of myself. I want to move to a city, maybe Seattle or Portland, work for a while and see what happens."

Hilario and Brandi looked at each other, perplexed. He was in fact perfectly fine with the idea. *Work will be good for her*, he thought immediately, but he knew at the same time this could be a real deal breaker. He'd witnessed Brandi's struggles to get Adriel to understand the importance of finishing school.

For Brandi it was simple: meeting Adriel's defiant eyes and confronting her about school was like looking at herself in the mirror. The image made her flinch. She could hear her own mother—Crystal—yelling at her and holding her fork in the air, the tines holding the last piece of her overcooked pork chop.

"Brandi, if you don't finish school, you might as well pick up your shit and get the hell out!"

This is how Brandi, with no direction, ended up working in cafeteria after cafeteria, until she'd worked at and been fired from every cafeteria in Pendleton and Baker City.

Noticing Hilario wasn't planning to say anything, Brandi turned off the television and made a conscious effort to remain calm.

"Honey, you're a minor and you have to finish high school. Just wait," she said.

Adriel pretended to be listening. The topic irritated her so much!

"I'm sure Papi can ask Alejandro to make another fake ID, showing me as an adult, so I won't get in trouble. You said it yourself when you wanted me to go to Mexico," Adriel said.

"There's NO way you aren't finishing school, Adriel, you got to und—" Brandi couldn't finish.

Adriel, volatile as nitroglycerine, rolled her eyes and interrupted Brandi in a mocking voice, saying,

"You'll regret it, if you want to get out of this shit hole, blah, blah, blah. I KNOW." And she disappeared toward her bedroom.

The arguments about school were the loudest. Adriel Gonzalez—this was her fake name—was a great kid. She loved every aspect of school, except for one: the studying part.

They'd followed the plan. Her hair was now black and very short. She looked nothing like that missing blond girl from Baker City, but she certainly didn't look like the blue-haired punk rocker living in Portland who came later. What Brandi hadn't expected was having to deal with a hormonal teen with no desire to finish high school.

It was difficult for Brandi. Hilario and she worked a lot and had no way to oversee Adriel's homework, if she did it at all. They didn't have the education to help her, or the resources to hire a tutor.

Report cards would arrive and Brandi would yell about the many Ds.

"I told you, Brandi. I do what I can, but teachers don't like me," Adriel always said, rolling her eyes, the way teenagers do.

Homeschooled, Adriel had never had to negotiate with a teacher or work under a deadline. More importantly, some of the high school subjects were completely new to her.

"There's a lot of stuff I don't understand and, I don't know, we have tests in real high school. In homeschool there were no tests. We didn't study much science, definitely never studied health, I don't know."

Brandi didn't believe it, in great part because she'd seen Adriel's school records. Leah had given them to her; straight A's, every year.

One of those nights, wanting to prove her point, Brandi went and got a few of the tests she'd seen that afternoon when they were unpacking.

Adriel looked at her own handwriting, and then began to inspect the documents page by page. She frowned and moved her lips, silently reading a question about how an earthquake travels through the layers of Earth. She kept going. The more questions she read, the more she realized she'd been living another lie. Her expression slowly transformed from one of pondering to surprise, sadness, and anger.

"Answer, Adriel: What about those tests?" Brandi said. But Hilario rushed to quiet her, signaling with his hand.

"Mija, you've never seen those, have you?"

Adriel turned her head toward him. Her eyes were teary and her lips were trembling lightly.

Adriel's struggles at school never ended, although her grades improved some once Hilario convinced her to get help from Juanita.

It was different with Hilario than it was with Brandi. Adriel had no defense against him. There was something about his calm; she just couldn't be smarmy with him. Every night, while Hilario watched Fútbol Picante, Adriel would come and sit with him. He talked to her about soccer, and every now and then, she would open up to him, and just like he had in that little lunch room when he first met Brandi, he just listened.

Adriel would have locked herself in her room if she'd known Brandi was coming behind her to resume the argument about finishing high school, but it was Hilario who came to get her.

He sat on the edge of her bed and brushed her hair.

"Tell me, Mija, what's the real problem?" he asked.

"I don't know, Papi, I just want to try. I feel I got to do it on my own this time," Adriel said. She was calmer, but couldn't articulate her reasoning very well.

He helped her up and then gently led her back to the living room, holding her by the shoulder. He understood. He knew right then he needed to let her go.

"Maybe we should let her decide, Brandi. It's her life," he said.

Brandi persisted. To her, the battle had many more layers; she had to let go her promise before she could set Adriel free, and she wasn't ready to do that.

An argument resumed, and, feeling she was losing control, Brandi did what she knew to do: she took possession of the conversation, getting louder and louder, demanding that Adriel finish school, until Adriel had had enough of it at last.

"You aren't my mother, okay? I'm not going to school anymore, period," she said.

Brandi stayed quiet, her mouth open. Blinking nervously, her eyes met Adriel's defiant gaze for a second or so, before looking down, defeated.

There was an awkward silence, long enough to allow Adriel to rethink what she'd just done.

"I'm so sorry, Brandi. I'm really, really sorry, please forgive me!" she said, holding Brandi's arm.

Brandi remained quiet, as if she'd fallen into a black hole.

"Brandi, I left home to work at fourteen." Hilario finally spoke again.

This ain't Zacatecas, Hilario. This ain't Zacatecas, Brandi thought, but didn't say anything. Head down, she thought about how to respond and found herself lost in an empty mental space, until one more time, the memory of her promise came to her.

"I ain't your mother, but I made a promise I was going to care for you, so if you're going to do that, you'll do it my way."

The car kept moving through the slow traffic. The cable car was gone from Adriel's sight, and even if it was there for her to see it again, her mind was still dancing with her feelings.

"Do you want some?" Kyle said all of a sudden.

He reached out and offered some M&Ms he was opening, and with that, swept Adriel's guilt out of her mind.

She waved away the candy and leaned against the window again, while Kyle resumed his conversation with Monica.

Through the window, Adriel admired the downtown buildings, standing like coconut trees along the Willamette River, at least until stubbornly, her mind delivered her back to where she was, replaying the past.

Brandi agrees to leave without her—her way. This story has been told; the new fake ID, staying with the Johnsons, ole Diesel the Bernese Mountain Dog, and Brandi finding a job for Adriel—at the bagel shop. But Adriel isn't remembering any of this. Instead, she's transported to Motel 6, where they stay for a few days and where she says goodbye to Brandi.

They're outside the motel entrance where guests park to unload their luggage and go to check in. The roof is protecting them from the rain. Today is another one of those unwelcoming wet, gray days in Portland that seem designed to expel unwanted visitors considering staying in the city for good. The taxi driver has already put Brandi's luggage in the trunk and now he's waiting for them to say their last goodbyes.

"Listen to me, darling, listen to me. Promise you won't do anything stupid. Promise me you won't do anything at all until you're eighteen. You know what I mean! Wait until you're eighteen. It'll only be safe then!" Brandi says, holding Adriel's shoulders.

Then comes the hug—one of those hugs that make you close your eyes when you don't mean to. They cry on each other's shoulder, and for this brief moment, they are one.

Brandi wants to say something else, and she's the first to let go, but Adriel pulls her back. Her mouth is against Brandi's shoulder, so when she speaks, her voice is filtered and quieted by the wool of Brandi's blue sweater.

"I don't want you to leave!" says Adriel.

They cry a while longer, until Brandi, in an almost incomprehensible mixture of words and tears, says,

"I'm sorry darling. I'm so sorry. But you know, this is such a great opportunity for us, such a step up. When's Hilario going to have another chance like this one? You know I'll visit you, darling."

Adriel, calmer now, stops her and wipes her tears with her sleeve.

"Stop, Mom, stop. I'm going to be okay. It's all good. We already talked about this."

Looking through the rear window of the taxi Adriel sees Brandi disappearing through rain and distance—an image that will stay with her forever.

In the car, with that picture of Brandi eating her alive, Adriel let the window be and typed another message to Brandi on WhatsApp.

13) 3:19PM. Richard.

Richard had hoped to be done with the numbers he was crunching for his client. But the computer system had been down for over an hour. To make matters worse, he was so hungry he couldn't think straight. All he'd eaten all day was a bowl of cereal in the morning and a day-old donut he found in the lunchroom, abandoned in its box.

Fearing for his job, he'd skipped lunch, hoping to get the whole estimate done for the client. He wanted to show his boss that he cared, even though he knew Mike didn't want to see his face, didn't want to hear his voice. And that, in fact, he'd left the office to wash away his ire in a nearby bar without telling Richard, who, clueless, stayed behind longer than necessary just in case Mike came back.

After looking at the time again and concluding that Mike wasn't returning, Richard saved the document, feeling resigned. Then he stood up, grabbed his jacket and keys and headed for the door.

"Guys, I'm going to Subway. Want something?"

Neither Larry nor Charles wanted anything. They'd both eaten.

When he opened the door, the intense sun surprised Richard. While Portland was grey and drizzly that afternoon, Eastern Oregon's sun was like a lamp in an interrogation room.

"It's November for God's sake!" Richard said out loud, using his hand as a visor.

He stepped into his truck and began driving toward Subway. His mind, however, wasn't focused on the road or the mechanical act of stepping on the gas or the brakes. He was on automatic pilot, unable to let go the loss of a contract he'd assumed was a done deal until the very end.

Minutes later, parked in a lot that Dairy Queen and Subway shared, he was eating a foot-long Italian sub. He dialed 101.1 on his radio to listen to the Lars Larson Show and escape from his self-inflicted torment.

He wolfed down the sub, his eyes—all his senses, really—fixed on the shrinking sandwich. Between bites, his attention drifted to the random people going in and out of the Dairy Queen. Here and there, the voices on the radio caught his attention.

"Look, he said grab 'em by the pussy. So what? It was locker room talk, a joke. Are you gonna compare casual locker room talk with Hillary Clinton's professional lies?" said Lars Larson.

This last sentence hit a neuron somewhere in Richard's brain, triggering a quick memory to come to the surface.

"I'm not lying, Richard! I swear!" Leah had begged him to believe her the night he discovered his daughter wasn't going to be part of his life any longer.

He swallowed the last mouthful of his sub with difficulty. Today was Adriel's birthday. In anticipation of the date, he'd been thinking about her for a week, but with all that was going on at work, he'd forgotten about it till now.

His relationship with Adriel had been suboptimal at best, but he still loved her. Secretly, despite their constant fights, she'd been his favorite. He missed her dearly. Although it had been three years since Adriel had escaped away, it still was difficult for him to accept she was gone.

What happened? he wondered. Anger followed him like a shadow, poisoning him with paranoid theories and an infinite number of "What ifs." He was angry because of the loss and the failure to have it his way, his inability to shape her the way he'd idealized. And because of the lie. Adriel had told him she trusted him; she'd said she was going to get married. At the center of his anger, there was Leah. It was simple; Richard was convinced Leah had everything to do with Adriel's escape.

A headache came to life, its heart pulsing in Richard's temple. He made a small ball with the Subway wrapping paper and put it in the paper bag, which he took outside and threw in the garbage, not without first making sure his seat was spotless. He wanted to throw his thoughts in the same garbage can. Instead, Leah's words came back to him.

"I'm not lying, Richard! I swear!"

Oh God, he had underestimated Leah so badly. In the driver's seat, but with his hands off the wheel, he began revisiting—for the hundredth time— that whole ruinous day as if it had happened minutes before.

"Richard, I'm really sorry to bother you at work, but I can't find Adriel anywhere," she'd said over the phone.

It was a little past eleven thirty and he was just getting ready to go home for lunch, something he did every now and then whenever it wasn't busy at work.

"I went for a walk with Jacob. She didn't want to come with us. She said her stomach didn't feel well. And, well, I spent more time than usual at the park. But when I came back she wasn't here. I waited a while, thinking that maybe she went to find us at the park, but it's been over two hours and she isn't here."

Reclining in his chair in the cubicle, Richard shook his head, exhaling his annoyance at Adriel. He could picture the argument he was going to have with her for leaving the house without telling Leah. It seemed not a single day went by that he didn't have to rebuke her.

"Did you go somewhere else?" he asked.

"No, Richard. I've been waiting here, and nothing," she said.

"And Jacob?"

"He's in his room watching TV."

Thinking Adriel would eventually show up, Richard drove home without rushing, and even stopped to get milk and eggs. The realization that something was really wrong came later on.

When his truck turned the corner of his street, he began playing—as he always did—a silly game of clicking the remote control for the garage door to see how far from the house it would work. He liked to imagine this game being a kind of competition or record-setting sport.

He clicked the first time, then the second, and bingo, he saw the door opening as he approached his house. It opened from as far away as the Browns' house! New record!—He smiled and turned to enter the driveway, but facing the garage, made a sudden stop. He frowned. He rubbed his goatee, and then his eyes, under his glasses. His other car—a Ford Fusion— was parked front first, and he knew he'd parked it backward. Tapping the front board, rapidly and without rhythm, he thought about the possibilities; Leah had told him she didn't go anywhere.

"Is she back?" he said to Leah as soon as he entered the kitchen through the garage door.

"No she isn't, and I just found this note. What should we do?" she said.

As Leah handed him the note, Richard tried to look into her eyes, but they avoided his as if his were a destructing laser, and he noticed. Little did he know she hoped to hide what was clearly written in her eyes: that she'd instructed Adriel to write the paper just moments before driving her to meet Brandi.

He grabbed the note with some concern. Once he read it, his body emptied inside, leaving just thin air covered by his skin.

I'm gone for good. Please don't look for me, the note said.

Reality began hitting Richard like a baseball bat, merciless. In the few seconds of silence, he envisioned a thousand things to do, one crazier than the next. Panic and the feeling that something was fishy began fighting for prevalence inside him.

"Tell me exactly what you did this morning, and when it was that Adriel disappeared," he said.

"Well, you left for work, and the kids slept until about nine. Then I fed them breakfast, and we went for a walk. I mean, Jacob and I went for a walk." Leah corrected herself, nervously. She looked up briefly and brushed her hair twice while finishing her sentence.

"Adriel stayed here. But when I got back, she was gone."

He believed her at first. Pacing around the kitchen like a maniac he began considering his options, although there was no space for rational thoughts. The harder he tried to focus, the more his emotions played him. He had angry thoughts of beating Adriel after he found her. Paternal thoughts of hugging her and telling her he was sorry. Panicky thoughts because she was just a child. What could happen to her? A storm was brewing inside him—one you couldn't see from the outside because his expression was stoic.

"Let's just wait awhile. I'm sure she'll show up. I doubt she's serious about this," he said, to get rid of Leah for a little while and organize the chaos in his mind. Walking down to his home office, little did he know that by then, Adriel and Brandi were cruising their way to a new chapter in their life, in Olympia.

Tick... tock... tick... tock.

Another hour passed. He went back upstairs and found Leah sitting in the kitchen, at her usual spot.

"C'mon, Leah. Let's go and find her," he said.

He opened the garage door and went to his truck. He sensed she was following him.

"Richard, we can't leave Jacob here," she suddenly said.

He stared at her, lost in a forest of doubt.

"Damn it!!!" he yelled.

Leah jumped, startled.

"Go get him. Hurry up, and come back fast," he said in a calmer voice, and Leah obeyed.

With Jacob in the back seat they went to the Amtrak station and the bus station. He asked every single employee about Adriel. They then drove around the outskirts of Baker City, and around the neighborhood. Of course, he didn't find her.

He was about to suggest it was time to call the police, but as time went on and dread began forming around him like a fog, random thoughts took over his mind once again. And one of those thoughts was the memory of driving back from the supermarket with Adriel.

"Okay, Father, I trust your opinion. I'll surprise Mother when you tell me to," Adriel had promised him that night.

She said yes way too easily, he thought.

He began recollecting the days following that conversation in the car. Leah seemed tight, quieter than usual, more obliging. Adriel didn't argue with him, even once. Suddenly, he recalled Adriel picking up his empty plate when he'd eaten the pasta. She was smiling. "Let me get it, Father. It's okay." It was probably a nice gesture on her part, but in that moment he imagined her turning to Leah for approval, and Leah subtly assenting, and then, as he was about to reheat coffee in the microwave, he spotted Adriel in the reflection of the microwave door. Believing he wasn't watching her, she was glaring at him, hating and despising him. Of course, none of this was real.

Slowly, he began developing a conspiracy theory. Distorted as the scenes in his imagination were, he began to see the possibility of Leah being a big part of his daughter's disappearance.

He saw that little white blue-eyed baby breastfeeding, looking straight at Leah and Leah looking back, oblivious to the world around them. At that moment, he entered the loneliness of fatherhood. The bond between the two women was stronger than he'd admitted to himself.

I never had a chance with Adriel, he thought.

"Adriel, I told you—you can't watch that movie!!!" He'd scolded her just a couple of days earlier, catching her watching Sin City on cable television.

"Okay, I'm sorry. I forgot," Adriel had said, cold as a realtor's calendar. She didn't even look at his eyes before going to her room. *She hates me*, he'd thought, more than once.

Immersed in these thoughts, he'd stopped looking, even though they were still driving around the neighborhood. Meanwhile, Leah played her part almost to perfection.

The scenes unfolded in his memory. He recalled the night Leah threw herself between him and Adriel, willing to be beaten before he could swing his belt to punish Adriel the way she deserved to be punished.

How did I miss it before? he thought. Adriel probably told Leah about the wedding. She hadn't kept her promise. He'd avoided telling Leah about the marriage he was arranging for Adriel for a reason, and now he could see why. And of course, a liar fears a lie.

The more he thought about it, the redder his pale face became. For the time being, the sense of emptiness and loss was replaced with anger. At this point, he was convinced his daughter had gone with the help of his wife. What he didn't know, at least just then, was that he wasn't going to be able to get her back—that she was truly gone.

A flood of other memories gave him the pieces he needed to support his theory. None of it made sense. Some of it wasn't even real, but by the time he had finished his introspection, Richard was about to explode.

"Can you tell me again where you were when Adriel left the house?" He finally broke the silence.

"As I said, I went to the park with Jacob, right Jacob?" she turned around and asked the child for support. "We were in the park for what, two hours, sweetie pie?"

"I don't know, Mamma."

"So Jacob, where's Adriel? Do you know?" Richard asked.

Leah was about to say something, but Richard raised an index finger in her face, and she stopped.

"I don't know. Mom put a movie on. I was watching the movie."

"A movie? Do you normally watch movies in the morning?"

"No, not usually."

Richard saw Leah freezing like a small animal hiding from a predator. Her fingers were holding the door handle so tightly the knuckles were white.

"And did you see Adriel this morning?" he said

"Nope."

The boy was answering the questions like any boy of his age: to the point, and minimally.

Richard began tapping on the steering wheel of his truck and shaking his head.

"But Father," Jacob added,

"I heard Adriel this morning. I just didn't see her." He smiled innocently.

Brandi had planned everything quite well. She made sure Jacob wouldn't be a liability. She had Leah put the movie on for him so, distracted, the boy wouldn't notice anything, not even the car leaving the garage. Brandi also made sure Leah went to the park with Jacob after Adriel was gone, to make the boy believe they were looking for his sister.

They arrived home. The garage door opened again. Wanting to get the child out of the conversation, Leah rushed to talk again. She told the same story, nervously with a kind of verbal diarrhea, talking nonstop and repeating herself over and over. But Richard wasn't even listening to her anymore. While her lips moved, he was making sure his memory of the car was correct. *Did I park the car front first?* he asked himself. He knew he backed the car in carefully, until it was barely touching that tennis ball he'd left hanging from the ceiling, to be sure that when being parked, the car didn't hit the tool stands on the back wall.

Even after Leah finished her version of the story, Richard didn't say a word. He was still thinking, and his silence made Leah rub her hands together. Nervously she said,

"You know Richard, I even ran around the block. But nothing!"

This time around, his eyes met hers, and there it was: one of those looks that only a married person can decipher, like an "I'm tired. Let's go" look at a dinner party. Somehow, Richard knew Leah was lying.

Leah went to the kitchen with Jacob. Richard went downstairs. It didn't matter how much he tried to focus, he couldn't think straight. Pacing from one corner of his small office to the next, he was making a trench in the floor.

I have to call the police, he thought, this time more decisively. He sat in front of the computer and began searching for their number on the internet, when the Stickies memo, always present in the corner of his screen, caught his attention:

Our submission to male leadership at home and churches reenacts Christ's submission to God His Father, it read.

He decided that calling the police wasn't the answer, but by threatening to he could get Leah to talk. He rushed back upstairs to the kitchen, ready to take Leah's head off, but Jacob's presence stopped him. The boy was sitting at the table waiting for his sandwich, looking at a Lego magazine Leah had subscribed him to.

"Here, Jacob, why don't you come with me? Let's find a movie on TV or something. Your mom and I need to talk, okay?" Richard said, taking the plate and signaling the boy to follow him. The boy was immediately glued to the screen, entering the marvelous world of Disney characters.

Back in the kitchen, Richard stood in front of Leah and began his act.

"The other thing, Leah, is this: child abduction is a very serious crime. You remember my cousin Jared? You know he's a cop, right? Well, I called him. He said that it's a ten-year deal.

So I don't know, maybe we should call the police. What do you think?" *Say something bitch. Let's hear your typical bullshit,* he thought.

Nervously, she began playing with a fork, rolling it over the table. The suggestion caught her off guard.

Insist you guys should call the police and go to the police if you have to. But don't worry, he won't have the balls to do it, she recalled Brandi telling her.

"I agree Richard. I don't know, you and Father know better. But I feel we should call the cops right now."

She looked at his eyes. He too looked tired. He slept even less than she did, and just as Brandi figured, this single statement changed everything.

You fucking bitch. Don't you think I know you're lying.

"Really? That's what you think we should do?"

Insist on calling the police, Leah. I'm telling you, honey—he won't have the balls to do it. He knows.

By now the fork was at full speed.

You never ask for my opinion, she thought.

"Yes! Richard, Adriel could be in the hands of a lunatic by now."

"Let's call the police, Richard, don't you think?" said Leah when he returned.

"Can you fucking stop playing with the fork, Leah? I can't think with that annoying noise."

It hadn't worked, and that pissed him off. He oscillated between picking up the phone or questioning her further and opted at last for the second option.

"What for? The easiest way to get her back is for you to tell me where the hell she is, because I *know*," he said, pointing to himself, "that YOU KNOW."

Leah began rocking her chair like she always had since she was little, with her knees together and her arms over her legs. In her hands, she hid her terror like a toy a child doesn't want to give away.

A theatrical game of accusation and denial lasted a little while, but Leah wouldn't give up. Over and over she repeated what she'd rehearsed. There was no way she would leave her young daughter on her own.

"Richard, you know me. You know my feelings about my children. Do you really think I would let my baby run away? That I would let Adriel go who knows where? She's only fourteen! I'm not lying, Richard! I swear!"

You know I was planning to marry her off, he thought, but said instead,

"I think you got bad advice from somebody at work and that at the same time, Adriel wanted out of here, because she hates me. And since you don't give a fuck about me and you do anything that spoiled child asks you to do, well, you did it!"

No, you're wrong. I just don't want my baby to go through the hell I've gone through, she thought and said,

"Richard, I want Adriel back here as much as you do."

He took off his narrow glasses, revealing the mark they left deeply stamped across the top of his nose. Looking at her with a cynical smile and sounding dead calm, he said,

"Where's my fucking daughter, Leah?"

Leah bit her lip so hard she almost broke the skin. Her hands were sweating badly.

"I don't know! How can I know? Please don't hurt me, Richard!"

Leah wasn't afraid of Richard hurting her; the words came out without her permission.

"Do you think I'm an imbecile? You took the car out, Leah. Where did you drive her to?" His eyes were wide and threatening as though he was yelling, but he kept his voice down, concerned that little Jacob would hear them arguing.

Leah stood up and went to the corner of the kitchen, un-settled.

"I'm sorry, I'm so nervous. I forgot to tell you! I drove to the park to try to find her. I was desperate! Please Richard, don't hurt me!" she repeated. She knew it. Richard had figured it all out.

More than the lie and the denial, what upset him the most at the time was her crying and begging him not to hurt her, as if he were an animal. As if, other than that one slap the night Charles and his wife came over, he'd ever hurt her. Leah's only concern was her own wellbeing. She didn't care about him, or how he felt about losing Adriel.

He took her by the arm, and forced her toward the door leading to the garage that was next to the kitchen, along a very short hall.

"Please Richard, don't hurt me!" she screamed again.

"Shut the fuck up!!" he said and opened the door.

He stepped down the two steps leading into the garage and once more pulled her as hard as he could, closing the door behind him. She was wearing sandals, and stumbling on the step with a sandal coming off her foot, she fell face forward, hitting her front teeth against the cement floor.

Feeling a cold, electrical pain in her front tooth, she felt with her tongue and found it had shattered. The piece, about a third of the tooth, was lying on the floor in front of her.

"Richard, my tooth! It broke! Stop hurting me! Please believe me—I want Adriel back as much as you do!"

"If you tell me not to hurt you again, I swear to God, Leah, I'm going to break every tooth in your mouth. You know very well I'd never hurt you! Get up!"

She did so, keeping her distance from him as though he was an angry cobra. But that wasn't necessary. By the time she lifted her head, he was already walking away, back to the house and to his office.

Unable to get any useful information from Leah, he was engulfed in a mixture of anger, desperation, and cluelessness. He had nobody to go to but Leah's father, who'd become his mentor after his own father died.

It was already evening when he called him for advice.

"Don't call the police. It's not worth it," Leah's father told Richard over the phone.

"We can get her back, Jim! There's still time!" Richard said.

"Remember, I lost a boy too. My David. Don't blame yourself. You've done your duty. You've done the best you can. It's Adriel's choice—she's old enough. And you know what? She may come back. Just wait—she'll be back. She's just a girl. Don't open a can of worms, Dick, you understand? Look, if Leah is involved, and we both know she is, then you can be sure Adriel is safe. Agree? I'm gonna head over there and help sort things out. We have to see about Jacob."

Richard was trembling and felt possessed, like an evil child inside him was kicking hard. Still holding the phone, he curled up like a cheese puff, holding his aching belly.

"But I only have two children, Jim. Just two," he said, hardly articulating his words.

"She's gone. I mean spiritually, Dick, you lost her."

And there it was. Jim's last words had haunted Richard for the past years. Parked in Subway, his eyes wide, the pupils floating in a growing ocean, he couldn't escape his thoughts, the last of them tormenting him—a memory of Adriel as a little kid.

"Higher, daddy, higher!!!" He remembered throwing her into the air at the pool at Sam-O-Swim Center, a place they visited every weekend until Adriel grew tired of it.

He sobbed and sobbed, and cried his soul out, as he had back then, in the darkness and cool of his home office. That night, he'd prayed when he wasn't crying, all night long. But Adriel would never come back.

14) 3:19PM. Adriel.

They'd been driving for about four hours. The grey sky was left behind.

It was nice to finally be showered with rays of sunshine, considering the old Honda's heater didn't function that well. It was definitely cold and crisp. Not even the blanket Adriel had brought for the trip was keeping her warm.

Anxiety had tightened her belly like the head of a conga, her pulse marking the beat like a metronome. Yet, it was the cold and the need to find a comfortable position to fight a dull backache that kept her preoccupied.

Monica was tired too. Not used to driving for so long, she found her vision beginning to blur. She saw light particles floating like snowflakes, in the same sleepy fashion one sees the sunlight squeezing between branches on a sunny day; out of focus. Rubbing her eyes, she turned to ask Adriel to grab her sunglasses from her bag on the floor in the back of the car, but saw that Adriel was lying in a weird position, eyes closed.

"I need to stop and get some coffee," she said.

Adriel didn't speak. It was Kyle who answered.

"Actually, do you see that restaurant sign with the big bear?"

It was an old metal billboard with a black bear dressed like a boy scout holding a plate with poorly drawn pancakes and bacon.

"A redneck eatery with a bear theme, really?" Monica said.

"It's actually a cool little place. What did the sign say, twenty miles? I ate there a couple of times when I was dating Susan. She played a tennis tournament in Baker City with her friends and we stopped there. It's a decent place."

"Four hours driving to play amateur tennis?" Monica said.

"Yeah, because they have the only grass courts in Oregon, although they're pretty bad."

Adriel wasn't paying attention to their conversation, but for some reason, the mention of a restaurant sign with a bear mascot rang a bell. She sat up, sleepy, and looked for the sign, but it was gone. With her face glued to the window she was fogging the glass.

An endless brownish landscape of low hills was all she could see. A sense of déjà vu woke her. She sat up to look out the window, until a memory leapt up like a fighting marlin into the air from the ocean depths.

"Here, listen to this: music heals all," she recalled Brandi saying just as they passed a sign advertising the same restaurant, but on the other side of the highway, heading west. They were driving away from Baker City, the day Adriel left home for good.

In the rear-view mirror, Monica watched Adriel getting up. She didn't want to impose a stop, but it wasn't just the sleepiness; she felt as though her bladder was about to explode.

"Hey, okay if we stop at that restaurant for coffee?" she asked Adriel.

It took Adriel a moment to answer. She met Monica's eyes in the rear-view mirror and assented before saying,

"You know the last time I was on this road was when I escaped? That weird bear sign you guys were talking about was like a flashback."

Adriel got between the front seats, resting her arms on them while she began telling the story.

"We were driving to Olympia. It was awkward. Think about it—I didn't even know Brandi. She was quiet. I think she could see that I was upset. I wasn't crying or anything. I felt like shit."

Nervous about the plan execution, Brandi was struggling to control the weight of her foot on the pedal. On one hand she wanted to get away as fast as possible. On the other, she worried Richard would call the police. Not until that point had she even thought about the consequences of getting caught. She couldn't afford the police stopping her for speeding, or any other reason.

"It was the beginning of summer and still, I remember feeling as cold as I feel now. I was probably shivering, 'cos Brandi parked the truck on the side of the road without saying anything and put her arm around my neck and said something like *it's gonna be all right, kiddo*. I was weirded out 'cos, as I said, I really didn't know her at all, and when she put her arm around me, I don't know, I wasn't used to strangers."

So then she got out of the truck and came back with a blanket and these grandpa-style headphones and an iPod. She handed them all to me, turned the key in the ignition, and began driving again. She said something like, *'Music heals everything.'* I think we were listening to Pearl Jam, or maybe it was The Cure. I don't know."

Adriel paused, trying and failing to remember what the song was.

"How exactly did it happen, Adriel? How did you manage to get the hell out of there?" Kyle asked, turning toward her.

Adriel rested her arms on the front armrests. She paused. Monica extended a hand to caress her cheek.

"You know, for a long time, I lied to myself believing the decision was mine and that I escaped. It felt good to believe

I had the balls to liberate myself from the whole thing, but it was my mom, and Brandi of course. It was my mom who had the balls and who truly made the decision."

Memories played in Adriel's mind, like movies at the old Laurelhurst Theater she and Monica frequented. The scenes presented themselves and she narrated them to Kyle, like a translator recording a dubbing sequence.

She wished she could recall everything in detail, but the movie she had stored in memory had been edited, cut into fragments, like a promotional clip.

"*Whatever I am; I am, and whatever I've done; I've done, but you are you, Adriel, you need to be yourself and be happy. I agree, you must leave this place*. This is what my mom told me."

Adriel shook her head in disapproval. Her voice got louder.

"I didn't know what to think. I'd written in my diary that I wanted to leave, but never truly thought about that prospect in detail. I never, ever thought of leaving my mom behind. So I asked her: 'What do you mean?'

She'd read my diary and apparently had planned the whole thing. She said it wasn't because of what I'd written, but because she knew what had to be done. Then she told me that I needed to be strong and asked me if I was ready to do it. And I told her that I was, but I wasn't of course. Who can be ready for that? You know what I mean?"

Adriel stopped and looked at Kyle for a response. He didn't answer although her silence prompted him to turn his head and look at her.

"So then came the morning, and what can I say? Asshole left to work and my mom came to my room to say we had to get going, no bullshit.

Okay sweetheart, we have thirty minutes to get a few things together for you and leave. Don't worry about clothing. I'll get that.

Just put whatever's truly important for you in here. She sounded so dry and decisive that it gave me no chance to even think about it. And just in case I had something in mind, she threw me this backpack so I couldn't stop to think."

Adriel took the old, worn-out Levis backpack she always carried and showed it to Monica and Kyle, as if they'd never seen it before. Then kept going,

"She took a small luggage and began packing some of my clothes. As you can imagine, I didn't put a thing in the backpack, because I was paralyzed. I couldn't think straight. So when she finished and looked at the empty backpack, she smiled and said, *It's okay, I have something for you.*

Then we went to the garage and we got in the car. That was our second car, but we rarely used it because my mom never drove, not even when she worked. My dad drove her in his truck after dropping me and my brother off at Mrs. Fuiten's where we did home schooling. Anyway, so there she is, my poor mom taking the car out of the garage. I could see she was nervous, but I just stayed quiet. Except that I realized my mom was leaving my brother behind, and so I asked her about him and she said, *If I bring your brother he'll be so excited he'll tell your father. Don't worry. I left him watching a movie, and this will take ten, fifteen minutes max.*

I started thinking about my little brother, the same brother I thought I pretty much hated all my childhood. And suddenly I realized how much I loved him."

Adriel paused. The image of little Jacob smiled at her, as if she was taking a photograph.

"Anyways, we drove for a little while and got to this parking lot. Brandi was waiting with her weird hair and her super tight everything, like she was picking up a guy right there in the parking lot. But she wasn't. That was her normal self.

My mom introduced us and then made me promise I would listen to Brandi. She said anything coming from Brandi was truly coming from her. Then she made me promise I would never, ever try to contact her or find her until I was eighteen. So here we are."

Adriel paused again. The car was silent like a tomb.

"I didn't know what to think. I know it sounds weird but I was, like, numb. I remember wanting to ask why, but all it came out was like, err, err, and then she gave me a big hug. I can still feel her trembling, like right before crying, but she didn't cry. And so I asked her, and I really meant it, if she could come, and she said she couldn't because of Jacob, and I said, like, I meant both of them. And she told me she couldn't do it, that it wasn't that simple."

Adriel paused again, and in the silence the radio was loud and clear:

"...Clear skies tonight in the cascades, the coast and the metro area, as Portlanders prepare for the eclipse. Right now the eclipse is scheduled to begin at about six o'clock tonight. This is OPB..."

"That is a ridiculously incredible story, Adriel. I'm so sorry," Kyle said.

"It's cool, I mean, here we are, aren't we?" she said.

"Man, I tell you what would be cool—seeing The Cure in an eclipse. Wouldn't that be amazing?" he said.

She remained quiet, as if she was thinking about it.

"Shit, you know what? It was The Cure. It was the fucking Cure that Brandi had me listening to! Charlotte Sometimes to be exact!" Adriel said.

Monica pressed a button on the stereo to switch from Radio to Media. Then she grabbed her cell phone from the compartment behind the gear stick.

"Siri, play Charlotte Sometimes by The Cure," she said.

"Here is Charlotte Sometimes by The Cure." A female voice came out of the speakers.

Monica turned her head toward the back for a brief moment and smiled at Adriel before throwing her a kiss.

Adriel leaned back. She needed this moment for herself. She stretched her legs straight and brought up her hips to remove her wallet from her back pocket. It was an aquamarine surfer-style wallet she'd bought at the Portland flea market a year before.

She opened the wallet and from one of the side pockets, slipped out a fragile photo. In reality, the photo cut from a larger photo to fit the wallet. More important—for Adriel— was that it was torn into three pieces, held together with tape on the back.

She lay down across the back seat, with her legs bent, and stared at the photo, feeling melancholy.

In the photo, in front of a nice rosebush, a young, tall, blonde girl stood with her feet together, waving and smiling at the camera. It was Leah at the Rose Garden, that day before the Metallica concert. The photo was torn, a white line traveling diagonally across her thighs. Her face was torn too, making it difficult to see she was narrowing her eyes because of the sun; it was a bright, beautiful day, one could tell.

Adriel put the photo back, put the wallet in her pocket and once more leaned back in her seat, closing her eyes.

Charlotte Sometimes had begun playing in the background. Adriel listened to the song as memories associated with the photo rushed into her consciousness.

The first image was of Brandi, kneeling on the carpet, hunting for shattered glass, moments after Adriel had thrown the framed photograph against the wall.

"Your mom is an angel, Adriel. Don't ever forget that," Brandi had said before taking the torn pieces of the photograph and giving them to Hilario, who'd also arrived in Adriel's room to see what was going on.

In anger, Adriel had thrown the framed photo against the wall.

Hilario looked at the torn pieces, and then turned to Adriel, who was sitting on the floor, resting her back against her bed. She'd thrown the frame so hard that the glass shattered and the photo flew out of it in the air, landing softly, face up against the carpet, before Adriel, enraged, seized it and tore it into three pieces. The photo was the one thing Leah had left her the day of the escape, inside the backpack.

"Why, Mija?" Hilario said, calmly.

Adriel hugged her knees. Head down, she looked up at him without moving her head, and said nothing.

Hilario waited, his gaze penetrating. He was waiting for an answer. His expression was serious.

"She is a coward, Papi, she is a coward. She should have come, and she should have brought my brother with her," she said, sobbing, in a scratchy voice.

"Mija. No child deserves to go through what you went through, but you have to be strong. Don't let sadness mess up your head. Your mom was everything you want to think she was but a coward," Hilario said.

Minutes later, he taped the photo together and gave it back to Adriel. They were sitting at the dinner table. He smiled and stretched out his arm, inviting her to come and hug him. She did, and hiding her face against his shoulder once more, she cried.

Sitting in the car seat, Adriel didn't let this memory bring on more tears. Instead, she let her mind drift back to the day of the escape. She knew Leah had read her diary several days before her departure. She knew that even before everything was planned, Brandi wanted to get away from Baker City, to leave for a different town in search of new opportunities. She knew her mom opened up to Brandi about her own predicament only when she discovered the diary. That it was Brandi who offered to help, and that it was Brandi who planned the whole thing. That it was summer, and that in summer her father went home a little after twelve to have lunch. That he went to work in the morning and that half an hour after, her mom drove to that parking lot as planned, to meet with Brandi. She knew Brandi and her mother never spoke again, as they had planned, in person. She didn't know of Brandi's attempts to reach Leah.

All of this she knew from Brandi. She also knew her face was on no milk container, or anywhere else they spotlight missing children. But there was way too much she didn't know.

Beyond wondering what had happened to Leah and Jacob, Adriel had questions stored in her subconscious as well. Those were the questions she'd never asked herself or asked Brandi, yet they were the ones eating her, for only her mother could answer them.

She needed to hear from Leah that Leah had been thinking of her every day, from the day she left her with Brandi, and that she wanted to hug her again as much as Adriel wanted to hug her.

There was more. There was the wish that her brother would recognize her and run toward her the day they met again. The wish that her father had somehow disappeared, that he no longer existed and never had. There was the wish that she could liberate her mother from that hell. She knew her mother'd been living through hell way before she escaped. Hell was the one thing she still believed from the bible, except her hell wasn't a dungeon of fire. Hell was life as her mother experienced it.

In the back seat, Adriel, feeling solitary and doubtful and mentally exhausted, let go, and with Charlotte Sometimes still playing, fell asleep.

Her mind stayed blank until, a minute or two later, old memories of her mother squeezed through in the form of a dream that progressively distorted into a nightmare, in which once more, Charlotte Sometimes played as a soundtrack.

All the faces
All the voices blur
Change to one face
Change to one voice

"Adriel, don't make that grumpy face, dear. Your brother is just a baby. He didn't know."

The first image of her mother consoling her about the toy Jacob had damaged took full possession of Adriel's mind. She felt Leah's warmth again, felt her hand brushing her hair and saw her eyes gazing at her intensely.

Prepare yourself for bed
The light seems bright
And glares on white walls
All the sounds of Charlotte sometimes

"There's nothing to be afraid of, darling. Mommy is always here for you. Call me if you need anything, okay? But you need to be brave. Light needs to go out, okay?" Leah said.

"But why?" Little Adriel asked, tucked under her blanket and scanning the room for ghosts, spiders, monsters, and other unwelcome creatures.

"If the light never goes out, you'll always be afraid of the dark. But once you're in the dark and see that nothing happens to you, guess what? You won't be afraid anymore. You see?"

Night after night she lay alone in bed
Her eyes so open to the dark

The streets all looked so strange
They seemed so far away
But Charlotte did not cry

Adriel saw herself that first night at the Johnsons, a victim of insomnia without her mother, without Brandi or Hilario. Not even the warmth of Diesel the dog could put her to sleep.

Sometimes I'm dreaming
Where all the other people dance
Sometimes I'm dreaming
Charlotte sometimes

"I have a little turtle, his name is Tiny Tim!" Adriel dreamt of that morning she was recording a video of her mother singing to Jacob. Leah and her little boy were holding hands and dancing in a circle. Behind the music of The Cure, Adriel could hear her brother's laughter. Her mother's eyes were shining with happiness.

Sometimes I'm dreaming
Expressionless the trance
On that bleak track
(See the sun is gone again)
The tears were pouring down her face
She was crying and crying for a girl
Who died so many years before

She pictured two scenes over and over, looping and repeating one after the other. The first scene was the memory of her mother hugging her while they lay in the old hammock. From above, she saw Leah humming a song, and saw herself curl up under her mother's arm. Then, the point of view shifted. She saw the hammock from the side, and about ten yards away. It was the second scene: an imaginary vision of her mother alone in the hammock, crying and calling for her.

Charlotte sometimes dreams a wall around herself

But it's always with love
With so much love it looks like
Everything else
Of Charlotte sometimes
So far away
Glass sealed and pretty
Charlotte sometimes

At last, Adriel pictured the grayish, dead face of her mother and her glassy eyes staring into the limbo. In the scene, she recognized her own hands shaking Leah's shoulders in desperation, trying to revive her.

The image stayed with her for some time, until, to her surprise, Leah woke, just for a moment, saying,

"Darling, stop building a wall around yourself. None of this is your fault; it isn't your fault."

Leah's face froze again. Adriel began calling out again, trying to revive her once more. Again she could see her own hands shaking her mother's shoulders and her tears falling on her mother's dead face, but to make the nightmare even more macabre, she wasn't calling Leah "Mom" or "mother" or calling her by name. She was calling her "Adriel."

"Adriel, Adriel, please come back. Adriel, Adriel, wake up!" she kept saying, until coming out of a deep sleep, she heard Monica's voice replacing her own in the dream.

"Adriel, Adriel, wake up!"

And just then, Adriel woke. She exhaled the dark visions as she sat up.

"You fell asleep and I guess you were having a nightmare," Monica said.

"Yes, yes, I did."

"What was it about? My mom says in Peru they believe if you talk about a nightmare you'll never have it again," Monica said.

"No, I won't talk about it," Adriel said, getting out of the car. They had arrived at the restaurant.

Monica saw the stress in Adriel's face. She was about to argue her point, but let it go.

15) 3:51PM. Leah.

Is it really Friday? Leah thought for a moment. She began putting together a mental summary of her week, but feeling rushed, gave it up, knowing that Nicole was on the other line waiting for her and that she still had to take care of the chicken.

The chicken was her biggest preoccupation. It needed to go in at least twenty minutes earlier, but deep in the long phone conversation with Nicole, Leah had forgotten about it. It was hard to know when Richard would be back, but she liked to have the chicken out of the oven by six so it could rest for fifteen minutes before she served dinner, assuming Richard was there.

After turning the oven on, she waited for the temperature to reach four hundred degrees, as if it was the New Year's Eve countdown. With her elbow on the kitchen table and her chin resting on one hand, she watched the temperature rise slowly. A minute can be painfully long when you're watching a clock. The fastidious obsession had kicked in; her legs began shaking rhythmically, eight times a second, synchronized like a Rolex. An irony considering that, in her state of mind, she wasn't able to keep track of time.

Searing the chicken the first ten minutes was a trick she learned from Emeril Lagasse, a man she considered a genius of the kitchen. She'd cooked the same juicy chicken for years and not once had it disappointed.

It wasn't that Richard demanded to be fed on arrival or anything like that, not at all. This was about Leah's own obsession for punctuality and the way everything had to be done in a timely way.

She'd learned this fastidiousness as a child. Having to sit at the table right on time (or else) was one of the many experiences that shaped this trait. Leah was a neat person; one of those addicted to daily calendars and organizers, who manage to empty a tube of toothpaste in a perfect progression from bottom to cap.

Confusing a day wouldn't be a big deal for someone who was distracted, but it was a big deal for Leah. Perfection was part of her functioning: perfectly held hair, perfectly white clothing, perfectly everything. Yet what bothered her the most about her confusion was that it was a reminder of a much bigger problem she wasn't yet able to accept; a lot of her memory was gone, particularly her memory of the events right after Adriel's departure, and the two years that followed.

"Oh, yeah, tonight is the eclipse. I completely forgot about it," she finally jumped to say once she remembered what day it was. But the truth was, doubt stayed with her like a thorn in her shoe.

She wanted to avoid talking about not being able to remember. And she still needed to answer Nicole's original question about her failing marriage. She had a strong need to explain why it wasn't simply a matter of domestic violence.

"But I want to tell you, the marriage didn't go down the drain because Richard hit me that time. I lived a lie for way too long, Nicole, although I was willing to put up with whatever it was. You have to understand, I believe marriage is sacred, and that you should only get married once. But when I discovered that Richard had given up, that he'd been seeing that young thing all that time, I realized our marriage was nothing but a formality for him. And then it was over. I mean, he could fool whoever he wanted but not the Lord, and I didn't want to be part of that sin."

Leah made a fist; her face growing darker with each word.

"I felt betrayed, and yes, I had a lot of anger, but as the days went on, I realized I had mixed feelings about the whole thing. I hated myself for being so naïve, hated him for his hypocrisy and all, but in a way, felt it was my fault and that this affair would be the beginning of the end, which is funny. I mean, ironic. I wanted it to end but didn't want it to be a failure. I felt he was looking elsewhere because I was a failure of a wife."

The day Leah found out about Liberty was a rainy, lazy Saturday in Baker City. There weren't many cars in the streets and the few establishments waiting for customers to fill their tables were hopelessly desolated.

The whole family was coming back from the movies. Inside the car, everybody was quiet except for little Jacob, who was talking nonstop, mimicking the voices of his new heroes, the Penguins of Madagascar, who just minutes before had saved the world from evil forces.

On special occasions—and going to the movies was a treat—the family went to a local Chinese restaurant named Rising Sun Palace, where they all enjoyed the chicken fried rice. But that day, a Penguins McDonalds' Happy Meal had caught Jacob's eye when it was advertised during the movie previews. He begged and begged to get his own so persistently that, fifteen minutes later, the family was ordering quarter pounders at the drive thru.

"So we got there and ordered a few things. It was raining and Richard was all worried about his new truck getting wet inside. Don't do this. Don't eat here. Be careful! You know, so annoying. Anyhow, there was an accident with the sodas."

The McDonald's worker, a middle-aged Hispanic woman, opened the drive-thru window. She was handling both the money transactions and the delivery of the food.

Richard opened his window and handed her his card, which she returned in a small plastic tray holding the card and the receipt. He signed it right there, in the air, between the two windows. Then she handed Richard a small bag with the Happy Meal inside along with a small Sprite, and told him the rest of the order would be out in a minute.

"Look Momma! It's Skipper!" Jacob said, excited after opening his meal.

"Wow! That's so nice, Jacob. What else you got?" Leah said.

"Jacob, you can take the toy out but don't eat until we get home," Richard said.

The woman took the board back and promptly handed Richard the rest of the order, beginning with a big paper bag with the food. Still holding his card, he passed the bag to Leah, hurrying to make the exchange as quickly as possible, to keep the inside of the truck from getting wet. Then the woman passed him a cardboard tray with three drinks, but between his haste, his eyes looking in so many places, and the fact he still was holding his credit card, Richard reached out and grasped it on just one side without accounting for the weight of the sodas. The weak tray gave up and bent, splashing the drinks into the groove in the doorframe that held the window. The plastic lids failed to prevent Coca Cola from running like a muddy river all down the outside of Richard's door.

"Shit! Are you stupid, or what?!" he yelled at the poor worker, who truly had little to do with the accident.

"I'm very sorry, sir. I thought you were holding it." Her accent suddenly worsened.

He began inspecting the damage frantically. At the same time and without looking, he attempted to put his credit card in the compartment to his side, to free his hand, but the card dropped in the narrow space between Leah's seat and the compartment.

"Can't you see I'm handing you the card, Leah!? Can you be useful for once?"

"Hey Skipper, should I go for the bad guy? No, no Rico, you stay here on the ship, I'll go and get them!" Jacob kept playing loudly, making the whole scene even more chaotic.

"Here you go, sir." The woman handed Richard a big pile of napkins, which he took and used to wipe down the door.

"Can you also give me some water? Or d'you think I want my brand new car to stay sticky?"

"But sir, it's raining," The woman said, doing her best to stay calm.

He stared at her for a couple of seconds without saying a word.

"Fucking bitch. Why don't you go back to your country?" he muttered.

"Richard, please," Leah said.

"Run, Rico! Run!!!" Jacob yelled.

And while Richard was busy cleaning the outside of the truck, Leah squeezed her hand in the narrow space to rescue the credit card.

"But instead, Nicole, I found this card with red lipstick pressed on the front. I didn't get it right away, but then I read the note inside. I remember this sour gut feeling, like when your stomach's empty."

Resigned, Leah shook her head as she told the story. She no longer felt the total silence and emptiness around and inside her that she'd felt at that moment of discovering the brutal reality. The card said: *The earrings are so beautiful! I can't wait until tonight. You better have energy, Liberty.*

While Richard was cleaning, Leah raised the card to her nose and smelled it. Perfume. Her lips began trembling. The scent passed from her cell receptors through the olfactory bulb until it reached the limbic system and then the cortex. In a flash, she was back in the laundry room. She'd smelled that scent before, but back then, she hadn't processed it. She recalled Richard's voice on the phone that same day.

"Don't wait for me tonight. I need to work on a contract. Mike's making me stay late tonight."

One by one, the images passed in front of Leah, until Richard's voice interrupted her tortured thoughts.

"Can you believe that stupid wom—" he began, but stopped when he saw Leah's eyes. He looked at the card for a fraction of a second, and then made an attempt to get it from Leah's hand, but she pulled it away.

"Pushhh, Ahhhh! Get him, Skipper. Get him! Look Momma, look, Skipper is winning!"

"My gosh, that's Larry's card, I can't believe that guy. He's so distracted!" Richard said with a forced smile before beginning a long tale about Larry's fictional girlfriend.

The more he talked, the more obvious it became to Leah that the girlfriend was his. She stared at him, then at the card and then back at him again, but didn't say a thing, until they were back home. It wasn't because the children were present. Everyone and everything had disappeared around her.

Later that night, Leah was standing at the bathroom door, dressed in sweatpants and a T-shirt. Her voice wasn't demanding. If anything, she was imploring Richard to give an explanation so she could understand.

"It just happened, okay? I didn't plan it," Richard said from the edge of the bed, where he was sitting, elbows on his thighs, refusing to look at her.

"And this woman, what can she give you that I haven't given you, what?" Leah said.

"Really? Do I need to answer that?" he said, lurching up violently.

The belt of his robe was loose and with the sudden movement, the robe opened completely in the front, uncovering his penis.

She avoided the sight as if it was a puppy being slaughtered. Turning her face so abruptly away from Richard, she found herself staring at herself in a mirror that was hanging on the wall, opposite the bathroom door. She wanted to argue, yell into his clueless face. He had no idea, no clue whatsoever why she was unable to give him the sexual pleasures he wanted so badly. But seeing his bloodshot eyes, she simply turned her back and grabbed her toothbrush.

In front of her was a weathered woman with dark circles under her eyes, and a vein between her eyes growing like a river in the middle of winter.

The older I get, the more I look like Mother. How sad, she thought.

A feeling of worthlessness invaded her. She questioned herself for her inability to be good enough for Richard. Anger came to the rescue, pointing out it wasn't her fault; it was Father's and Mother's for making her marry this horrible person. It was Richard's fault, the fault of his sinful selfishness, weakness, and hypocrisy. Adriel and Jacob joined the party, to remind her of her value and true purpose in life. All these thoughts flew in and out of her mind like pigeons on a church roof. At the vortex of the mental tornado, the possibility of divorce poked in, and a fierce battle began between her faith, her fear of the unknown, the many social and economic disadvantages forced upon her from childhood, and the well-established cultural myth that divorce destroys children. All these confronted her anger and the basic human need of freedom.

In the morning, putting waffles on Richard's plate, she still smiled to distract him from looking into her eyes, so he wouldn't discover the infernal war going on inside her, the two infantries—divorce and no divorce—throwing everything they had at each other.

Her desire to leave Richard was strong, but she didn't know where to begin. The hours passed and no winner was called, but the war faded away. The more she thought about it, the more sense it made to stay put. She had her children, a roof over her head, and three meals a day, and now, with all cards opened, she knew Richard wouldn't ask for sex ever again.

Nothing changed in her punctual routine, really, except that she turned a switch off. Maybe she wasn't sure about divorcing or not divorcing, but she was certain Richard was nothing other than the person who fed her and her children. In return, she was his maid.

Nicole, who'd been listening in silence, wondered what made Leah pick up the phone and call her.

"So what made you decide to leave him?" she asked. "I thought it was his cheating—that you didn't want to be part of that."

For just a second, Leah watched Richard taking off his belt to beat Adriel savagely. It wasn't just the way he swung the belt, or even the way he removed the blanket covering Adriel. It was his eyes. There was something in those eyes that triggered the deepest mammalian instinct, a mother's need to protect her child at all cost.

"I guess I spoke too quickly, you're right. Things could have stayed the same indefinitely if it wasn't for how his relationship with Adriel changed.

Richard had been a good father to Adriel and Jacob. He was playful and tolerant with them, took them to movies and other children's activities whenever he could. He was by far a better father than Father was to me. But that all changed with Adriel as soon as she was a teenager.

And after I found out about the affair, even just a couple of weeks later, he decided he had a free ride. He began distancing himself to the point the man sitting at the table was nothing but a food-consuming mass with little to say *and* no longer a better father than my own, in fact the worst of fathers for Adriel. So what for, Nicole? What for?"

Leah looked again at the oven temperature—it was almost at four hundred—and then at the chicken. *All this cooking... what for?* she thought.

Just weeks after the discovery of the affair, Richard decided Leah could work part time. This was his way of saying he was sorry, and his way of giving her something else to think about. But she knew that the distance between them was growing and that by having her working, he was acquiring more freedom. His kindness was selfish at heart. Still, in practical terms, the idea was attractive to her too. Working at Safeway was in many ways returning to the swimming classes she was once denied. Being able to go out by herself and have friends was plenty for her to ignore his deeper motives.

In the long run it was a different story. Richard's strategy ultimately backfired on him because his wife developed a friendship he would have never accepted, a friendship that opened Leah's eyes and that led to Adriel's escape.

"Ohhh, he shushed me, Nicole, he did, every time I tried to talk about it. And I tried a lot, at least until Adi left with Brandi because as you can imagine, that was so traumatic and it all happened so fast that all of a sudden I wasn't concerned about divorce or no divorce. I think in a way it was the same for him. He changed once Adriel left."

Leah stopped, as if wanting to remember what happened then. There was a gap. Her issue with memory was deeper than just confusing Friday with Monday; she knew that.

"It took a long while for me to talk about divorce again. I just didn't have the courage before. To be honest, I began asking again just a few weeks before I called you for the first time. I was worried about his reaction, so I waited until dinnertime, to get his full attention."

That evening, it was Richard who was sitting at their laminated kitchen table, Leah's usual spot. On the opposite side of the table was the stove, one of those standalone electrical stoves made of steel, painted white, with four burners on top and a small oven, from which Leah was taking out the macaroni and cheese they were having with a beef stew.

The heat and the sweet smell coming from inside the oven felt good on her face. She breathed deeply and stayed still, close to the heat. She wondered if raising her body temperature would stop the cold feeling in her gut, but it didn't. Even though her hands were shaking a little, she managed to remove the tray, with a towel in each hand, being careful not to burn the top of her hand on the upper rack, something she'd done so many times.

"He was on his computer, working on some client contract or something. I remembered him saying the food smelled really good and I thought, *well, this is a good start*. I knew he loved my macaroni and cheese and Jacob really loves it too. It's his favorite."

"Was Jacob in the kitchen when you were going to talk divorce?" Nicole interrupted her. She tried to hide her amazement, but couldn't.

"Oh no, no, of course not, Jacob was with my parents. He's spending a few weeks there. I guess I didn't tell you that, right? And funny you asked about Jacob because I did the same. I asked him when was Jacob coming back, but he didn't say anything. He just took his glasses off and looked at me as if I was crazy."

Resting the tray on the counter, Leah began searching for a spoon to serve the macaroni with the stew. She moved around the kitchen like a beaver building a dam, then struggled with the worn wood cutlery drawer that always got stuck and never closed properly.

All she could hear was the breathing of the old Sears refrigerator. Nervously, she began putting the plates together and changed the subject, Mother's voice resounding inside her. *When your husband gets back from work, make the evening his. Remember, he had a much more difficult day than yours.*

"Gosh, honey, I didn't ask you: How was your day? Any new clients?"

Silence. Richard didn't even acknowledge her this time around. As pale as he was, and under the kitchen light, without glasses, he seemed like a ghost.

"I was nervous. I don't know why, but I remember the kitchen suddenly felt foggy and I was a bit sweaty."

Leah served dinner in silence, everything on one plate. She also poured Richard a glass of Minute Maid lemonade, leaving the rest of the bottle on the table.

As she was serving, she looked at him and smiled. But without acknowledging her, he closed the computer screen, moved his plate next to the computer, reopened it and began eating, staring at the screen.

She too began eating, looking at him between bites. She knew what she needed to say next, but fearful of his response, waited until she found enough courage to talk. After taking a final bite, she gulped a big drink of lemonade to get the food down. Her mouth felt very dry.

"Anyways, I sat down and said something random about Hawaii Five-O, a show he really likes and I recorded for him. But you know, as I said, Richard had no interest in any conversation with me, which was my point, and I told him that. I told him that he doesn't even look at me anymore. But right away he banged the table, really hard.

This is my chance, I thought, but I was wrong. I hurried to tell him he was happier with her, that it would be easier for everybody if we divorced."

This wasn't easy for Leah. Countless times she'd tormented herself with images of the "young thing," but the reality was that she'd allowed the relationship to take place, in great part because deep down, she didn't care.

So hard and loud had Richard slammed the table after hearing Leah's divorce proposition that she almost dropped her fork, startled.

"You know, Richard, my intention is not to bother you. I mean, you wouldn't need excuses to see her, and I think you'd be happier, don't you think?" she insisted.

Richard closed his computer, before saying in a dry, cynical tone:

"The food's wonderful. Thank you very much. Leah, I wish all I had to do was this silly job of yours, you know? If my job was to make sure meatballs don't burn, my life would be so much easier. But it's not."

When Leah saw him unplugging the laptop charger, she tried to make her case, but that simply prompted him to leave the kitchen faster.

"I told him he could keep it all, Nicole, that I wasn't asking for a thing, but he simply stomped out, down to his office in the basement."

16) 3:53PM. Leah.

"So what happened next?" Nicole asked.

It was the beginning of summer, a few days after Adriel left her family. Leah's parents had gone to Baker City to help sort things out. The grieving silence and ochre-colored mood of the first days following Adriel's departure were replaced—at least in Leah's eyes—by tension. It was only in the shower she could let her guard down and give in to her feelings of loss and to fears and doubts about Adriel's future.

Upon their late night arrival Leah's parents hugged her and told her how sorry they were about the whole thing. Despite the "you look too thin, honey" type of comment, she felt supported and even a little guilty for causing so much pain.

The next morning things changed drastically. At breakfast—and this was to be the status quo through all the meals they shared—the air Leah breathed seemed thinner, like the thin air at the top of Mt. Rainier. She heard her parents and Richard breathing it in as they—she could swear—watched her and spoke between them with only their eyes.

Father speculated about Adriel's whereabouts and even suggested that someone must have helped her—and that someone would likely end up in jail. Leah stared at her pancakes, then cut a piece and brought it to her mouth. She knew they were looking for a sign; they suspected her.

Finally she lifted her head. "Can you pass me the syrup, Mother?" she said.

Leah could swear she saw Mother's lips tightening. She couldn't stand Leah being in control, that she wasn't giving an inch—or at least that's what Leah thought.

The tension only broke after breakfast, when Mother began her agenda, the to-do list, the let's correct this, let's correct that. Leah's parents had taken over. They'd arrived with a clear purpose. Everything they did was predictable. She was prepared for it, except for what happened the last night. That was something she and Brandi hadn't imagined throughout the endless calculations they made when they planned Adriel's escape.

Leah's mother was a skinny woman. Her eyes seemed closer set than normal, a feature that added character to a face that although it was weathered by age, was otherwise perfect. Unfortunately, her natural beauty was hidden behind the dark circles under her eyes.

Like her husband, she was pale. Her bones, like Leah's, were long and thin. She had full lips that once attracted eyes from all directions, and a small mouth that very rarely smiled, partly because secretly, she hated her teeth worn down and shortened by a severe case of bruxism, a condition caused by stress that made her grind them severely when she was asleep.

As soon as breakfast ended, she told Leah to go outside with her. They needed to work on the garden, she said. It looked awful.

She was wearing her usual jeans and a cream blouse. She rolled up the sleeves before putting on gardening gloves. Next to her were big bags of soil from Home Depot, an empty heavy-duty trash bag, and a hand shovel.

Leah's small front yard was a green sea of dry, dead patches of grass. Resting her hand on Leah's shoulder, Mother pointed at the patches and spoke in a nurturing tone that surprised her.

"The front of your house, Leah, is like the front of your soul. You've got to water your plants more often during the summer, dear. And you have to change the soil yearly. Here, let me show you how it's done."

She took some of the dirt from one of the larger pots and then, using her hands, mixed the new soil with it, making sure the soil was nice and loose.

"Go on, Leah. Go ahead and water this one while I go to the next one," she said.

Leah followed the instructions with a certain apprehension. She listened and did as she was told, but inside she was calculating her answers to the interrogation she suspected was coming at any moment.

Leah, also wearing jeans and a green T-shirt with Oregon printed on it in yellow went and got the hose and began watering the large pot.

"You have to wet it really well. Make sure it's all wet," Mother said and approaching Leah and patting her on the shoulder.

"It smells kind of nice," Leah said and smiled.

She inhaled deeply, smelling the fresh soil. She felt her mother's hand on her shoulder, and now patting her on the back in that loving way she'd been missing for so long.

"As for the grass, you've got to get on your knees and dig up the weeds, daily. But at this point, I'd say get it all out and spread some fertilizer on top, then water it often. You can use weed spray too. I can buy it for you later. You wouldn't know what to get. But it's not enough on it's own. It's like washing laundry without soap."

Gardening wasn't Leah's thing. She enjoyed having a few plants, but the idea of the perfect garden wasn't something that attracted her. She wouldn't even spend the money to hire a gardener if she could afford to. *I'm never gonna do this ever again in my life, but how can I tell her?* she thought. But as boring as she thought the whole thing was, her biggest preoccupation was still the questions she was expecting.

She was used to Mother's mood swings—being playful one moment and mean and abusive the next. And between the two, Mother the victim could appear at any moment, complaining of a migraine, begging Leah—although they both knew it was really an order—to take care of things while she rested. But this was different. Leah had felt true concern the previous night, and though breakfast was what she expected, in her mind, it was extraordinary that Mother wasn't blaming her for Adriel's disappearance.

Once she'd watered the first pot, still unsure of what was coming, she joined her mother to work on the second one, a small lavender bush. Mother removed her gloves and handed them to Leah.

"Go on, dear, see what you can do with this one." Mother smiled at her and even patted her arm.

There it was again. This was unusual. It had been years since Leah had felt Mother as a mother. The nurturing days and unconditional support had ended long ago. But somehow, subconsciously, this unexpected connection had liberated the warm memories of Scrabble and Ovaltine stored somewhere inside Leah. With some hesitation, Leah looked back in time in search of her true mom.

"You know, Mother, the problem is that I have little time for this. It's overwhelming," Leah said.

"Don't be silly," Mother said.

Leah kept working on the soil, nervously spreading it throughout the pot. She opened her mouth but stopped before she could say anything else. Mother noticed. She held Leah's hand and looked her straight in the eye.

"A woman can heal her marriage by obeying every reasonable and unreasonable word. Are you doing that, Leah? Be honest. Because I know you're not. We all know you're not."

The motherly tone was gone. Leah hurried back to digging, wanting to hide inside the humid dirt, like a worm. She knew what mother was referring to. But interestingly, this first fearful reaction was replaced with passive anger.

She wanted to scream. *Yes, Mother, I helped Adriel escape. I don't want my daughter to be as miserable as we both are!!!*

"But Mother, it's too much. I mean, I'm miserable. I was miserable even before Adi left. And now Richard isn't going to let me work anymore. He already told me so. So what else is left for me? What?"

"Stop!!!" Mother yelled, blowing away Leah's anger and bravery.

Leah shrank away like a puppy after an accident. When she looked back at her mother she saw the same eyes she'd seen the night she was locked in her room, the day they took her out of swimming.

Leah related this story to Nicole while she waited for the oven to heat up. By now, her hand was beating impatiently against her leg.

"She yelled at me really loud, Nicole," Leah bleated.

"I remember looking at her eyes and thinking, *Mother will never understand.* So that's the closest I ever got to asking her for help. I wanted to tell her that I didn't love Richard. How could I? I would have shouted at her that the only love I ever felt was for Daniel. And that *she* shut that down when they made me stop swimming. I never saw him again. And that was cruel."

At that moment, the oven bell rang, announcing it had reached four hundred degrees.

"But did you ever tell her about your marriage?" Noting Leah's tone, Nicole insisted.

"Hold on, Nicole, I need to put the chicken in the oven. Let me use the speakerphone for just a minute," Leah said.

She jumped out of the chair like a racehorse at the Kentucky Derby, and began moving as fast as she could to finish her task. She kept talking, louder now.

"Of course I did, and of course that didn't help. Mother knew about Richard's affair, but all she said was that I needed to beat his lover at her own game. You know? She was clueless about what was going on around here, and didn't care how I felt."

Sitting down again, calmer, she switched off the speakerphone before saying,

"You know, the irony is this: I really thought they had come to support the family, in the sense that Adriel was gone. But no. The truth was, we had no relationship. Throughout the years, we'd only gone to visit them twice, when the children were old enough to fly. That's it."

Terrified of those eyes, Leah evaded them by hurrying back to the pot, but Mother'd had enough. She took Leah's hands out of the dirt as if Leah was a ragdoll. The nervous digging annoyed her as much as Leah's words did. Then she grabbed Leah's chin, forcing her to look into her eyes.

"A job? Are you serious? You blew your chance big time. Your husband gave you a privilege and what did you do? Tell me, Leah, what did you do?"

There was a pause, as if her mother was waiting for her to confess. *Here it comes*, Leah thought. *Oh my God! Oh my God!! Oh my God!!!*

"*Servants are to be subject to their masters, always. It doesn't matter if the masters are perverse or unfair,* and we both know Richard is a good man, Leah. What you've done is going to take a lot of healing," Mother said.

Her eyes stayed on Leah's, which kept blinking until Mother let her go. She took the trowel from Leah and walked toward the house, not without first patting her on the shoulder and saying,

"Let's resume this later, darling. I'm exhausted and have a terrible headache. I need to lie down for a while."

Leah breathed at last. At that moment, Father appeared at the door, shirtless.

"Woman, I thought you were going to iron my shirt?"

"Oh, I'm sorry, honey, I completely forgot. I'll do it this evening, okay?" Mother said as she walked toward the door.

"I need you to do it now, sweetheart. Richard's taking me bowling and I want to wear that shirt."

Mother said nothing but turned and looked at Leah. Leah looked away.

She stayed outside finishing her task, not without realizing she'd have to direct her effort toward Father. Their parents would stay three more nights; she had to find a moment to talk to him.

The mood and the tension never went away. Mother neither relaxed nor seemed maternal again, although she helped Leah make meals and was especially attentive to Jacob. Despite everything, Leah enjoyed watching them playing the same games she'd played as a child, listening to the same words and the same little stories, eating the peanut butter brownies she loved so much that not surprisingly, Jacob loved too.

While Father and Richard spent most of the time together, downstairs at Richard's office and in front of the TV, he too took his time to enjoy being with his grandson as much as he could. He played catch with him and even got down on all fours to be his horse, something Leah didn't remember him doing with any of her siblings.

Days passed and Leah's fears of being confronted with questions about Adriel dissipated. Strangely and to her relief, even Richard stopped asking questions as soon as his in-laws arrived. Other than Mother's subtle insinuations, that was one thing she could stop worrying about.

Paranoia on the other hand, grew and grew until she felt overwhelmingly afraid. Precisely, it was the calm before the storm, the silence at the table and the eyes on her that seemed to multiply day by day that increasingly troubled Leah. In a way, she felt they were all avoiding her somehow, although in reality they weren't; what they *were* avoiding was the elephant in the room.

By the time their last day arrived, she'd have thought she was silly to be so worried about nothing. But her worst fears began surfacing again that morning when they all went to McDonald's with Jacob but suggested she stay home.

"I think it's best you stay here, Leah. It's important that one of us always stays home, just in case Adriel shows up, don't you think?" Father said.

The idea didn't sound crazy. But it was Richard's cynical smile at the moment Father made the suggestion that made Leah wonder if they were scheming. Later that night, she would discover that indeed, they were orchestrating something—and that was her parents' true and only agenda. And when did she find out? At the same time she was finally able to talk to Father while they were eating burgers in the back yard.

Mother was sitting at the picnic table by herself, nibbling carrots and vegetable slices with ranch sauce, and watching Richard play catch with Jacob. Father and Leah were at the grill, chatting while they made the burgers. He seemed more approachable than in days past, a good sign.

Superficially, the scene seemed beautiful. Up close, though, it wasn't.

"This is a great family tradition, isn't it Peanut? Do you remember how you and I used to make burgers at White Oak Lake? Those were the best burgers, don't you agree?" Father said.

How could she not?

She remembered what her father had said at the park when she handed him the cheese slices for the burgers. "Peanut, you know you're Mother's big helper, right? And that means you're *my* helper too."

Looking at the spatula moving the burgers randomly to prevent them from coming into contact with the flames, Leah's mind jumped from past to present. It was the same scene, except back then, she was looking forward to the burgers and to sitting between Father's legs to eat hers, sharing a bag of Doritos and a bottle of cold Pepsi.

Wandering, her mind landed on a night she'd nearly forgotten.

"Father hit me yesterday, Mother."

Mother was stroking her arm, but the feeling of that sweaty hand that stank of garlic touching her was unbearable to Leah.

"He means well, darling. And it's a bit your fault too. You know that."

Father's order to bring salt and pepper liberated Leah from the memory. She went to the kitchen to get it, and in the process thought hard about when would be the best time to ask him about her predicament. She returned with the shakers without resolving her dilemma.

"It's a shame, Leah. Adriel should be here, learning how to make these burgers, you understand? I mean, wouldn't it be great if Adriel could be here?"

He stared at Leah with his small blue eyes and finished his sentence.

"Tradition's everything, Leah. Everything."

Looking for an escape, she hurried to pass him the cheese slices, but feeling nervous, dropped the first one on the ground.

"It's not time for cheese just yet, Leah, you know that," he said.

His eyes were lifeless, like an open, rotten clam. Leah stared at them wondering what happened with those sweet eyes that had looked at her when she was little.

"You have to put the cheese on it at the right time, Peanut, so it melts just right."

The only thing remaining of those glorious days was the beautiful, charred, sweet smell of the burgers. Truth was, those burgers were still the best Leah had ever eaten.

"Look at your husband, poor guy. He's like a zombie. May the Lord be with him, the undeserved hell he is living."

Just a breath away from screaming at the top of her lungs, she put the cheese back where it was and longing for the awkward moment to end, began organizing the few things that were on top of the small table next to the grill, to avoid having to look at Richard.

Father persisted. "Look at him Leah, look at him."

Believing they were still playing catch, she turned her head to where Richard and Jacob had been throwing the ball. Her eyes found him head down, seated close to the cooler. He seemed trapped in a dark cloud and somehow afflicted. Yet the chill Leah suddenly felt came after she directed her eyes to the other side of the table. Her mother, holding Jacob, was staring right at her. The child tried to squirm out of her arms, wanting to go and play, but Leah read Mother's lips: "No Jacob, stay with me a bit longer, dear," she said.

"Mother, he doesn't like to be held for long. Let him go," Leah yelled, uncharacteristically.

"Pass me the cheese, Leah. It's time," Father said.

Leah obeyed, but kept her eyes on Jacob and her Mother, who purposely didn't react.

"Mother, please let Jacob go."

"You know Leah, Jacob wants to come and spend some time with us. Isn't that right, Jacob?"

"Yes, grandma!!!" the boy said.

Leah felt a lump the size of a melon grow in her throat. She tried to speak, but couldn't. An urge to run to her child invaded her. She took a step or two forward, but just then, Mother let the child go, and Father said,

"Let it be, Leah. Pass me the 57 Sauce. I wanna put some on the burgers before we take them out."

Mother stared at Leah, confronting her with a half smile.

"Leah?" Father said again, impatiently. At last Leah let it go. She passed the sauce and a little brush and with a forced smile said,

"The secret ingredient, like the old times."

He smiled and reached out and touched her. They both must have thought the gesture normal, but from the outside, he looked as though he was petting a friendly, but dirty, stray.

All Leah could think about was the idea of Jacob going to her parents. She wanted to address that, but her father's gesture gave her the courage to finally speak to him. The words came out without her permission.

"Father, you have to know, I'm miserable here. I'm truly miserable. Please help me, I need to leave Richard."

He flung the large spatula down.

Telling the story to Nicole, Leah remembered the pain of him slapping her hard with the back of his hand. It wasn't physical pain; she felt the pain in her belly.

"If you want a father at all, don't even think about what you just said. And should you ever decide to stamp your way to Hell, know that you won't get any help from us. Is that clear?"

"I guess that was the end of that, right?" Nicole said, interrupting.

"Right away he tried to correct his outburst. He began saying how it wasn't my fault, really, that I was probably fed lies at work and that he and Richard had decided I couldn't go to work anymore. And you know, Nicole, I saw that coming, of course, from the moment Richard began interrogating me. But anyhow, he kept going on and on, telling me how everything was gonna be fine."

Telling the story to Nicole, Leah was reliving that day— her father's hand coming at her. She tensed her muscles out of fear, but this time he didn't hit her. He just grabbed her shoulder and told her,

"Leah, sweetheart, please, accept God's gift to you. I don't want you to feel we're forcing things on you. We just want what's best for you. You know how much we love you."

In the kitchen talking with Nicole, Leah heard the words coming over and over from difference voices; first, her father's:

We just want what's best for you.

And then, Richard's:

I just want what's best for you. You know how much I love you. I'll come back tomorrow to get you.

She replayed the images in her head; she knew there was something more to them. Engaged in the effort, she abandoned the phone on the table, trying her best to pull more out of the scene. What she remembering happening with her father was complete, but all she could remember about Richard that day was his voice, which she played in her head over and over, until abruptly, in her mind's eye, she saw the door closing violently in front of her.

WHAM!!!

Once more, the door was bright red, but this time, there was a small, cream-colored poster hanging on it, mounted under glass with a simple brown wood frame. The poster seemed to be a quote written with nice, old-fashioned calligraphy, but Leah couldn't make out what was written on it.

She frowned and tried again to see the door, but it was futile. At last, she realized she hadn't heard Nicole for a long time. She finally rushed to get the phone, only to realize Nicole was gone.

"Hello? Hello!! Hello!!!" she yelled, desperately and in the absence of any response, looked at the phone screen to verify the call had ended. She felt trapped and as though she couldn't exhale, as if a cork had been squeezed into her airway. Lost, she made a gesture as if to throw the phone against the wall, but instead, she screamed as loud as she could. The cork popped, she screamed as long as there was air in her lungs. She was about to explode into tears when the phone rang again. It was Nicole.

17) 3:53PM. Richard.

By the time Richard returned to his office, Larry and Charles had both left to meet with clients. Mike wasn't there, but Richard didn't want to take chances. He checked the estimate he'd worked on and then sent it to Mike by email, so he could review it before sending it to the client. Fearing for his job, he wanted to be sure he had his boss's approval in writing.

He checked the sent box to be sure the message had gone through successfully before giving his attention to a bogus series of tasks designed to prolong his stay at the office. This was his way of impressing Mike and showing him that despite the loss of that contract, he wasn't giving up.

He cleaned the desktop on his computer, deleted junk emails, ran the anti-virus program he'd been waiting to run for months, went over and over his to-do list and reorganized his in/out paper trays, shrinking the amount of paper inside them to almost nothing.

The last task was a useless reorganization of his top drawer, an exercise he performed mechanically, moving little things in and out of small containers, but without thinking about it. He couldn't get Leah's phone calls and the conversation he'd had with Leah's father out of his mind.

"Let's chat about that later. It's been difficult for her. Let me talk to her, okay? But in the meantime, you better wake up," said Leah's father over the phone.

It's gotta be an attorney. She must be talking to an attorney, he repeated. *How many times has she asked me for a divorce by now?* He tried to compute a number. Memories of their arguments in the kitchen flashed through his mind. But his calculations failed. His memories were superimposed, for brief moments, by memories of his own recurrent nightmare of a fictional, well-dressed, fifty-something woman attorney with white hair, a nice figure, and one of those butthole feminist faces: it's like they've gotta take a shit but there ain't a bathroom nearby, he liked to say.

"Love, that smells really good. What is it?" he'd told Leah the last time she suggested a divorce. She was taking the macaroni and cheese out of the oven. This was one of his favorites. The tangy, sweet smell of melted cheddar took him back to his childhood. But that wasn't why he said anything. It was just a game. He could see her trembling, looking at the ceiling when she was lying, the angle of her mouth when her smile wasn't sincere. For God's sake, he'd known her for so long, he knew every single one of her moves; she couldn't fool him.

"Oh, before I forget, I recorded Hawaii Five-O," she said, forcing a smile.

Then came the blaming, it was all so predictable, so pathetic:

"Richard, you don't even look at me anymore."

And then all this bullshit about him and Liberty and how all of a sudden he wanted a divorce for his own sake. How nice of her!

He recalled that evening so clearly. Sitting at the kitchen table with his laptop he was browsing Major League baseball results, pretending he was busy with work. He knew she'd ask for a divorce next. Pretending to be busy was always the easiest way to get rid of Leah.

"You wouldn't need excuses to see her," she said. It was all a manipulative scheme to make him feel guilty. That's why he walked away from her. The best way to get an idea off Leah's mind was to shut her down at once. *You can only kill a snake by its head, son*, his father always told him.

Yes, he knew all of Leah's tricks; when she'd started crawling he was already running. That was a fact. How or why he had underestimated her motherly instincts was the one thing he couldn't forgive himself for.

Resentful, he made a fist when the music on the radio stopped and the loud voice of the DJ brought him back to his office.

"It's going to be a gorgeous evening as we prepare for the eclipse," the DJ said, and then there was an endless station break that annoyed Richard to the point he got up to turn the radio off.

Back at his desk, he looked at the time: 3:53PM, it said.

Richard got up again, just for a moment to peek through Mike's door. He wasn't there. He went back to his seat. *I guess I'll leave now. I'll be home a little before four thirty. Who knows, maybe I'll catch her on the phone if I get home early*, he thought.

He gathered his belongings and got ready to walk out. When he reached to grab his cell phone he saw a new text message on the screen.

"I'm working today. It'll have to be tomorrow," it said.

The text upset him. But not the way Leah would infuriate him. Now he was just disappointed. The text message wasn't from Leah; he had to stay silent. He had no choice but to wait, for he had no control over Liberty.

He hadn't seen her in five days. She'd gone to Boise to the wedding of a childhood friend. And in less than two weeks she'd leave again to visit her parents for Thanksgiving.

Liberty was an addiction; once she was in Richard's mind it was hard to get rid of her. The good news was that, most times, he could stop at her place on his way home because being a bartender, she worked the night shift at least three times a week. But now she'd be gone for so long, she'd work double shifts to make up for the lost income.

He'd texted earlier. "Don't worry about money. Don't work this afternoon. I have to see you." It took her half a day to respond.

Walking to the car, he read the text. He was tempted to call her just then. He waited a couple of minutes to start the car. But after a moment of indecision, he found himself driving away from his office.

They'd met at Barley Brown, a local brewery where she bartended. Richard was there with Larry and Charles celebrating a contract. They stayed the whole afternoon. As usual, Larry and Charles drank till they were drunk, while Richard focused on the food and his usual diet Pepsi.

Larry, but especially Charles started hitting on Liberty after the first few rounds and then got more and more obnoxious.

She didn't care. She was used to it. It was like a game with a puppy. She had a string she let the puppy sniff only to take it away from him just when he was about to take a bite. More interesting to Liberty was the nerdy, timid guy who didn't drink and didn't seem interested in her at all.

She joked with Richard a little and pushed her breasts forward whenever she served him. He kept apologizing for his friends, a gesture she found cute.

Everything would have ended right there if it wasn't for the size of the tip Richard had given her. He wasn't trying to impress her. It was an embarrassment and the realization that such a hot girl was paying so much attention to him, even though he wouldn't have noticed if Larry hadn't pointed it out to him. She'd made his day.

"Call me anytime, cutie," she said after taking the tip, touching the tip of Richard's nose and handing him a piece of paper with her number. Two days later, he went back for lunch, and then again, and again. For her it was another one of her little games, at least at the beginning, until one day she mentioned her troubles with paying rent, and he offered to help out.

Still, nothing would ever have happened if Liberty hadn't invited him to her apartment, to thank him for all his help. It had been a slow seduction, swimming in cold wine and broth that, simmering slowly, gradually grew piping hot. Only when Liberty thought Richard was about to explode, saturated in his own boiling juices, she removed him from the oven to devour him from head to toes, to his complete satisfaction.

After that night, he couldn't help going back, over and over. It wasn't just sex. Beyond everything else, what made him go back to her at the beginning was the adventure, the getting away with it, the adrenaline and endorphins flowing through him as he drove to her apartment.

At first, by giving her money to pay the rent, he thought power had shifted, that he was the one holding the hot pan handle. Soon he found the payments weren't a power-giving device but a pre-condition for her to even consider spending time with him.

For a man like Richard that was something very difficult to accept. But even after Leah discovered the affair, and as a result the adrenaline was gone, his relationship with Liberty grew deeper. He was willing to take the shortest stick. He thought he loved her.

"Piggy"—yes, she called him Piggy—"you look tired. Why don't you lie down and I'll rub your back?" she'd say.

Every day it was the same. But the predictability didn't dampen his desire to see her. He'd lie back and talk for hours—about work, marriage, even Adriel; it didn't matter. All he knew was that Liberty listened to him like nobody ever had. God, she was such a good listener. She never asked about Leah. She didn't want him to leave his wife. Her position was well understood. She just listened for as long as needed before rubbing his belly, reaching lower, slowly. He left feeling invigorated and rejuvenated after another day at a job he hated in the knowledge that Leah was the next stop.

Liberty had been so good to him. But things were changing: Liberty was cooling down. He could sense it. And the more she ignored him, as she did at times, the more he wanted to be with her.

There were times when she was short with him, even rude. He'd thought of leaving her, especially after Leah's father confronted him. The thought went through his mind as he headed out on highway I-84 to Baker City. *How rude is it to wait six hours to answer a simple text? And to be short with me like there's no room for discussion?* he thought. *My texts are a whole lot longer than hers, every time.* But he knew he wouldn't be able to break up with her. Only Liberty could end it.

He pictured her naked on the bed. She was slender and full breasted, and had a butterfly tattoo on her shoulder. She always lay with her legs crossed and her arms hiding her light-colored nipples as if she was posing for a soft porn magazine.

Suddenly a long, desperately loud horn blast jolted Richard out of his daydreams. His truck was swerving into the next lane.

"Oh my God," he yelped, before re-establishing control of the truck. Embarrassed, he waved to the driver next to him and waited until she could pass him. Then, impulsively, he took out his cell phone to call Liberty. He wanted to complain to her, wanted to see her so badly.

Phone in hand, he hesitated. She definitely was like Penny, Leah's cat, who didn't like to be touched unless she wanted to be petted, and if you tried to pet her when she didn't want you to, she'd leave a scar on your arm to remind you: pet me only when I ask you to pet me.

When he finally dialed, the phone rang a few times. He hung up before the voicemail kicked in and then dialed again. This time she picked up right away.

"I told you not to call me. I'm working," she said. He could hear her snapping the gum in her mouth.

"When will you be finished?" he asked.

"I'm working, okay? Call me tomorrow," Liberty said and hung up.

Is she with somebody else? Fuck! he thought. He considered taking the next exit to head back to the brewery and wait for her there. It was a desperate move; he knew. She was working, period. He pictured her getting upset, like the night he showed up at the bar where she was celebrating a late birthday with her girlfriends, just to have her tell him the relationship was over, that he was too possessive and didn't give her space.

Still holding his phone, he was about to dial again. The urge to see her hadn't disappeared, but he knew she'd just reject him. *Sleep with babies, you wake up with a wet bed,* Larry had told him. He was the only one at the office who knew about the affair.

Resigned, he set the phone on the passenger seat and accelerated, distracted by thoughts of Liberty's naked body. He was horny. After a day like today he'd have loved a good session of raunchy sex, but that wasn't going to happen. Leah wasn't Liberty. When she was willing to do it, she'd lie there like a corpse, and then whine about how much it hurt.

The memory of the last time they'd fucked came to him. More than a memory, it was a nightmare he wished he could forget.

"I know what you truly need," he said that very last time they did it, holding her hand and guiding her to the bedroom. He couldn't even put it in the context of time, it had been so long.

Leah held his hand to stop him, forcing a smile. Caressing his arm with her free hand, she said,

"I'd really rather not. I have a bit of a headache. I just need to move around a little bit. Maybe I should go cut the grass."

He enjoyed her hand on his arm. Aroused, he began caressing her face, but very quickly moved his hand down to her breasts.

"Why not? Adriel and Jacob need a brother. I'll be gentle," he said playfully.

"Because it hurts, Richard. It really does! Remember the bleeding?" Her voice was low, as if they could be heard.

"So what are you saying? Once a semester's good enough?"

"Please lower your voice. Jacob might still be awake."

There she goes again, he thought. Her affection for the child made him madly jealous. The love between mother and child blossomed in a way his couldn't and never would. He'd learned this already with Adriel. He insisted; he prevailed, but things always went the wrong way. Her body turned so rigid.

Seeing her face distorted by the intense pain was like an ice cold shower, literally. He pulled off and watched her burst into tears, at last. He felt bad. He didn't mean to hurt her. He apologized and tried to comfort her. He never tried again.

He drove onward. Apart from the car that had passed him, I-84 was emptier than usual, almost deserted. He'd driven that highway so many times he could probably do it with his eyes closed. The sun was bright and shining in his eyes. He squinted and drove on past the same traffic signs, billboards and pine trees. Telephone poles passed him, heading in the opposite direction, as fast or as slow as he drove.

Bored with the landscape, he reached that strange moment of wakeful dreaming people sometimes reach when they sit still for too long; when thoughts invade our minds and take strange forms and get mixed all together like a vegetable scramble.

Boredom revived an old dilemma. The idea of a divorce came to knock at the door of his thoughts—and not for the first time. He'd thought about it many times on the drive back home from Liberty's after a wonderful youthful night, free of bad memories, breathing the hope of having a new family with her. *A new beginning!* He'd surely be forgotten if he were able to create what he couldn't with Leah. He'd be forgotten because at the end, everything was Leah's fault. How often had he begged her to go to a doctor to fix the problem, but she wouldn't go. As far as he was concerned, he'd done all he could. He'd never felt sexually wanted by her. He didn't think she could feel sexually attracted to anyone, she couldn't please anyone; really, she was a real sack of potatoes in bed, if anybody was.

But whenever he remotely considered the idea of leaving Leah, irrefutable obstacles came to the defense of the sacred marriage. He grasped the wheel tightly before the first obstacle; the memory of his sick parents reminded him of his obligations.

He remembered what his father had said. *I know the family, son. Leah's perfect for you. The Lord sent you this beautiful bride; marriage is his gift to both of you. Don't forget, you aren't a man until you have a wife and a family to guide.*

He had serious doubts about marrying—and he'd gone to his mother for help. "But, Mother, she's a lot younger than I am. We have nothing in common."

Son, nobody's born with things in common. You make it happen. She's younger than you are, so show her your world. She'll embrace it.

In the end, Richard reluctantly agreed.

He was still driving on autopilot and unaware that the car was going faster. As usual, the whole hypothetical divorce picture was spiraling down to the same bitchy woman attorney, nailing him at court with his hands pressed together like Jesus Christ's were. And with Leah laughing at him in the end.

He imagined himself knocking at Liberty's door after the defeat, with a pocket as empty as a dirty sock. She was the consolation he could count on, except that in the next imaginary image, she was opening the door and telling him,

"You're a loser, you know. I should have known. What are you good for if you can't help me pay the rent?"

He put his foot on the accelerator and moved into the fast lane, re-energized by fear and resentment. Refocused, he began organizing his ideas. Leah was gonna tell him who she'd been talking to. She was gonna surrender her phone. He was going to lock her up again.

18) 4:05PM. Leah.

"Hello! Hello!!" Leah said.

"Yes, Leah. I'm here."

When Leah heard Nicole's voice she sighed loud and deep, and walked toward the bathroom, smiling.

"My Lord, I'm so glad you're calling me back, Nicole! I apologize; I know you waited for ages. I got caught up in my own thoughts and forgot all about the phone. I guess what happened is the memory of that red door came back to me. It's weird, but now I'm sure the door existed somehow, and that there was this small poster hanging behind it. I can see it right now, but can't make sense of it."

Nobody trained me for this, Nicole thought. What she'd uncovered so far was disturbing; a world she'd never understand. But the idea of somebody insisting it was Monday on a Friday or leaving the phone in the middle of a conversation was too much. To make matters worse, Leah so far had done her best to avoid getting a referral to either a professional or a hot line.

Overwhelmed, between calls, Nicole texted her supervisor for advice. She didn't know what to do; she didn't think she could help Leah.

"*You have to stay with her, Nicole. Clearly you're her crutch,*" the supervisor texted back.

With this in mind, Nicole listened to Leah. It was getting late and it was Friday.

"I understand, no worries, I'm here for you, Leah, I wouldn't just let you go. I've only got about ten minutes, but I'll be happy to talk with you next week or refer you to a hotline right now, Leah."

While Nicole was going on about the advantages of having a local referral set up, Leah went back to the kitchen to look at the time. It was 4:05PM.

Oh God, what have I done? I have to hurry, she thought. She rushed to the living room and began organizing it, ineffectively.

Between the long phone call and her earlier preoccupation with the question of Adriel showing up or not showing up, she'd neglected the house. She was late with the chicken, and still had to prepare a side dish and fold the laundry that was on top of the sofa, along with dealing with Mother's card and present.

Like her obsession with punctuality, anxiety before Richard's arrival was an aspect of her personality seeded in childhood.

Leah, it's your fault your father is so upset. No one else but yours, lady. Don't ever forget how to receive a man when he comes home from work. Remember, he had a hard day, much harder than yours, always.

Scolded by Father, Mother had spit her resentment on Leah and left the room without giving young Leah a chance to explain herself. Leah wanted to say that all of what Mother had passed on to her was too much; that David and Bethany were fighting about a toy car, that when she went to see what happened, she'd realized it wasn't just one toy, but a whole Toys' R Us store spread over the floor; that Adam had left a mess in the kitchen after preparing a simple sandwich, that Aaron was literally feeding cereal to this gorilla doll of his; that in view of it all, she wanted to wake Mother from her nap, that she really needed the help, but worried Mother would get upset. She knew about Mother's migraines and knew Father was interviewing for a job. She'd tried to get it all ready before he arrived, still jobless.

"So what do you think? Should I look for somebody in your area?" Nicole said, hoping she had convinced her by now.

Leah didn't even hear what Nicole had proposed. Overwhelmed by the thought of Richard arriving and finding nothing was ready, she interrupted Nicole abruptly.

"Oh my God, look how late it is! I need to finish dinner; Richard will be here any time! And I'm a mess, the house is a mess!!!"

Holy shit. Poor woman, Nicole thought.

"Leah, Leah!" She raised her voice. "It's not even four fifteen yet. You told me Richard would get there at five at the earliest. You have time!"

It took a moment for Leah to recover from her panic attack. Nicole helped her take a deep breath and let go the futile rush to organize everything. They agreed to hang up by four fifteen so Leah could finish her tasks.

The conversation continued. Calmer now, Leah went back to the bathroom and managed to urinate without making it obvious to Nicole; that would have embarrassed her big time. She covered the phone's microphone with one hand and once she was done, didn't flush or wash her hands.

"Does this happened to you often? Do you get this agitated a lot?" Nicole asked.

"Not at all," Leah said, slightly ashamed, and knowing she was lying.

"Are you safe, Leah? What would happen if your husband were to arrive and see the house isn't in order?"

Nicole would have to call the authorities if she knew her client was in danger.

"Oh, no, no. I mean, yes, of course I'm safe." Leah dismissed her right away.

"To me it's more about picking my battles. I prefer having Richard on my good side, if you know what I mean. The last thing I need is an argument tonight."

She continued mumbling incoherently and then paused.

"I miss my children, that's all."

Her voice cracked.

"I need to ask Richard again when Jacob's coming back from my parents. It's been weeks! It would have been helpful for me to have him around today because I really, really thought Adi was going to show up. I really thought I'd hear from Brandi too."

As she said these words, Leah looked at the clock again. *She isn't coming*, she thought, but then her hope took a second breath: There's time; Brandi wouldn't do it any other way.

Leah had imagined Adriel living happily with Brandi. She'd also found herself in desperation, imagining Adriel living on the streets, like those youngsters she saw the time she visited downtown Portland. These fictional, pessimistic images kept torturing Leah until a real-life memory came to her: Adriel's tearful eyes, the day they said goodbye:

"Can't you come?" Leah always remembered Adriel saying the moment she sent her away with Brandi.

She felt the chill air on her skin and, battling tears, forced a smile. She looked at Brandi briefly, as if asking for help, when Adriel added,

"I mean, you and Jacob, Mom, both of you!"

That's when Leah lost the battle and tears began rolling down. She looked her daughter straight in the eye and, tightened by the rope of her own limitations said,

"I'm sorry, Adi. I know this is hard, but it's complicated. I can't do it."

With this image haunting her from day one, it became difficult for Leah to stick to the plan. She followed all the details religiously, except for keeping herself from calling Brandi.

After a few days, she tried to call, but Brandi had disconnected her phone and changed her line just a couple of days after the escape, as they'd planned.

Even when she heard the message from the operator saying Brandi's phone was disconnected, she tried two, three more times. Unable to connect, she felt a dark cloud form above her head. Doubt rained down on her like a tropical deluge. The only connection she had with Adriel was gone.

How could Brandi do this to me? Leah thought back then, but the memory of urging and begging Brandi to stick to the idea, to never, ever contact her, and to instruct Adriel to do the same came to Brandi's rescue.

Brandi's voice spoke to her often, in her head. It wasn't a whisper; Brandi was incapable of whispering. It was more of an obnoxious loud, nasal voice speaking to her.

"Honey, where have you been the past fifteen years? You don't know Eddie Vedder?" This was something Brandi had told her once. It was one of those random memories that stay with people.

Their relationship began when Leah started working at the supermarket. Brandi was assigned to train Leah to use the cash register and learn food codes.

"Brandi, this is Leah. Leah, this is Brandi." Marvin, the store manager said.

They looked at each other with distrust. The difference in their attire said it all. Brandi was wearing a red mini skirt about halfway up her thighs and a tight white T-shirt that said Baby Doll in sparkling pink. Her hair was loose, highlighted, and straightened with a dryer, and she was wearing her usual heavy makeup. Yet, what impressed Leah the most were the nipples clearly visible through Brandi's thin T-shirt; she almost never wore a bra.

In return, Brandi looked at Leah wondering if she was auditioning for a role as Laura Ingalls at a play put together by the local church. Chewing gum, Brandi saw Leah staring at her breasts and, annoyed, said,

"Honey, you can touch them if you want to."

"Brandi, please. Don't start," Marvin said. He was used to Brandi, although that didn't mean he agreed with her demeanor.

"Hey! I'm serious, I know they're a work of art, aren't they Marv? I've seen you salivating at them too, honey," Brandi said jokingly, pushing Marvin gently.

The manager shook his head and raised his arms, leaving before Brandi said something worse. *I'm not going there*, he thought. Despite the awkward start, he knew they'd figure things out, as they did.

"There's no code on these plums, Brandi. What do I do?" Leah said a few days later while working at the cash register. An elderly lady was waiting in front of the cashier belt. She had short, silver hair one could tell she'd done herself with a dryer, and was holding it together with a flowery, black-and-white headband she'd made herself.

"Honey, remember! Would you mind ma'am? She's in training," Brandi said.

"That's okay, no rush," the old lady said.

"First, look at other plums and see if one of them has it. Otherwise, you can always look at the code here, see? Enter fruit and kind of follow the lead, you know?"

Leah smiled and followed the instructions promptly.

"Yippee!!!" she yelled and pumped her fist in the air once she got the code entered.

Brandi looked at Leah as if she was just out of the sanatorium.

"Honey, this ain't the lottery," Brandi said.

"I just love it, I love so much being here," Leah said with a big smile.

"Honey, I'll pay you if you get me out of here, just name the amount," Brandi said jokingly.

"One must like her job to be good at it, that's for sure," the old lady said.

It was supermarket beltline talk, but Leah and Brandi talked all day for the few days Brandi was in charge of the training. Layers began getting exposed and before they knew it, they'd grown dependent on each other.

A few months later—and weeks before Leah discovered Richard was planning to marry Adriel off—she was in the break room having some coffee with Malike, a young black man from Tennessee who worked in the meat department.

This was a very small room with no windows, a refrigerator, a water dispenser, a large coffee machine and a medium-size table where people mingled during their break.

"You got to tenderize your ribs if you don't have a smoker. It ain't barbeque without a smoker, but it still pretty gooood," the man said.

"What you do is this: put your ribs in a deep tray. Put salt and pepper on both sides, then add water until you fill the tray about one inch, half a cup of vinegar, a few garlic cloves and a few bay leaves. Then cover them with foil and put in the oven at whatever lowest temperature you can, ideally one hundred and forty or less, eight hours. You turn them at hour four, and that's it, then you grill them the next day with the sauce, baby, and ya'll will be licking your fingers, believe me."

Malike was going on and on about his rib recipe when Brandi entered the room. She touched Leah's shoulder and greeted Malike. She made coffee, washed the dishes somebody had left in the sink, trying to make time. Once she ran out of tasks, she sat in silence with an old People magazine, until Malike finally said he had to get back to work.

Brandi stood up and made sure nobody was coming to the room, then set her chair close to Leah's.

"Honey, I did some investigating for you."

"What do you mean?"

"Honey, I don't care what they told you, but I'm damn sure you can leave that piece of shit anytime you want. The problem is Adriel and Jacob and how much money you'll get, but you'll make it. It just ain't gonna be that simple. I mean, I think you'll get full custody but you'll need an attorney."

"I don't have money for that, you know it, and even my parents told me they won't help me."

This wasn't a rebuttal; Leah's eyes shone and stared at Brandi. She knew Brandi was her only hope. Her eyes were pleading for answers.

"Honey, I know it's hard, but you need to do something or Adriel is gonna end up like you. You know it. If you get custody, he won't be able to do anything without your approval, understand?"

Envisioning the idea of Adriel's early marriage wasn't easy. Even before reading Adriel's diary, Leah knew that outcome was inevitable, but avoided the vision; it was too painful. Instead, she focused on the idea of being divorced and with her children. It was such a wonderful feeling, a feeling that didn't last. The momentary optimism was crushed by her fears of failure; that she would ultimately lose Adriel and Jacob.

She hid her face behind her hands and sighed deeply. Brandi took her phone out and after a brief search, took a napkin and a pen, and wrote a number she'd saved in her phone. She handed the napkin to Leah.

"Take this, honey. Don't put this in your phone, he'll find it. This is a group in New York that helps people in your situation. You can call them and they can help you. They have therapists and lawyers and the whole bananas. They can help you, Leah."

Leah took the napkin and laughed.

"Adriel has better handwriting than you do, Brandi."

"You don't survive in this world writing pretty, honey. You just don't," Brandi said and they both laughed.

No. *There was no way Brandi would let me down*, Leah said to herself. *Brandi's just following the plan; she knows what's best to protect Adriel. I'll hear from her, and from Adriel too, if not today, someday; I just need to be patient. Brandi will know when is best*, she thought.

The day of the agreement they were sitting at Mad Matilda's Coffee Shop, a place they went to during their break at Safeway Supermarket. They could hardly afford it, but Leah, in particular, loved to go there. It was the one place she could go without Richard knowing about it.

This time it was different. Leah had read Adriel's diary. *The Lord guided me to it*, she concluded. It was very unusual for her to lift Adriel's mattress, but she was having a difficult time tucking the sheets around it. She'd seen the small notebook before, of course; she'd bought it for Adriel. Adriel always hid it in her underwear drawer, underneath a disorganized bunch of panties and socks. *Why here?* Leah wondered when she saw it. She'd never opened it to look inside. A rare curiosity led her to browse through the pages. Ironically, it wasn't the writing, but the interesting drawings Adriel had made at the beginning of each day that fascinated her and kept her going until she arrived at that bizarre tree with the cat and the long tail. The word "marry" appeared in the corner of her eye, and then she read. The sound of the notebook hitting the floor woke her from the shock.

The coffee shop was small and homey. The floor had a nice decorative pattern of flowers. The furniture, sofas as well as tables and chairs of all sizes and shapes, seemed stolen from the set of an old country house. Leah and Brandi liked to sit on the sofa right at the entrance, but that day, they were sitting at a table in a corner of the coffee shop, leaning forward to speak, close to each other and in secret, as if they were planning the next bank robbery at the local bank.

"Honey, I'm telling you, I'm moving to Olympia. I got a cousin there who is going to help me out finding a job and all. I got to get away from Baker City. I need a change. I got to get away from here. I want nothing that reminds me of Jerry. I really thought he was the one," Brandi said and lowered her head.

The feeling of failure wrapped her like a blanket, which she tossed away just a few seconds later. An eternal optimist, Brandi turned to focus on Leah as soon as she could.

"But let's talk about Adriel, honey. Let's talk about you."

She reached out to hold Leah's hands in hers.

Leah smiled. An old memory exploded from the depth of her soul like a champagne cork, appearing in front of her just for a second or two, but long enough to make the experience even more enjoyable.

The memory started with the school's merry-go-round spinning fast, the children on top screaming for joy, while four boys kept it going.

"C'mon, Leah! Come with me!!! We'll hang on the border of the merry-go-round, like Melissa and Curt, with our hair loose, okay?!" said Shirley Clemens, that wild girl with the funny voice.

Little Leah hesitated. She wanted to do it. Rubbing her hands, she stepped forward once or twice before stopping.

"But Shirley, that looks scary. They're going too fast! And my mom will get mad if I take my hairpins out."

"Don't be silly, silly! I know how to put it back," Shirley said, believing she could put Leah's hair back together, in the same way one knows how to wrap a present.

Leah thought about it, bouncing a little, nervously. Shirley took Leah's hands in hers and smiled at her.

"Faster!!! Faster!!!" Sitting in the coffee shop, Leah saw herself on top of the merry-go-round, her hair lashing her face wildly.

At the coffee shop, Leah smiled. Brandi's hands were cold, like Shirley's. Looking up, she found Brandi's eyes staring at her. For whatever reason, she trusted this woman.

Waiting for an answer and seeing Leah's hesitation, Brandi insisted.

"Honey, if I tell you I'm taking care of her, I mean it: I am," Brandi said.

She was chewing a chocolate chip cookie and some of the crumbs flew toward Leah, who moved sideways like a boxer to avoid them. They both laughed; Brandi made her laugh even during the most stressful moments.

19) 4:05PM. Adriel.

Still sleepy, Adriel rubbed her eyes before opening them. The bright sunlight hurt a little, and it took a few seconds for her vision to adjust. She noticed there was just a single car parked outside the restaurant.

She wondered if the place was closed. Only when she looked at the open sign hanging on the door and was ready to walk toward the entrance did she realize that Monica and Kyle were ahead of her.

She rushed to catch up with them. It was so sunny that they all could feel the fight for preponderance between the sunrays and the cold breeze on their skin.

The restaurant was one of those old-fashioned diners that served breakfast all day. A wood sculpture of a big brown bear welcomed them holding a plate with a tower of pancakes. The carved bear was there in case clients missed a large board in a small grassy area next to some bushes and a couple of hungry trees in front of the dining room windows.

Inside, there was an unattended small store selling cheesy memorabilia, kitchen utensils, country cookbooks, local honey, and branded products for cooking "as good as Papa Bear!"

"A table for three, please," Kyle told the waitress.

She was a blonde teenager who in Kyle's mind needed a lesson or two about make up. Although she was fuckable—or a *yes*, as he and his friends would say, the sparkly blue around her eyes and the ridiculous amount of that thick, black stuff women put in their eyelashes made her an atrocity. He smiled, and the girl reciprocated politely, thinking it was a smile at her, although he was just laughing at his own immaturity.

The yes/no game was something he and his friends had practiced for years when out drinking. They'd stand at the bar and qualify girls with yesses or noes. It was a predictable boys' game whose overall statistics were highly influenced by the amount of alcohol consumed at a given moment of the night.

"Can you tell me where the restroom is?" Monica asked.

The girl pointed to her left without taking her eyes off the computer screen in front of her, as if she was resolving a calculus problem. The restaurant was huge and practically empty, but she took her time.

Monica ran toward the bathroom, disappearing through a dark wooden hall.

"Just a moment, please. I'll just get your table ready," the girl said, and went to find a table for them. She insisted on acting as if the restaurant was busy, even though from Kyle's point of view, there was no one there but a couple of old timers sitting at a table near the entrance.

He turned around and approached Adriel, who was looking at some fruit spreads and jerkies that were for sale. Behind her were all sorts of clothing with the bear logo on it. He went around Adriel and picked out one of the T-shirts and a beach hat that had bear ears. He put the hat on and held the T-shirt open in front of her.

"What do you think, Adriel? Maybe Cyanide Roses can wear this for the next gig?"

They were laughing and fooling around with the hat and a scarf Adriel picked up, when Monica returned from the bathroom. Watching Adriel doing a silly dance wearing the hat and scarf made Monica laugh out loud.

"Wow, sweetie. You look so hot!" she said.

Adriel shushed her; eyes wide open in disapproval gesture.

"Don't sweetie me here, fuck face! This is Trump land, you'll get us shot!"

Monica laughed and began to kiss the air in Adriel's direction while chasing her with her arms open. They circled around the main merchandise stand until with embarrassment; they found themselves in front of the server, who had been watching them with amusement, secretly jealous of the fun they were having.

"Your table is ready," she said.

They followed her, passing next to the old couple table. For the second time in a day, Adriel recognized the penetrating smell of cooked bacon. Kyle glanced at the old man's BLT sandwich thinking he could eat something.

The girl sat them at a nice window table facing the grassy area next to the entrance of the restaurant. From their table, they could see the back of the large advertising board as well as the highway and the dry, deserted area on the other side of the street.

The girl had inadvertently left on the table a small plate with a few coins and a dollar bill that had seen better days. The dull, greasy and slightly corroded aspect of the coins didn't discourage Adriel from playing with them. First she made a small tower before she began flipping them like a spin.

"Are you guys okay if I eat something really quick? I am starving!" Kyle said.

"Damn you, Kyle. Do you ever not eat? We have to get going," Monica said, looking to Adriel to have the final say.

"No, no, it's okay. Go ahead, Kyle, go for it," Adriel said. Her first internal reaction was to say no, but how could she say no to Kyle?

Kyle ordered a BLT with fries, while Adriel and Monica ordered just coffee.

They both went to use the bathroom and once back, Kyle began to tell one of his many stories about his bouncing experiences. He went on and on about how DJ Blas had filled up the place to the roof and there was this drunk girl running around topless, but he couldn't catch her because she was small and fast and could squeeze between people like a chipmunk.

Adriel wasn't really listening. Tired of the coins, she was staring at the window in silence. She hadn't let go her Charlotte Sometimes dream.

"Hey, are you okay? Are you sure you don't wanna keep it going? I can cancel the sandwich," he said.

"It's all good, really, I was just thinking that—"

Adriel's phone ringing interrupted her statement. She looked at the screen and her eyes brightened. She began squeezing out the booth instantaneously, signing Monica to get out, so she could too. In that process, she swiped the screen to get the call before it would go to voicemail.

"It's Brandi," she told Monica, moving her lips but without making a sound.

Walking toward the entrance, Adriel laughed out loud. Brandi was singing Happy Birthday, and then explained at length why she couldn't call earlier. Adriel stepped out to the grassy area in front of the restaurant. Monica and Kyle could see her from inside. She was holding the phone but wouldn't talk. Brandi had taken control of the conversation.

"Hilario's been working late almost every day for the past couple of weeks. Remember I told you? So his boss gave him the afternoon off. And I switched shifts with this new girl, Paula. Nice girl. She's struggling with a new baby. She's only twenty, you know? Anyway, she was happy to take the shift because of her daughter."

As always when she was nervous, Brandi began randomly shuffling between subjects. She had wanted to be with Adriel. While Adriel hadn't said a word about going to try to find Leah, Brandi had no doubt that Adriel would. Brandi felt it was her responsibility to take the trip with Adriel. She worried about her safety and what the emotional outcome would be if Adriel couldn't find her mother.

Secretly, she'd moved heaven and earth to get back to Portland on time, but the truth was that the Mexican adventure didn't turn out to be the paradise she had envisioned. Life was good. Their quality of life had improved, but Hilario's responsibilities were much greater than at Olympia. As a manager, he worked until late every day, including Saturdays. Her work was also much more demanding. It wasn't like the deal she had in Olympia, punching a clock and running groceries along a belt. She was in charge of ordering merchandise for a whole store, a job that wasn't about hours, but about completed tasks. Wishing she could procrastinate, and overwhelmed by the amount of work, she was having a hard time liking what she was doing.

At the end of July, she began looking at the possibility of going to Portland in time for Adriel's birthday. Looking into ticket prices she found the first surprise: the high season for travel to Mexico began precisely in November. The brutal reality hit her. Sure, they were making better money than they had in Olympia, but in dollars, they weren't making enough to pay high airfare and hotel fares. In view of all this, she decided it was time to use her savings; she just had to do it without Hilario knowing, because he was adamant the money was untouchable. Yet she hit the final and most decisive wall when she asked for vacation time. Vacation from October to December just wasn't an option, especially for the person in charge of ordering merchandise. Who was going to order the toys, clothing, and whatever else people buy for Christmas? Christmas is a holiday for all except those working in retail. It's the busiest and by far most profitable time of the year.

She could have planned the trip for January. She was going to get a nice bonus then, but what was the point of that? Plus, who wanted to deal with Portland rain? So she decided to wait until Easter. Tickets would be cheaper; the weather would be much nicer; and with some luck, Leah and Adriel would be waiting for her, together.

Remembering her promises to Leah, she wished she'd planned for this better. Pacing in her kitchen while talking with Adriel, she almost asked the obvious question: Are you going to your mom? But she was also afraid of hearing the answer. Instead, still with the visit in mind, she decided to bring it up.

"Hey, guess what?!" she said.

"This was gonna be a surprise, but it's just not practical. We are going to Portland for Easter. *Finally!*" she said.

From the table, Kyle and Monica watched Adriel jumping with excitement. A giant smile exploded across her face, as if she was a child opening a present. Seeing her smile, they wondered if it was because Brandi had come to Portland. This wasn't a crazy thought.

"I just hope things go well," Monica said.

She'd seen the anxiety of the past two weeks. She knew Adriel's expectations.

"Fuck, dude, what a life. It's unreal. Can you imagine what she's feeling right now? I'd be shitting my pants," Kyle said to Monica.

"Yeah you asshole. Yet you still ordered a sandwich."

"I'm sorry, I didn't think about it."

The sandwich arrived as if Monica's words were magic. She shook her head half smiling. Kyle began eating it as fast as he could.

"That woman Brandi, she needs a statue, dude. I mean, would you do for anyone what she did?" he said between bites.

Monica didn't think about it. She just thought back to how each time Adriel needed a shoulder, Brandi transported herself through the cellular signal right to their apartment, to lie in bed with Adriel and hold her, to console her and lift her up.

She also revisited their twice daily, sometimes three times daily phone calls. Brandi's silly excuses to call Adriel were worth a comedy show, and many times so were the phone calls: from laughter to endless arguments, to music talk, and Brandi's irrational demands for faithful descriptions of Adriel's day, every day.

"Watch, Kyle. I bet you anything Adriel's going to start pacing at any moment. They'll argue about whatever. I guarantee it. It's funny to watch."

Outside the restaurant, Adriel was leaning against one of the posts holding the main advertisement board in front of the entrance.

"Hey, you'll be happy about this, I'm gonna start going to night high school pretty soon," she said.

In a way, Adriel wanted to give back to Brandi the feeling of receiving good news, but more than anything, she too was prolonging the light conversation for as long as she could. In her anguish during the past few days, she'd forgotten about Brandi and dealing with Brandi. Secretly, she wouldn't have wanted Brandi to be there. It would have been too much to deal with her on top of everything. She was glad she wasn't going to have to fight that battle.

"Oh my gosh, that's such good news, Adi. Hilario, did you hear? Brandi's back at school!"

She walked from her room to the living room, where Hilario was waiting for his turn to talk. Speaking to whoever was in the room while she was on the phone was another bad habit Brandi had.

"I know you didn't hear it and that you aren't on the phone, Hilario. Why do you have to be so literal?"

"Brandi, Brandi!" Adriel said to bring Brandi back to the conversation.

"So where are you? I hear a weird sound. Are you outside?" Brandi paused before asking the next question. She exchanged a knowing look with Hilario.

There was no sound, really, but Brandi was bracing herself to talk about the elephant in the room.

Adriel looked around. *I'm in the middle of nowhere*, she almost said, but made up a story about being at the waterfront with some friends. She switched back to the topic of the upcoming visit so Brandi wouldn't detect the lie. In the end, even over the phone, Adriel was sure Brandi would drive her insane if she knew she was on her way to meet her mother.

Ironically, hearing that the visit was going to take a few months disappointed her some. She'd dreamt of having Brandi and Leah in the same room, at the same time. She'd seen them attending one of her Cyanide Roses concerts, walking together on a visit to Forest Park, and running around Cannon Beach.

They began working out the details and soon enough, an argument exploded when Brandi insisted she and Hilario were going to stay at a hotel during the visit. Hearing this, Adriel paced around and swirled her arm emphatically.

"Fuck, Brandi, it's my birthday. Let's do what *I* want for once and not what *you* want. You're *not* staying in a hotel; you're staying with us! No, I said, no. Look, let me talk to Papi, I'm not arguing anymore. What? Dark side of the moon? What are you talking about?"

"I'm asking if you listened to Dark Side of The Moon yet today. The eclipse is tonight," Brandi said.

Pacing, Adriel was now facing the window where Monica and Kyle were watching her. She directed her eyes toward them and made an incredulous gesture, in response to the sudden change of subject. *She is crazy!* she signaled them, pointing at the phone and making little circles with her finger next to her ear.

"Well look, can I talk to Papi?" Adriel said.

"¿Cómo estás, Mija?" Hilario spoke.

Hearing his voice after speaking with Brandi was like changing from a radio station playing Cindy Lauper on cocaine to Tom Jobim.

"Hi Papi. Can you please tell Brandi there is—"

"I know, I know. Don't worry," he said, interrupting, knowing it was about where they'd stay during the visit.

He walked away from Brandi toward their balcony and closed the sliding window door behind him to be sure she couldn't hear him talking.

"Forgive her. She's nervous. She couldn't sleep yesterday, but—"

This time it was Adriel who interrupted him.

"Papi, let's stop the bullshit here, okay? I'm on my way. In fact I'm less than twenty minutes away."

There was a long silence.

"Please tell me you're not alone."

Adriel told him about Kyle. She reminded him of Kyle's size and looks, and the times her friend had saved her. Suddenly, she felt empowered; she was ready to face her father. It always was about reuniting with Leah and Jacob, but right now, for the first time, her resentment surfaced. She was ready to teach her father a lesson. This time she was going to be the one holding the belt.

"I'm very proud of you, very proud, Mija. And remember, if your father gets out of control, call the police immediately," he said.

"He's not my father," she said, pausing briefly, and added, "You are."

Her eyes filled with tears. She felt a multitude of ants running through her veins, but realizing Monica and Kyle were watching her, she turned her back and kept on with the conversation to give herself time to recover. Just once she looked at them sideways.

Once the phone call had ended, Adriel approached the window and waved to Monica and Kyle to come out. They were pretending they weren't watching her.

Kyle had finished his sandwich, inhaling it at fast as he could. He rushed to pay the bill.

Outside, waiting, Adriel finally realized that the moment had come. She began walking toward the car and once again, the thousand possibilities that had tormented her all week came back in a merciless assault: fear, hope, excitement and doubt. Now, the sun was lower in the sky. She wrapped her arms around herself. Seconds later, Monica's embrace rescued her from anguish.

When they got into the car, the world stopped for a moment. All three remained silent until Monica sighed loudly and deeply. She spoke first.

"So what's the plan?"

"We all go to the door. Let me do the talking. If the asshole doesn't let me talk to Mom, or if he tries anything stupid, you kill him, Kyle," Adriel said.

Monica turned on the car and just then Adriel's phone rang.

She looked at the screen and refused the call, but just seconds later it rang again. She refused the call again and the phone rang again, and again.

Adriel looked at the screen. BRANDI, it said. She clicked the "message" option, followed by "can I call you later?"

"Should I guess? You only told Hilario, right?" Monica said.

"I'll text her. I really prefer not to talk to her about this right now."

20) 4:12PM. Richard.

Richard was now heading home with a purpose.

His wish to see Liberty surfaced into his awareness one more time, but he shooed it away. "Fuck her," he said out loud, bitterly. "She doesn't deserve what I've done for her." Besides, there would be time for her later. Now, he had to decide how he was going to deal with Leah.

His first impulse was to sit down and have an actual conversation with her and get his marriage back in order. The constant vigilance was exhausting.

I can't keep doing this, he thought. *It's going to drive me mad. What happened four weeks ago was insane. Leaving the world in stand by to drive all the way to Baker City like a lunatic. What for? To find that everything was okay. I have to stop.*

Richard was right. Wanting to maintain control over Leah was going to kill him. That day, he was checking Leah's location through her iPhone's Share My Location feature. He did this every day at random hours, and always found the little dot blinking on the map, right on top of his house, except for that morning. Offline, it said.

He immediately called the home line, which he'd bought and was willing to pay for, for the sole purpose of being able to call Leah and check that she was home. He'd instructed her to always pick up, but she didn't. She was taking a shower.

What an irony. I get her a phone so I can track her—and now what? Who's she talking to? he thought.

He knew it was all crazy. It had to stop, or else he had to do what he'd done for over two years after Adriel's disappearance. Oh no, I can't do that to her again. *I can't!* he thought and sighed. His brain paused for the first time.

The practicality of going back to that again was even more difficult. But that wasn't all. The truth was, he felt terribly guilty about it. That was the one thing he had done without telling anyone, not even Leah's father, a mentor and in a way, a replacement for his own father. *How did I allow myself to do that to Leah—and for so long?* he kept asking himself. The whole ordeal had gone on much longer than it should have. He'd fallen into an emotional abyss, which to this day, he didn't know how he'd got out of. One thing was certain: over two years was a long time, and the damage, very hard to repair.

No, what I need to do is to reason with Leah. I need to get her back, he concluded.

What he wanted was his marriage the way it used to be, but better. He wanted the Leah who would get into bed with him and would never even consider the prospect of divorce. Instead of contemplating reality, he fantasized this wish becoming true.

Imagining himself chatting with Leah and resolving it all provided him with a moment of peace. In his fantasy, he was sitting on the sofa with Leah. They were chatting and laughing about the early days, the great fun they had. And as it turned out, Leah never spoke with an attorney; she was just trying to find a job where she could work from home, to help pay the bills.

Be real, Richard. This will never happen, he thought. *You have to get her to tell you who the hell she's talking to.*

This time around it was different: he had concrete proof of the phone calls. How could Leah deny them? The shortest of these phone calls was about seven minutes, but a couple were almost forty-five minutes long. There was no way she could say they were marketing phone calls of some sort.

He imagined sitting on the sofa with Leah again, but the mood this time was very different. He imagined manipulating her, scheming, promising her whatever she dearly wanted in exchange for the truth. What could it be? He held a royal flush: allowing her to work again? Telling her he was going to leave Liberty for good? He chuckled.

In this fantasy he saw something much closer to reality, the "she says this, but this is what she really means, and then I say that, but it's as much bull as what she says and she knows it too" type of thing.

He could have gone on and on, but his phone sounded an alert that wasn't just any alert. It was the one assigned to Jacob's text messages. Richard had assigned individual sounds to all of his family, Adriel included. Jacob's was the train.

"Hi Father. I wanted to tell you, Grandpa and I are going to see Captain America tonight. I'm really excited. Have you seen it yet?" Jacob texted.

Time flies... Jacob was now a young teenager. Guilt landed on him, even heavier than before. *I can't do that to her again, and I have to bring her Jacob back*, he thought.

Richard missed his son; he wanted to share with him the love the child had for the magic of cinema—something Richard didn't really understand that well. Movies were the only thing Jacob could talk about. He loved them all, although action-packed movies were his favorite. *It would be so great to go to the movies tonight with Jacob*, Richard thought, wistfully. A whirlpool of grief began bubbling up in Richard like shaken soda.

Yeah, maybe bringing Jacob back will help us all, he thought. He'd been coordinating with Leah's father when and how to bring Jacob back. He wanted to go to Little Rock and pick up the boy by himself, but if he was going to do that, he needed to wait until the holidays when he could take time off. Jim and Clarice had no interest in coming to Baker City, and Jim in particular was vehemently opposed to sending the boy on an airplane by himself.

But there was another detail: he didn't want to leave Leah by herself in Baker City. The circle was closed. He was back to the first issue: he didn't trust his wife.

I have to take the phone away this time around, he thought, but he couldn't think up a plan. Organizing his ideas was a little overwhelming.

Without many more answers, he kept driving. A minute or two later, the phone sounded a second time, as it always does when a message isn't read. This time Richard took it. Not only did he want to talk to Jacob, he needed to talk to Jim and see what his opinion was about Leah and her phone calls.

His strong relationship with his father-in-law began right before the death of his own father, Jay. There never was a formal transfer of parenthood or mentorship, although Jay had told him to listen to Jim just weeks before succumbing to an aggressive pancreatic cancer.

"Look up to Jim, son. When I'm no longer around you'll still need guidance before making big decisions. You know that. Jim is a deeply pious man who'll always do what's right."

Jay was right. Shy and insecure, even as an adult, Richard yearned for somebody to guide him. After giving birth to him, his mother was unable to have more children. A few days before the birth she began having horrible headaches. *Keep the light off and close the curtains. Light makes it worse*, she'd said to her husband. They didn't act until she began experiencing blurred vision. Preeclampsia, they called it at the hospital. They had to induce labor, they said. To make it worse, they couldn't stop her bleeding. You have to have a hysterectomy or you'll die, they told her at last. The emergency procedure was performed, killing any chance of Richard having a sibling to play with.

If there was ever a stereotype of the only child, Richard was the perfect model for it. He was spoonfed from his first year all the way until his mid twenties, when he was graciously asked to open, and he did, eyes closed, so Leah could be fed to him, flying to his mouth accompanied by a soothing lullaby. Overprotected by his mother and micro-managed by his father, he found it challenging to make decisions on his own.

It was hot in the truck with the heater on. Richard opened his window and drank the last of his soda. Then he picked up the phone, hit the home button, and followed the steps until he reached his favorites contacts, a short list of four people that included Jim and Clarice. He did all of it believing he was in complete control of the vehicle, and that the phone wasn't a distraction at all, like most people do.

As he waited for Jim to pick up, he closed the window. The phone had already replaced the radio in the speakers. Richard took his glasses off to rub his eyes when finally, Jim picked up.

A gruff voice answered. "Hello?"

They greeted each other and talked a little about the weather and the upcoming eclipse.

"Maybe you guys can take Jacob somewhere to see the eclipse," Richard said. "How is he? Can I talk to him for a minute? He just sent me a text telling me you're taking him to a movie."

"Oh, he's fine. As I told you the other day, hormones are kicking in, but he's a good boy. Anyhow, they went to Costco. I'll have him call you back in about thirty, or so, okay?"

"Sure, no biggie," Richard said.

They spent another minute making meaningless, polite chitchat, until silence arrived. Richard hadn't organized his ideas before making the impulsive call.

"Well, I also called you because I'm having a bit of a tough day and, hmm, I need to finish this massive amount of paper-work and something has come up."

"How are things going? How's my daughter these days? Is something wrong?" Jim said this cynically. Lately, he only got phone calls from Baker City when things were going the wrong way.

"I hate to bring this up, but Leah keeps asking about him. And you know, at times it's as if she's delusional or something.

I mean, she talks about him as if he's still a little boy and, you know, she says thing like: 'Well, Richard, I am going to make this pie or whatever that Jacob likes this afternoon. He's going to love it.' I mean, what do I do with that? It's hard, Dad, it's hard."

The guilt Richard had felt moments before was gone, replaced by the annoyance he felt that day in the kitchen, when Leah brought up Jacob and the possibility of a divorce. It was the divorce part, of course, that had done the trick. He was once again thinking about the mysterious phone calls.

"Well, I guess I wanted to talk to you about something else."

"What now?"

"I think she's into something. I don't know yet, but I can see her phone calls through the Family Plan with Verizon, you know? I mean, I get like a report. Anyway, there's this eight hundred number showing up daily."

"Hmm, that's strange."

"Indeed. I did some digging. I'm worried it could be some kind of government hotline."

"Oh Lord, last thing we need is the government telling her what's wrong and what's right."

"Yeah, that or maybe an attorney."

"An attorney. Is she still talking about divorce? You ended your affair with that girl, correct, Richard?"

Richard shrank behind the wheel and remained silent.

"Oh c'mon, Richard, you got to quit fooling around with that other girl. You got to stop that right away. As a man I understand you, but this is my daughter we're talking about here. You got to stop right now," Jim said, rebuking him.

"I know, I know. I feel embarrassed, you know?"

Silence. Still shrunk in shame, Richard jumped to add,

"I want to have a normal family, Dad."

He waited for Jim's response. He was seeking approval.

During Richard's teen years, the pendulum had swung wildly from side to side in the face of the question: What's normal? The ambiguity originated in the clash between what he was being told at home and what all his friends were telling him. Contrary to Leah's experience, he was allowed to finish high school, and he could have gone to college if it wasn't for not being able to afford it right after high school, and while working and making good money, losing interest. He'd questioned his parents and his faith many times. He doubted the specificity of the roles his family assigned men and women, but whenever he talked about it, he was scolded, beaten, or worse, taken to their faith community to be—figuratively at least—stoned to death.

The worst came during his last year of high school when he dated Ashley, a lively girl with opposite beliefs who ultimately broke his heart.

Like Leah, he was confronted by feelings of inadequacy when he was around others. In front of friends, he was able to hide his indoctrination and to be accepted, but in the intimacy of his relationship, he had no choice but to choose. He truly loved Ashley—the only true love he ever felt. But the seed was planted early and deep inside him. He fought with his parents, argued with Ashley, and stayed silent in front of his friends, until Ashley had enough and broke up with him.

He'd grown up on the other side of the table, raised, like Leah, with very specific roles. But there was a big difference: with several sisters and brothers, Leah's childhood at home was her university for later life, with tons of practical courses and seminars. Richard, on the other hand, was exposed to lots of theory and no practice, trained for a world where he was king.

He had been given a recipe with no in-depth explanations about what to do if something went the wrong way with his relationships.

The pain of losing Ashley was washed away with girl after girl thrown at him, but he rejected one after the other; none were Ashley. It took years before he could finally let go, although like Leah, the feeling of social inadequacy didn't leave him, at least not until she was pushed upon him, and he got a chance to figure out what his role was about.

"Well, if you want a normal family, you have to do your part." To Richard's disappointment, Jim rebuked him one more time.

He shook his head. This was like the meeting with Mike at work that morning. He felt like speaking his mind: *Well, your daughter doesn't give a fuck about me*, he wanted to say. Another trigger was pulled. He took his glasses off again and wiped his forehead, even though it was dry.

"So, what do you think we should do?" he said instead.

"I think you have to intervene right away, of course. I mean, you never know with Leah. We already learned that lesson, didn't we?"

Here it was. Richard stayed silent again. Just thinking about that "lesson" made his face turn red. The whirlpool inside him began swirling faster.

"Listen, you need to confront her right away as soon as you get home, and no question, disallow the use of any phones. That's a no brainer."

"But she is gonna lie about it, she'll lie like she lied about Adriel" he concluded out loud before rushing ahead.

"But what do I tell her? How do I get her to tell me what's going on?"

He heard a sigh of impatience at the other end of the line. This upset him even more.

"Wake up, Richard!"

"What do you mean?"

"Do I really have to tell you? I mean that you have to take her phone and watch her very closely. Again, did you learn the lesson or didn't you? WAKE UP. I'll have Jacob call you later. Bye now." Jim hung up.

Richard began to speak, but stopped when he realized Jim was gone.

He put the phone on the passenger seat. The sound from the radio returned to fill the cabin of his truck.

Wake up, Richard. Think! he said to himself. "Attorneys usually don't function with eight hundred numbers, do they?" he said out loud. *Although, of course!* he thought. *An attorney hired through one of those liberal groups. It's got to be an attorney. That bitch has been asking for a divorce. That's gotta be it!*

He drove home on autopilot; the images of him sitting and chatting with Leah were burnt to ashes now by his anger. It was time for a reality check. He imagined himself again on the sofa, yelling at Leah and demanding that she tell him the truth, or else.

OLD GRUMPY BEAR DINER, HONEST COUNTRY FOOD FOR THE SOUL, COMING UP.

This familiar sign interrupted for a moment the erupting volcano of his introspection. Usually he stopped at this place to get their famous apple pie before heading back home. But not this time. Any appetite was suppressed. He wasn't going to stop, but something—actually someone—made him slow down.

In front of him and to his right was the restaurant parking lot. Two cars were parked out front: an old but well maintained Buick Century and a very old, rusty Honda Accord Hatchback. Yet what caught his attention was this weird-looking girl he spotted next to the Honda. He noticed two things: 1) She was cold, hugging herself with her arms, and 2) *She had blue hair.*

Fuck, what's wrong with people today! he thought, before accelerating again to get back on the wild highway of paranoia and anger he'd been cruising before.

"You better wake up, you better wake up, you better wake up…" The words looped inside him as he drove.

The usual brain salad of anger, sadness, paranoia, memories, resentment and his deep desire to know what had happened to Adriel began forming inside his head. Memories flowed by, just like they had while he was eating in the parking lot at Subway; the rest of the universe barely existed. He kept driving, although his mind was on the road just enough to keep him from having a fatal crash.

The whole self-destructing cycle began once again, the same memories and nightmarish fantasies passing through—a feminist attorney, Richard losing everything and so on, ending again with the image of him carrying little Adriel at that water park.

His whole body began shaking; the whirlpool at full speed, the urge to cry rising from his gut, tearless weeping that made his whole body convulse.

Fuck!!! He yelled as loud as he could to expel the need to cry, banging at the wheel and losing control of the truck briefly. Having to concentrate on the road gave him his composure back.

His eyes dried like the fields surrounding him. He accelerated again. No doubt the phone was a mistake: Leah would never, ever change. His initial desire to talk to Leah and repair his marriage was gone. Guilt had definitely melted away.

When he was nearing a hundred and ten miles an hour it came to him: He had to do it again. His mistake wasn't having done that to her for over two years; his mistake was stopping.

He slowed down abruptly and moved into the far right lane, where he stopped. He grabbed his phone. 4:12PM it said. He texted Leah:

I know what's going on. I know who you've been talking to. You're going back downstairs.

21) 4:11PM. Leah.

Nicole didn't interrupt Leah. Even after Leah finished her story she stayed quiet. Having no children, she couldn't completely relate to Leah's predicament, although she thought she did. In her silence, she began remembering the day her little nephew Michael got lost at the beach for a few hours. Her sister's desperation became her own in the same way she was absorbing Leah's feelings like a sponge. She was exhausted.

It was Leah who spoke.

"Are you there, Nicole?"

"I'm sorry." Nicole cleared her throat. It took her a moment to decide what to say. All she wanted by now was to hang up, but knew she should bring something positive to the conversation before it ended.

"We only have a couple of minutes. Why don't you tell me a little about Jacob? How many years apart is he from Leah? You were saying he's spending a couple of weeks with your parents. You're probably excited to have him back soon, right?"

"Five years. As I said, I had a few miscarriages between them. Anyway, he's been there pretty much the whole summer and, yeah! I'm super excited to have him back."

Leah smiled as if Nicole was there. She had began to put dried plates away, to at least get the kitchen ready so she'd have more time to get the laundry and the rest of the dinner done on time.

"Summer? Leah, it's November! I don't know about Baker City, but it's pretty cold here!"

Leah froze. She was caught between drying a plate and putting it away. Plate in hand, she had to think about what she had just said, although it didn't bother her. What troubled her was *knowing* she had no idea how long Jacob had been away.

"Well, yeah, I know that. What I mean is that he's been there for a while," she said.

"That's cool, and I guess it's great the hormones haven't kicked in. That would be rough for his grandparents. Frankly, considering how you describe your folks, I'm surprised he likes it there. But I'm sure they have softened up, haven't they?"

Leah frowned.

"What do you mean by hormones? Jacob's just a baby! He'll be eleven next month," she said.

"Hmm, maybe I'm confused," Nicole said and looked at her notes. She added,

"I thought you said you had Leah at fifteen and that they were five years apart. You were born in eighty three, right?"

"Yeah, that's right."

"Well, that means you had Adriel in 1998 and Jacob in 2003. Jacob is fourteen."

If there is such thing as dead silence, there it was. Leah put away a coffee cup and began pacing. Her mouth was open as if she wanted to refute that fact.

"It's okay, people lose track of time in—" Before Nicole could finish, Leah interrupted her violently.

"STOP!!!"

Surprised by Leah's reaction coming from what seemed like nowhere, Nicole stayed silent while Leah desperately tried to make sense of it all.

In the middle of her own calculations, to be sure Nicole was right, everything came to Leah like a bucket of ice-cold water thrown over her head. By now she knew exactly what had happened. The memories that followed came only to torture her.

She'd told Nicole the story surrounding the first image in her mind. Mother forcefully holding Jacob that night in her backyard, the night they were making burgers. Mother's smile suddenly seemed more cynical than ever.

A forgotten memory came next. Leah was speaking with Mother over the phone just days after Jacob had left for Little Rock with her parents.

"But, Mother, please! He's ten!" Leah had begged, but Mother replied impassively.

"It's decided. Father and Richard feel this is the best for the moment, dear. You have to accept that. Besides, as I just said, this is temporary, just until things get sorted out. You'll talk to him as much as you want. Don't worry."

There was no mention of Adriel. No suggestion that taking Jacob away was punitive. They even left a window open and made Leah believe the boy would be away for just a few weeks.

Nicole thought it was prudent to ask again what was going on, but Leah didn't respond. Blurry memories kept coming. It was hard for her to know what was real and what was panic punching her in the face. She wanted to believe it was all a misunderstanding.

"Oh my God. Oh my Lord, please help me!!!" she finally yelled. Impotence laughed in her face.

"What?" Nicole was lost—and worried.

"It's been over two years, two years! You're right!! They took him away, Nicole. My God!! My baby, I want my baby back, Nicole. Please help me!!!"

"Hold on, Leah. What do you mean they took him away? That's child abduction." Nicole's tone, as forced as it was, and despite her inexperience, sounded as if she was collected. But behind the phone she was pacing in her cubicle like a nervous wildcat in sudden captivity.

"It can't be true. Nicole, please tell me that's not what happened, please do!!!" Leah said between choking spasms. Still pacing rapidly, she reached the corner of the kitchen and turning, dropped the phone accidentally. Hysterical as she was, she left it there.

She stopped in a corner between the wall containing the heavily scraped, white cabinetry, and the wall where the old Sears refrigerator rested.

Nicole heard the "tock" sound without knowing Leah had dropped the phone, but worse, that she'd left it there. She too was trying to make complete sense of the situation, and in the process, frantically typing a text to her supervisor. She should have gathered Leah's address during the first call; she knew this was a novice mistake.

Leah leaned into the corner and slowly, keeping her back against the wall, slid down into a fetal position on the floor. The tears and mucus all over her upper lip didn't seem to bother her. All she wanted was for Nicole to tell her that everything was going to be fine, that indeed, her sudden realization wasn't the truth.

In the absence of this answer, Leah, by now sitting on the linoleum floor in full fetal position, covered her eyes with both hands. The phone still lay on the floor. Tall and long as she was, she barely fit between the wall and the small dinner table.

"Leah, it's imperative that I get your address so I can help you. Please, calm down and tell me, what's your address, Leah?" Nicole said, but her words sounded in the abandoned phone and evaporated in the dense kitchen air, already impregnated with the smell of baking chicken coming from the oven.

"Leah, are you there? Leah?" she said repeatedly.

Meanwhile, the eye-opening memories let Leah take a breath. Her throat dry, she got up to grab a glass and fill it with water. She opened the small freezer at the top of the fridge, but struggled to remove the ice tray that was trapped in the frost that grew around it like bacteria.

The familiar images were replaced with a swirling vortex of hypothetical situations with both optimistic and pessimistic outcomes. At the core of this mental turbulence was a simple question: Now that she knew the truth, what should she do next?

Leaning against the kitchen cabinet holding the glass of water, she fantasized about confronting Richard and her parents. She saw herself yelling at her mother, and saw her mother asking for forgiveness, something that in reality, Leah knew too well, would never happen. She saw herself cuddled in front of the TV with Jacob, watching old repeats of Get Smart. The sudden warmth of her son resting on her chest was removed just as suddenly, like a blanket being pulled away by an angry sergeant to wake a lazy conscript. "You won't see him again, ever!" her dad told her in the next scene. Mentally, she shook him off, like one of those nasty flying roaches one finds in the tropics.

Inevitably, memories of Adriel came next. It was her birthday and Leah felt so guilty. *She has to be okay. She'll come back. I can feel it*, Leah thought. *I have to confront Richard. I just have to!* she thought next. She imagined doing it, and even right there, without his presence, she lowered her head. And the thought came to her like a whisper, so nobody would listen to it. Confronting him would be futile, she knew, and just the thought of it scared her to the point she almost dropped the glass of water—practically speaking, a good thing, because it pulled her out of what was a self-destructive mental state.

Instinctively, she sat at the table and tried to calm down, drinking the water and looking through the kitchen window. She could see the sun behind a cloud, sleepy, in that cold November air. It was a beautiful scene that Leah didn't often get to enjoy. Next, her conversation with Nicole, which prompted her to discover the true depth of her predicament began playing in her head:

"...My baby. I want my baby back Nicole, please help me— It can't be true, Nicole, please tell me that's not what happened, please do!!!"

"Oh, Gosh! Nicole!!" she said out loud. Realizing she'd completely forgotten about Nicole, she jumped out of the chair to get to the phone.

"Nicole! Nicole? Sorry, are you there?" she said. But Nicole was long gone.

She returned to her chair, rested her elbows on the table and her head between her hands. She took a deep breath and then placed the phone in front of her, to be able to rub her forehead and scalp, pushing her hair back repeatedly.

What had transpired in the past three years was too much to handle. Her breathing worsened and her stomach tightened. She gulped and was about to yell when a familiar sound, the Aurora Sound Alert Tone from her iPhone, interrupted her thoughts. Any other sound from the phone and she would have carried on, but there was only one person assigned to that sound: Richard.

She hurried to pick up the phone but, victim of her nerves, couldn't control her grip and the phone slipped out of her hands like soap in the shower. She rushed to pick it up again and look at the screen. As soon as she saw the words her lips began to tremble like a dry autumn leaf hanging on for dear life in a cold breeze. The screen read:

I know what's going on. I know who you've been talking to. You're going back downstairs.

Her first reaction was to quickly erase all previous calls from her phone. But almost immediately after, reality came crashing down on Leah like a giant Hawaiian wave, breaking her spine and forcing her underwater. In a momentary state of shock she heard the inescapable silence and saw the reality she'd avoided for so long—what had truly happened to her, an experience she'd wish on no one. An experience she was about to live through again.

The light burnt her eyes. Richard did this every morning. He turned the light on so she would wake immediately. Her body felt heavy, as if she was swimming in mud. Lost between dream, numbness, and reality, she looked around. It took her a second to recognize where she was.

In front of her were Richard's desk and the table he had improvised for her. She looked for that hideous plastic plant, but now completely awake, remembered Richard had gotten rid of it. Richard's office hadn't changed much since the days Adriel had come down there, clandestinely, and discovered porn on his computer.

"Get up," Richard said, expressionless.

He had a plate with a peanut butter sandwich and an apple, which she put on the table next to a small jar of water.

Leah sat on the edge of the bed. Suddenly, she saw two; no, four; no, three desks and two tables floating around her. Closing her eyes always got rid of the morning dizziness and this time it did the trick again.

Like every night for the past six months, Richard had kept her locked in since the previous night. She'd completely lost track of time, and had no idea how long Jacob had been gone.

During those days, Leah was already going down to the room without offering any resistance at all. It seemed as if she'd given up for good. Yet that particular morning, she was dreaming of Jacob when Richard woke her.

"Richard, this is enough. I don't mind being locked in here, but Jacob needs to come back. He needs to be with his mother."

"Jacob's doing very well, Leah. He's at camp. Let's see when he gets back."

She despised him, but she very specially hated that little smile of his and the madhouse nurse voice he used when speaking to her, the "I wanna make sure you know I'm pretending I care when in fact I don't give a fuck" voice.

"You're lying. Where is my son, Richard?" she said, eyes wide open.

"Leah, don't be silly, you just need to rest. Get up, use the bathroom and get back here so you can sleep a little more."

He took one of the pills from his pocket and then filled a glass with the water he'd brought with him.

"Here, Leah, take your pill. But don't drink too much water."

"I don't know, Richard. I really don't like how those pills make me feel. They make me feel bad."

She changed her tone, hoping that would have an effect on him, but it didn't. She insisted,

"No, of course not. But you make me sleep too much, Richard."

"Don't be silly, Leah. Here, take the pill."

She opened her mouth to say something, but still slowed down by the previous dose, obeyed.

It was a cold morning; he could see her erect nipples through her pajama. Noticing this, she covered them with her arms and sat back on the bed.

"I know there are things you don't enjoy about being locked in here. I ain't a fool. But that's gonna change, and you know how?" He paused. The cynical tone was gone.

"The same way you're gonna get back upstairs, and perhaps the same way Jacob may come back. You know how?" he said. And repeating the question, he raised his voice. "You know how?" Pointing at the poster hanging on the bright red door, he said,

"Everything will change when you truly understand this. So read it!"

WHAM!

The red door slammed behind her. Richard had forgotten to take her to the bathroom.

She had a thousand things to say, but he gave her no opportunity to speak. "A man always has the last word." She'd been hearing this ever since she could remember, verbally and by example.

Ignoring the poster, she thought back to her dream about Jacob. This saddened her. She would have gone back to bed if she could, but her senses were returning and suddenly she felt an urge to go to the bathroom.

"Richard. Richard!" she called up. She thought he couldn't hear her—but he could.

The trigger was released. She rushed to the door and began banging it. She could almost feel Mother standing behind the door; she could see her poster with the Save By The Bell characters smiling at her. She looked up, only to find the only poster was the one Richard wanted her to read:

A woman married to a command man has to earn her place by proving she will stand by him, faithful and obedient.

Reading the message infuriated her even more. So she began pounding on the door as hard as she could while yelling:

"Richard! Let me out of here! Let me out of here now!!"

Enraged, she kept banging on the door and calling for him, louder and louder. A rare feeling invaded her. She wanted to tell him that she wanted out, and that she was going to her parents' home, walking if necessary to bring Jacob back to her arms.

She pounded the door so hard that the poster fell to the floor, torn. But she got no response from him. He was standing at the top of the stairs, unsure about his next step.

Just then, she took the chair from behind the desk and threw it at the door, twice, screaming as loud as she could:

"I need to go to the bathroom, Richard. Open the door!"

When he heard the chair hit the door he finally went downstairs, not to open the door, but to threaten her:

"Leah, if I have to open this door, I'll take you to the bathroom and watch what you do, and if you don't do anything, I'll tie you to the bed. And if you make one more noise, I will tie you to the bed for a week. Is that clear?" She knew he wasn't joking.

Most of her memory was gone, but not the memory of him tying her to the bed so she had no way of moving. That she'd done her business in the bathroom made no difference. The damage to the door had infuriated him.

The marks on her wrists and ankles didn't bother Leah, not even the one on her left ankle, which he'd secured too tightly and was raw and open. But her neck—the inability to move at all gave her the worst stiff neck, and the worst headache she'd ever experienced.

She cooperated with him without crying. She didn't want to give him that pleasure.

"It's for your good, Leah," he said.

The chicken was ready; the kitchen was filled with the smell. Even the oven timer sounded, but Leah had ignored it all. Other images began to appear in her mind.

"Richard, I have this terrible nightmare. You're locking me downstairs all day and telling me Jacob is never coming back." She saw herself saying this to him many times in the moments he let her go upstairs: at the kitchen table when they were eating dinner, in their back yard and in the living room. Even in their bedroom. And every time he answered the same way, sarcastically: "You had a nightmare? My whole life is a nightmare."

The routine was simple; he locked her in every night. He let her go to the bathroom in the morning. He even brought her breakfast—Eggos, or yogurt, or a peanut butter sandwich and some fruit—before locking her up again until noon, when he came all the way back from work to let her go to the bathroom again, to then lock her in again until he was back. Often, he didn't bother to return at lunch. Those days he doubled the dosage of Valium, Percocet, or whatever he found online. He reassured himself many times: *Must be the real thing—she sleeps like a rock.*

Numbed with narcotics, and perhaps as a defense mechanism, Leah's brain began to show her only one reality: the moments she spent upstairs, when Richard was home. In that reality, Jacob was coming home soon.

The red door was one of the first things to go from her consciousness, partly because Richard replaced it with a wood-pattern door the weekend after Leah damaged it. It took Leah about seven months to develop the parallel world her brain adopted as her own. It took a little over a year from that point for Richard to stop locking her up.

With the next memory Leah understood what had happened in the past few months, after her release from downstairs. She also understood the nightmare Richard claimed to be living. She revisited the scene in the kitchen, the very last time she'd asked him for a divorce.

"I made chicken breast with Ragú sauce and potatoes—Jacob's favorite! Can you imagine if he was here, Richard? He'd be yelling 'More, Mother, more!'"

Again, she recalled Richard's forced smile before returning to his laptop and his annoyance when she asked,

"When is Jacob coming back, sweetie? Have you asked my parents?" she said.

She could see it so clearly this time. The way he took his glasses off and stared. It wasn't about her bothering him while he was working. It was the guilt, because he was his child's father too.

22) 4:29PM. Richard.

The garage door began opening like the curtain of a theater stage, exposing—in Richard's mind—the moment of his arrival the night Adriel left. His Ford Fusion no longer existed, but he saw it there, parked the wrong way. So clear was this memory stamped on his mind, that he parked his truck as close to the wall of the garage as he could, to avoid scratching the imaginary car.

He turned his truck off and grabbed the keys. With a hand still on the wheel, he paused and considered for a moment what he was about to do.

There was no guilt, no doubt, just calculation, clumsy, rage-driven calculation.

He never stopped to think about the consequences. All the anxiety he had the first time around about being caught locking Leah in was forgotten. He had been most fearful of Jim. He didn't know how his father-in-law would react, but the impulsive decision had been made. Fuming as he was, the only questions in his mind were practical ones.

It wasn't going to be so easy this time around; he knew that. He visualized the possibilities, dragging Leah downstairs by force, or her going voluntarily and submissively. *Hmm, that won't happen unless I give her a drug,* he thought.

Three years back, he had devised the idea of drugging and locking Leah in the day his in-laws took Jacob with them. After getting up early in the morning, with no time even to drink a cup of coffee, he left to drop his in-laws off at the Boise airport. On their way, Jim and Clarice spoke to him at length. Reflecting on their own loss of David, who never contacted them after running away, they concluded it was best for Richard to let go and focus on what he still had, on getting his marriage back on track, so Jacob could return to him sooner than later.

They talked and talked. Richard pretended to listen, but there was one thing and one thing only occupying his mind, and that was the funny little guy sitting in the back seat of the truck, wearing headphones and watching a movie on his iPad. Between listening to his in-laws' words, Richard watched his son through the rearview mirror and wondered when he would read to him again or take him to the movies. Already missing his son before saying goodbye, he turned his head to the window more than a few times during the ride to hide his trembling lips and stop tears from forming.

He cried almost all the way back. His loss was as big as Leah's. Through intermittent moments of clarity, he remembered Jim's words about repairing his marriage, but couldn't let go the idea that everything was Leah's fault, and that if somehow he were able to convince her to bring Adriel back home, everything would go back to normal.

Upon returning, he found Leah picking up and cleaning the backyard. There was still a mess from the previous night's burger making. It was almost noon, hot and dry.

"You know what I'm thinking?" he said, and sat at the picnic table.

"What's that?" she said, without interest. Adriel had left with Brandi just days before, and now Jacob was gone too. She had enough on her plate.

"I didn't want to say anything with your parents here, but the more I think about it, and the more I watch you, Leah, the more I'm convinced you're hiding something from me. Are you sure you don't know anything about Adriel? Because I'm telling you, man, if Adriel was back, I think we could just go to Little Rock right now, get Jacob here and shit, maybe talk about things and get it right this time. You know what I'm talking about?"

She was holding a garbage bag and was on her way to the kitchen, but she stopped, letting the bag fall to the ground and sighing.

"Richard, you just decided to give our son away to my parents. For the thousandth time, our daughter's gone. I wish she could come back. Please, I beg you." She hit the target right at the center point. Lost in the urge to run and hug his son one more time, Richard stayed quiet.

Leah took the garbage bag and escaped to the kitchen, proud of herself. He recovered a moment later and followed her.

She had begun washing dishes. He watched, wanting to keep pressing her, but hunger had kicked in. He took cereal and milk out to get breakfast, even though it was close to noon.

He didn't say anything else. Just filled his bowl with cereal and began eating it, with his elbows on the table and his arms guarding the bowl like a bear guards a freshly caught salmon on a riverbank.

The only sounds in the kitchen were the sounds of Richard crunching the cereal, his loud slurps and, now and then, his lips smacking as he ate with his mouth open. Leah just watched him, wondering what his next move would be.

You look really tired. Did you sleep at all?" said Richard, convinced he sounded sincere.

"No, *of course* I didn't sleep well. I barely slept at all!"

"You know what?" he said between bites, making an effort to sound calm. "I think you're hiding something from me. You're gonna need to tell me right now."

"No, Richard! I swear. Why would I do that? I don't understand why you would think this," she said, interrupting him, and he stopped her.

"All right, that's cool. It's all right," he said, raising his hands in the air. He was boiling, yet was able to control himself and kept his mouth shut. After all, he was on a mission. Shaking a little, he helped himself to another bowl of Honey Nut Cheerios.

Leah kept running, this time to the best hiding place of all—the bathroom.

Richard knew what she was doing. He let her be. *You bitch, you're getting nervous. I'll give you time. This ain't new to me. You were fucking fifteen when you began this bullshit. I know you!* he thought.

An hour went by. Richard ate and even watched a little TV. In his mind he was playing the cool guy, the one in control. Reality was different. The clock kept ticking and he still got nothing. He was supposed to have this woman eating from his hand—but the reality was, he didn't. Facing reality was tough. He started sweating. He could have blamed the weather, but it wasn't the weather that was making him sweat.

He stifled the impulse to force her to say what he wanted to hear. Instead, he went to find his bass guitar. He wasn't a great bass player, but he wasn't bad. He just didn't have any range. All he listened to was hard and classic rock.

He considered playing Sweet Child O' Mine, but this exercise didn't last more than a minute. Frustrated, he placed the bass on its rest and rushed to knock on the bathroom door.

"Leah! Open the fucking door!"

"I can't right at the moment. I got conditioner in my hair. I'll just be a few minutes!" she said and got up. She'd just been sitting in there under the running shower. The water was beginning to get chilly. Very soon it would be plain cold.

Before the end of today you'll be telling me everything, Leah, he thought and said,

"Are you sure? I mean, tell me again what happened. I still don't get why you took the car out, Leah. You barely know how to drive," he said.

Leah took a deep breath, and began telling her version again—shouting really. She was careful not to make a mistake. Her whole body looked like cold chicken now, covered in goosebumps as a result of the cold water, which she at last turned off.

Outside, Richard raised his fist as if wanting to punch the door. He bit down hard on his lip, then said,

"Yeah, you're right. This is silly. I'm sorry, I shouldn't doubt you at a time like this."

An hour later, Leah was in bed with the door closed. He entered the room and after sitting on the other corner of the bed, initiated another attack.

"Leah, if you tell the truth, I guarantee everything will be better for everybody," he said, but thought, *You fucking bitch. Tell me where my daughter is.*

"My God, Richard, please let me pray. I want to pray for my children." Leah lied to get rid of him again.

These confrontations continued for the next two hours, intermittently. The two sides recharged in between. Richard tried, but to his surprise, he couldn't get Leah to say a thing. He began to doubt himself. But knew his wife too well; he knew she was lying.

Fuck, my head, he thought and went to the kitchen to get a Tylenol. He opened the medicine cabinet and took the container out and doing so, uncovered one of those small, orange plastic containers with a white lid they use at pharmacies for prescription drugs. On the white label it said: Percocet 7.5mg/325mg.

The idea came to him almost instantaneously. He knew too well about this medicine. It was his something-something lumbar disc med—a prescription his back doctor refilled monthly. He didn't take it nearly as often as he had a year back, but he took it now and then. He knew how it felt to take one of those pills. For God's sake, he knew how it felt to take *two* of those pills.

There was no considering or analytical exercise. He just took the pills with a glass of water and went back to his room, where Leah was lying in bed.

"You know, Leah, you look pretty tired. You need to rest," he said, putting a hand on her shoulder.

His hand created a slight shock against her pajamas, but this wasn't what made her freeze. Feeling his hand touching her body was almost repugnant to her.

"Ohhh. Did you feel that?" he said, joking. He'd withdrawn his hand instinctively feeling the brief shock, but immediately put it back.

She didn't dare to remove it, even when the hand began rubbing her shoulder.

"You know what? I'm going to give you these pills Dr. Phillips once got me for nerves, you know, for work," he said, and with this, another mind game began. They both knew what was going on, but they each pretended otherwise.

"I think I'm okay. I prefer to stay awake, in case we hear about Adriel."

"Don't be silly. This has been hard on you too. I'm sorry for being on your case all afternoon."

"I don't remember you ever getting pills for your nerves, Richard. When was this?"

"Woman, I don't tell you everything, especially things about work. You know that!" He made an effort to sound jovial. He took two tablets and offered them to her.

He watched her stare at the pills and hesitate, but in the end, she took them. He *knew* she *knew* it was a farce, but he didn't care. She wasn't walking out without taking the pills.

He watched closely, making sure she was swallowing. He made her drink more water to be sure she'd swallowed the pills.

You're not going anywhere until you tell me everything, he thought while he was waiting for the drug to take effect. When he saw her distinctly dizzy and out of herself, he took her downstairs to his office for one important reason—his office's red door was the only door in the house with a lock.

A mix of relief and euphoria took possession of him, and relaxed his mind. Finally, when he was able to sleep, he slept like a baby, mind clear and white like an endless snow-covered savannah.

The next morning he went downstairs and opened the door. He let her be for about an hour, until it was time for him to go to work. Then, in the kitchen, he watched her swallow two more Percocets. A pattern had been established.

"I feel good Richard. I don't think I need another pill," she said, trying to refuse them.

"Don't be silly," he said, forcing the pills on her.

It was game over. He was going to lock her downstairs indefinitely.

Richard was still in his truck. There was no doubt he was going to need Percocet or Valium or whatever. "Oh well," he said aloud. "Meanwhile, I'm going to lock her in, period."

But he'd missed one small detail.

"THE KEY!!! Where did I put the FUCKING key?" He almost yelled.

It had been months since he'd allowed Leah to come back up indefinitely. There were only two places the key could be: 1) in the garage, in a small drawer labeled "assorted screws" where he hid things of value, like that pendant he once bought for Liberty, or 2) the top drawer of his desk, the most likely place he'd have left it, hidden under random papers. He couldn't force Leah to go anywhere without a key. He could take her phone away, but that was about it.

He rushed out of the car to try option 1, in the depths of the garage. Going around the narrow space between his truck and the wall, he reached a wooden table where he'd left all his tools and several old files in boxes. He was moving as fast as he could when suddenly, he tripped over his old softball bag. He'd left it there the night before, as he was making sure everything was there: his bats, gloves, and cleats, as well as his batting gloves.

Fuck!!! He spat all his anger out.

He reached the cabinet and looked frantically for the key. But it was nowhere. He was about to explode when in a trice, the memory of putting the key inside his desk drawer came to the rescue.

Shit, that's right! he thought, balling his fists triumphantly.

He was about to go into the house. Taking a deep breath, he hit the switch to close the garage door. More calmly, he went up the two wooden steps leading to the scratched white kitchen door. His plan was to go straight downstairs and find the keys, but to his surprise, the first thing he saw when he opened the door was Leah's eyes.

PART II

November 03, 2017
4:34PM
Baker City

23) 4:34PM. Confluence.

The car approached the corner between Church St and Valley Avenue. Adriel moved forward so she could see through the windshield. There was something strange about returning to her street. Somehow, the colors looked different. The images were familiar but the place felt foreign. The tones of the trees and the hues between them, the colors of the decaying houses all seemed less intense, like the colors in an old Polaroid. Somehow, she couldn't connect what she smelled or the way the air brushed her cheeks with the past.

As the car turned down the street, she expected to see that old oak in front of the second house on the right side of the street, where she used to run and hide from Leah on their way to the park.

BOOOO!

"I got you again Mama!" Adriel would shout. Leah always acted surprised.

The tree wasn't there, but the patched asphalt was the same, cracked and whitened by sun and age. The chain-link fences were also the same, and so were the several tin ornaments Mr. Bannister proudly displayed "for sale." When Adriel spotted them, she could have sworn they were the same ones she had left behind years ago.

"It's the fifth house on the right," she said.

They parked and got out of the car. The sunlight was just beginning to fade away, although it still was bright. Adriel felt the dry, cold breeze burning through her nostrils, as if she was sucking on a mouthful of those strong menthol candies. She wrapped her arms around herself in an embrace.

Kyle and Monica waited for her lead. She acknowledged this, but looked around her street before making a step. She imagined how Jacob would look now. This was an image well developed over the years, through so many of her wishful fantasies. His hair had gone a bit darker, a dark brown to be precise, and he'd grown slightly chubby because, in the end, there were not going to be any swimming lessons, Mom's food was incredibly unhealthy, and Jacob was Richard's son.

"Why didn't you bring me with you, Adriel?" The imaginary boy confronted her. He was floating in the air, surrounded by a black space.

"I couldn't do it, Jacob. I'm so sorry! I am!" She'd apologized to that dream image so many times in the past and did so one more time. Feeling she was about to cry, she hurried to take a deep breath.

"It's complicated, darling. I can't. I need to stay with Jacob." The memory of Leah came to her next. This image had never changed. What had changed were her feelings about Leah; up and down, left and right, in and out, and back in circles to the very beginning.

She had imagined how things were going to turn out. This was a movie that had kept her awake all night for the past two nights. It was a horror movie at times, a Disney movie at others, or even one of those surreal movies where Richard would turn into an ugly, slimy, amorphous thing she'd stomp on. At the end, she always confronted him. She was brave, she was firm, and she prevailed.

The one portion of this story she couldn't touch was the story of Leah; she simply didn't dare go there. She knew what she wanted to say and what she wanted to happen. She was terrified of the outcome; she couldn't imagine one more day without her mother. She couldn't accept the possibility of Leah not even being there—the chances that some random fat redneck was going to open that door wondering why in the hell a stranger was knocking at it. Or worse, the possibility that her father, smiling cynically, would open it and tell her he had no idea where Leah was.

"So how exactly you want to do this, Adriel?" Kyle asked.

"We're just going to knock at the door. It's not five yet, so I doubt Asshole is there yet. Things may have changed, but this guy was Mr. Routine."

Adriel clenched her teeth and rearranged her hair nervously. A thousand butterflies escaped from their cocoons inside her belly. The flapping of their wings spread all that coldness trapped inside her gut toward the rest of her body till it reached the extremities.

She covered herself again until Monica came to the rescue. She first held Adriel's hand and smiled at her, then flung an arm around her shoulders as she walked next to her. More than the warmth of her sweater, it was her smile and her brown eyes looking straight into Adriel's that stopped the trembling. They smiled at each other but neither of them could fool the other. In their eyes they both could see the tension of the moment. They could hear the leaves on the trees moving, at least until the ringing of Adriel's phone sounded loud.

Thinking it was Brandi, Adriel was ready to hit the "Sorry, I can't talk right now" button. She almost did, but the call was coming from Hilario.

"Hey," she said.

"Mija, where are you?"

"I'm about to walk to the house and knock on their door, Papi," Adriel said.

Hilario responded, but she had a hard time understanding him because Brandi was yelling hysterically next to him, so she was hearing both of them at the same time:

"Listen, I'm a little nervous. *Let me talk to her!* Can you do us a favor? How about this? Can you just hold the phone and keep the call going on speaker? *Let me talk to her for a minute, Hilario!* You don't have to say anything or talk to Brandi now. *What?! Let me talk to her right now, Hilario!!!* Just keep the call going, okay? *Adriel! Adriel! Call the police!!!*"

"Papi, I can't hear you that well, but listen, Kyle is probably larger than your refrigerator. Tell her to relax," Adriel said sarcastically.

"Okay, great, Mija. *Unbelievable!* Give the phone to Monica then, and just keep the line open, okay?"

"Here, Monica, don't hang up," Adriel said, giving her the phone. She took a deep breath and began to walk toward the entrance of the house.

When Richard entered the kitchen he smelled the penetrating smell of roasted chicken. The first couple of seconds was the most intense. With the garage door opened, some air entered the room, pushing the smell away from him.

Leah was sitting, knees together, and hands hiding in terror between her legs. When she saw the thunder in his eyes, she began rocking the faulty chair, side to side, as she always did when she was anxious. The hair on her arms standing on end was pulling the skin into fat bumps, like the skin of a chicken. The air coming from the garage was cold. But Leah was used to the cold, wet winters of Arkansas; fear was causing the goosebumps.

Richard rushed toward her and grabbed the phone. She had turned it off.

Neither of them said a word. He turned on the phone and waited patiently, a minute or so, for it to come to life; still, not a single word was exchanged between them. Although for different reasons, the waiting time felt like an eternity to both of them. Richard paced around a short loop of two steps forward, one step to the left, another step to the left and two steps back, over and over, until at last, the home screen replaced the white apple at the center of the screen.

The first surprise was that the photo of Mount Hood had been replaced with one of Adriel and Jacob. He remembered the photo. He'd taken it the Christmas before the year Adriel escaped. Both kids were in their pajamas, sitting next to the front window in the living room. They were holding an improvised poster Leah had helped them make that said Happy Holidays at the top and Merry Christmas on the bottom. A thick red line crossed over Happy Holidays.

1-4-1-1-2-2. He punched in the password.

Incorrect password.

He tried again, and again, the phone didn't accept the password.

"I changed the password." She was the first to speak.

"You what?"

"I changed the password."

"Did I ever say you could change the password of MY phone?" he said.

"The phone wasn't working well. I had to reset it. Anyhow, it's Adriel's birthday, so just type it." She knew what she was doing. She thought of him as a wild, dangerous animal. She was afraid of him, but she was ready to confront him.

He saw Leah's certain defiance. He wasn't ready for it. He stuttered but no words came out.

"I'm sorry. I thought you would remember. It's today's date," Leah said with the calm of a monk.

She didn't sound sarcastic. Looking down at the tabletop, she simply stated a fact, like a physics professor.

He tightened his grip on the phone to keep from throwing it in her face. Pain stopped him from biting his lips any harder. Then, he took a deep breath. He had to think for a moment. Of course he knew the password. He too had felt the weight of this date for the past few days.

After entering the password he checked on the "recent calls" archive. That it was empty didn't surprise him.

"You think I'm stupid, don't you? Are you so stupid that you think I'm stupid?"

Leah didn't respond. She simply raised her head to look at Richard for a couple of seconds before lowering her gaze again. The rocking of the chair had stopped moments before. Unconsciously, she began shaking one of her legs up and down, in a very fast and short-range nervous movement.

"I'm talking to you, Leah!!!" he yelled and walked farther into the kitchen. To his eyes, Leah had suddenly become that innocent, young girl he'd corrected so many other times. She no longer was a grown woman, the mother of his two children. Raising his voice was always effective; he'd learned this early in the marriage.

He stood behind her, so she had no option but to turn to look at him.

"I know you've been talking to an attorney, or somebody from an eight hundred number all week. I got all the calls. I'm going to ask just once. Who are you speaking to, Leah?"

She looked in his direction, but didn't meet his eyes. Behind him, all blurry, she could spot her blender, old and faithful, the toaster oven where she'd toasted so many Eggos for her children, and that fancy wooden knife holder Richard had given her as a birthday present, several years past.

She focused on the knife holder. She could only see the handles of the knives, but could recognize each of them anyway. The bread knife, the small one she used to work with raw meats, the weird, curvy one she didn't know how to use, the sharpener and of course, that big one she used for almost everything, but specially for tomatoes because it was so sharp.

In silence, she imagined herself pretending to be ashamed, asking for forgiveness. In her fantasy, Richard had a smile of satisfaction in his face, one she'd seen before. But next, there he was, lying on the ground in a pool of blood. She could recognize the curvy knife in front of her; she was holding it, feeling the blood from the knife dripping and flowing to her fingers.

"You coward!" She imagined herself shouting, feeling the knife going in and out again, repeatedly.

"Answer!!!" Richard's demand brought her back to reality.

She wanted to tell him about Nicole, about Brandi, about how miserable she was, and how badly he'd ruined her life. And how fearful she was the Lord would never forgive her. But the words that came out of her mouth were ordered from a deeper compartment of her brain.

"Richard, what have you and my parents done with my child?"

She finally met his eyes again, in a penetrating way she'd never looked at him before.

He stuttered for the second time.

"He's with your parents. There is nothing else to add."

The way she'd asked the question shook him a bit. He turned around and opened the medicine cabinet without thinking much; he just needed to remove himself from the sudden confrontation. He remembered about the Percocet on the spot, and hoped to be wrong and that there was Percocet left, but there wasn't. Refocused, he said,

"You're going back downstairs, and I swear to God, you're telling me who you're talking to, one way or the other."

Doing her best to hide her trembling, Leah said,

"Richard, I want to talk to my son. Please let me talk to him. That's all I ask."

He approached her violently and without much ceremony, grabbed her by her hair around the temple, and pulled her up.

The sharp pain made her stand up. She said nothing, just screamed in pain. There was no time to think. She just tried to keep up with his rapid pace as they left the kitchen and were about to cross the dining room toward the stairs leading to his office.

"You lost your son. It's over, and it's your own fault. You bring me Adriel back, you take your place in this marriage, and maybe we can talk, but for now, you're going downstairs!" he said, but stopped when, unable to keep up, she fell on the floor.

Struggling, they didn't hear the knocking on the front door, twice.

She yelled again. He felt something in his hand; it was a tuft of her hair. He shook it off with disgust and then slapped her face as hard as he could. Her legs buckled and she fell.

"Please Richard, let me talk to my son!!" she yelled again, on her knees, but ignoring the intense redness of her cheek, he just grabbed her again by the hair and forced her up.

"Get the fuck up!!!" he yelled and began to drag her again, until they reached the top of the stairs.

She put her hand against the wall and resisted for a second or two.

KNOCK KNOCK!!! This time the knocking, loud and unmistakably urgent, interrupted Richard.

Richard froze and released Leah. He could barely feel his legs. She too remained quiet, as if waiting to see what would happen next. Less than a second later the knocking resounded loudly again, and this time it didn't stop.

"It's the police!! Open the door, now!!!" Kyle improvised.

"Listen, you bitch. We're going to open that door, and you're going to act normal and let me do the talking. And if you say anything at all, I swear you'll never see your son again. Do you understand?"

"I just want you to let me talk to my son."

It was too late for a fake apology, but he needed her to cooperate.

"And you know, as I said, that if you obey me and if things turn around here, you will. So I'm telling you again: you'll say nothing, understood?"

Confused and a little dizzy, she couldn't think straight. With no time to put her thoughts in order, actually, incapable of putting any thoughts in order, she did all she knew, she assented.

He turned and began walking toward the door.

"Coming!" he said, in a friendly tone.

Leah followed him with some difficulty. She rearranged her hair a little and hid her cheek with her hand. Feeling the heat emanating from it, she concluded it had to be red. Within the limitations of the moment, she thought of her options. She felt tempted to ask for help, but as had happened other times, her fear of losing Jacob, her dogma, and her ignorance were greater than her desire.

Richard opened the door. His fake, insurance salesman smile disappeared as soon as he realized there were no police. Kyle looked so scary; Richard didn't notice Adriel, or Monica.

"Who are you?" Richard asked. Leah came up behind him, to see who it was.

"ADI!!!" she screamed as soon as she recognized her daughter. No longer worried about showing her face, she pushed Richard away as if he was one of those inflatable toys the shape and size of a man.

"Momma!" Adriel yelled. She too had jumped forward at the same time.

The women embraced tightly. At last, Adriel released the tears she'd been reserving for almost four years.

Nobody said a word for a long minute.

Richard couldn't even connect that this was the same girl he had seen at the restaurant parking lot. He felt lost; he hadn't had a chance to look at his daughter, but was confused by the blue hair. Where was that sweet blonde girl who'd smiled at him at the pool? He felt the slightest impulse to join them. He too wanted to hug his daughter, but raw paternal instinct was defeated by resentment.

"I'm so sorry, Adi! I'm so sorry. Please forgive me!" Leah said.

Adriel released herself and wiped her eyes with the Siouxsie And The Banshees shirt.

"Mom, you have nothing to be sorry about. You're the bravest person I know," she said, and turned her head toward Richard, but just for a brief moment. Only then did Richard have the chance to look at her.

He stood incredulous. His daughter looked like one of those before-and-after makeover shows gone wrong. It wasn't just the blue hair, but the whole gothic-punk look; the piercing, the boys' boots, and the tattoos.

She wasn't a little girl anymore. She was a woman; a woman he could hardly recognize, until he found her blue eyes, and all of a sudden, again, he too wanted to hug her and tell her that he loved her, plead with her to come back to him and God. He made a gesture, a hesitant movement to approach her, but refrained, fearful of rejection.

Adriel turned her attention back to her mother, who polite as always, was acknowledging Monica and Kyle.

They were just standing there, Kyle with his bouncer attitude turned on, waiting for Richard to make the wrong move, and Monica crying as if it was her reuniting with her lost mother.

"Mom, this is my friend Kyle, and this is my—hmm." She chuckled. "I'll leave this for later. This is my good friend Monica," she said.

Adriel was so excited she could almost hear her heart beating. In the awkward silence, impulsively, she kissed Leah and hugged her again, just for a brief moment.

"Are you okay?" Richard asked. He didn't even mean to say that, it was just what came out. But Adriel ignored him, more than anything because Monica had showed her the phone, making a "don't forget about these guys" gesture. Adriel took the phone.

"Papi?"

"Papi?" Richard frowned.

On the other end of the line, Brandi took the phone from Hilario like a rugby player takes a ball from an opponent.

"Leah! Leah!! It's Brandi, girl!! I'm here!!!" Brandi's unmistakable voice came through the iPhone Monica was holding.

Leah grabbed the phone from Monica. She was shaking with happiness.

"Thank you, thank you, thank you. I'll never be able to repay you for this, Brandi." Blissfulness wasn't a feeling that commonly visited her. She hasn't experienced it for such a long time. Overwhelmed by the moment, she'd forgotten her whole past, the whole existence of anything in the world other than Adriel being there.

"Ah, hmmm, wait a minute. Brandi?" Richard frowned again, and mumbled a few words. He knew who Brandi was. Under any other circumstance, he would have figured everything out by then, but he too was overwhelmed and couldn't think straight.

Adriel gestured to Leah to hand over the phone.

"I'll call you later, okay." She didn't give Brandi a chance to reply. By this time, she meant business.

"Are you coming back home, Adriel? Are you here to return to your home?" Richard said. He wanted this to sound like a question, but he was pleading. This time he even extended a hand to touch Adriel's arm, but she recoiled as if he was a deadly virus.

The rejection caused Richard's emotions to flip. His desire to hug his daughter disintegrated like dust in a flutter. His sweet blonde girl, the one he felt guilty about and wanted back so badly was suddenly replaced by this naughty, weird-looking brunette with an attitude that reminded him of the same rotten teenager he'd rebuked so often. With this thought, he began connecting the dots, and once he did, yet another layer of emotion exploded inside him. Leah had made a fool of him.

Adriel didn't even acknowledge he had spoken. She directed her eyes to Leah.

"Where's Jacob?" she asked. Her eyes suddenly shone.

Leah's face changed. She began rubbing her hands and as she responded, her eyes shifted toward Richard and back again.

"Well, hmm, well, he's with your grandparents at this moment," she said.

"When is he back?" Adriel asked. This was the first time she actually looked at Richard.

"Well, sweetie, it's complicated, you know, I wasn't well and so, Jacob has been living with them, you know, the thing—" Leah said, but Adriel interrupted her.

"Mom, go and get whatever you want to bring with you. You're coming with me." Adriel said without taking her eyes off Richard. She added,

"When's Jacob coming back?"

Leah didn't move. Still, two large tongs grabbed her forcefully. It was Richard.

"First, she isn't going anywhere and your brother ain't your business, young lady," he said, sounding reproachful, although deep inside, he wanted Adriel to go to him, penitent.

There was a short moment of silence and various glances exchanged.

Leah looked at Adriel with a pleading expression that wasn't new. A look that said "Don't contradict your father. Don't stir the pot." Kyle and Monica looked at each other like two accomplices getting ready to rob a bank. But the most intense exchange was between father and daughter, icy and fixed, like cats testing each other.

"Please Adi, leave it—" Leah began talking, but Adriel interrupted her, still not taking her eyes off Richard.

"Leave her alone."

She turned her eyes to Leah.

"Mom, go and get your stuff."

Richard began moving in front of Leah and in response, Adriel moved forward to grab Leah's hand, but Richard grabbed her hand and yanked her toward him.

"Listen young lady, you've caused enough pain here, if you aren't here for—"

He had no chance to finish his sentence. Adriel tried violently to twist out of his grasp, so he focused on keeping control of her. This struggle lasted no more than a second because, out of nowhere, Kyle did his usual thing. In a flash, the giant, gentle brute was holding Richard by the neck against the front wall.

"Listen, you piece of shit, you touch her again and I'm gonna get medieval with you. You're gonna pay for the pain *you've* caused." Richard had no option but to freeze with Kyle's words resonating inside him.

"I'm going to call the police! Leah, call the police!" Richard screamed.

"YOU are gonna call the police?" Adriel asked, sounding sarcastic.

"Please, Adriel, stop," Leah said.

"You're going to call the police? YOU???? Really?! Where's Jacob, you asshole?! And how come a grown woman can't decide if she wants to come or not?! Monica, call the police," Adriel said.

"What's that smell?" Monica said. She'd ignored what Adriel said about calling the cops, thinking she hadn't meant it.

The forgotten chicken was burning in the oven. Leah became more agitated.

"It's the chicken. I have to go and get it out of the oven," she said, looking at Adriel, as if asking permission.

"Mom, forget the chicken for a minute. It's up to you at this point. I know you're miserable. I'm here to take you away from this hell," Adriel said.

Monica turned around, Kyle turned around, Richard directed his eyes as far as he could toward Leah, and Adriel, a child again, presented Leah with the same look she had that day she escaped, the moment she'd asked her to bring Jacob and come with her.

"Woman, call the police I said," Richard demanded.

Leah looked at her daughter and her husband alternately, then in the direction of the chicken. Her movements were indecisive, like a cornered ant.

"I have to go and get the chicken!" she said, lifting her hands, palms up.

"Please let me go. You're assaulting me!" Richard demanded of Kyle, who didn't let go.

Everybody but Leah ignored Richard. All eyes were fixed on her.

"Mom, forget about the fucking chicken, and stop looking at him. This isn't his decision. It's yours!" Adriel pleaded, sounding annoyed.

Leah tried to forget about the chicken, but she couldn't. She even tried to imagine leaving with Adriel. But in reality she couldn't think, and she couldn't answer. All she could see was her husband being held by the neck by this big boy, her daughter's demanding eyes, and the image of the ruined chicken going to the trash.

"Leah, go and get the chicken and call the police!" said Richard.

"Mom, don't worry about Jacob, you'll easily get legal custody. You will—"

"IT'S A SIN!!!" Overwhelmed, Leah finally shouted, interrupting Adriel. She looked at her daughter's shocked expression and rushed to amend her statement.

"Darling, hold on, give me a minute, please."

Everybody was startled, but especially Adriel. Leah screamed so loud that even Kyle let go of Richard, and Richard just stood there with his mouth half open.

Leah didn't want to upset or disappoint Adriel, but she couldn't stop thinking about Jacob and what would happen to him if she left with her. And with that, a battle began in her head between her fears and her desire to please Adriel and ease the gargantuan guilt that had consumed her from the very day she'd let her daughter walk away.

"A minute? A minute?! Where's Jacob, Mom? And what exactly happened to you that he isn't here? Since when?" Adriel said after she recovered.

Leah began crying.

"I have to get the chicken. I have to!" She ran like a fire-fighter to the kitchen.

"Whatever's going on with Jacob stopped being your problem the moment you—" Richard was going to add "the moment you left this house," but Kyle raised his hand and pointed at him. He shut up.

"You stay here," Kyle said with a menacing tone.

Adriel's phone rang. It was Brandi, but Adriel signaled Monica to ignore it.

In the kitchen, with no eyes pressuring her, Leah resumed her internal battle. She tried to be rational, but couldn't get Jacob out of her head. She needed to know she was going to have her son back. And couldn't conceive leaving without some reassurance that she'd see him again soon. Trying to picture what he would look by now, but realizing that she had no way of imagining him saddened and infuriated her all at the same time. She had the impulse to run to the entrance and tell Adriel to take her away and get Jacob back, but her usual fears stopped her.

What would happen to Jacob if I leave with Adi? she asked herself and sat at the kitchen table, momentarily forgetting about the chicken, oblivious of the burning smell.

Mother, Father and Richard are capable of anything. She knew that too well. But she could also see that Adriel wasn't going to allow Richard to get away with anything.

The words "custody" and "you'll never see him again" kept floating in front of her until, overwhelmed, she closed her eyes and drifted back in time to hold her baby and watch Get Smart one more time.

Blinding smoke coming from the oven startled her out of her reverie. She took the chicken out. But it was ruined. She opened the garage door and the kitchen window to ventilate the room a little. Resting her hands on the counter, she took a deep breath, then another one, before returning to the front door, but instead of coming out, she stayed behind the door, timid for she still had no decision to offer Adriel.

Noticing Leah was back, Adriel immediately resumed her arguments.

"Mom, when we got here, you were screaming. I'm not leaving you here alone, not without calling the police myself. Look." Adriel showed Leah the phone screen. "That was Brandi again. You're not alone, Mom. Everything will be okay."

Adriel stared at Leah. Her eyes, her whole expression was incredulous and desperate. She was silently begging Leah to realize what was so obvious to her. In the lack of a response, Adriel's first reaction was to shake her, to slap her face like they do to people in the movies, to bring them back to their sense, but of course she didn't. She wanted so badly to grab her and tell her she couldn't leave her alone, that she couldn't handle losing her again.

Richard just stayed there, lost in an abyss. As far as he was concerned, it didn't matter what Leah decided anymore. His brain had begun to play reality check. He no longer had control of anything. With luck, nobody would press charges. But that didn't matter to him. Liberty didn't matter to him. It was the full realization of what he'd done that was chilling his spine.

I had to do what I had to do, he thought. He even tried to come up with a scheme, not just to get out of it all, but to get out victorious. He would be calling his father-in-law, he would claim Kyle hit him, he would prove that Leah was an unstable, delusional drug addict. No need to make up too much about Adriel, her look would ruin her in front of a judge. The plan came to him in bits, but the bits were always interrupted by defeat. The feeling of defeat took over him and he couldn't hide it.

Leah noticed. She'd never seen him look this way before. And now the memories came flooding back, filling her with confused feelings for her husband—the man who'd hurt her and humiliated her so many times and in so many ways. She remembered him at the picnic the day they met, asking, "Do you like mustard?" He seemed so friendly then. Fragments of memory kept coming. She winced at the most painful ones or pushed them out of her mind altogether, preferring to remember the dedicated father she once saw, when the children were much younger, on his hands and knees playing horse with Jacob and Adriel, carrying them on his back. The young man who introduced her to so many movies and took her to her favorite Italian spot, even if seldom. So many times she'd wanted to leave him, wished she'd never married him. And then she thought of Daniel again. How could she forget Daniel? The days they'd gone swimming, and the day he finally kissed her? The memory developed like it always did, Leah imagining a life with Daniel, the happy life that had slipped out of her grasp. She imagined walking with him around the Eiffel Tower on a cold night. But this time— for the first time going over this fantasy, it came to her that they were with other children. That Jacob and Adriel weren't there. And she looked at Richard. *This is why I married you*, she thought.

Adriel waited, and then insisted,

"So are you coming with me? Or should I call the police? Mom, you can be happy if you want to."

Feeling all eyes on her, she closed hers to escape. She needed to see what was inside her, clear as water.

"Give me a minute, Adi," she said.

Looking up at the sky, her eyes encountered a beautiful Oregon sunset. The sun was hiding behind red and orange curtains that contrasted with the dark, dry, cold blue sky.

This instant brought her back to the dream she'd imagined so many times; escaping, at least for a heavenly moment, from the hell that was her life.

She saw herself driving down to that secluded Hawaiian beach, once more, with Adriel and Jacob. But this time, no doors closed in front of her to interrupt the dream. They kept going along the dangerous road, all the way down to the beach. At the beach, they ran and ran. Adriel was in front and Jacob was second. She was the first to stop and turn in Leah's direction. The warm water brushed Adriel's naked feet. She smiled at Leah.

"Come with us, Momma. Let's get in the water!" Adriel said, holding Jacob by the hand once he reached her.

She still had no answer, but the memory had calmed her down. Her own smile opened her eyes again. They found those of Adriel; so confident, so full of life, so reassuring that at once, what she had been looking for so long came to her mind.

Of course she was terrified of losing Jacob if she were to leave with Adriel. And yes! In her mind, leaving Richard behind was a sin she was going to have to take with her to face God. But her biggest fear was disappointing her daughter, losing her again.

She isn't you, Leah, she reassured herself. She is strong.

Any sign of anxiety dissolved from Leah's face. A mysterious tranquility had invaded her. She walked forward from the shades of the entrance to the full light of the front yard.

She approached Adriel with a smile and hugged her, feeling an electrical splashing that began in her belly and spread all over her skin like a firework exploding into tiny lights in the sky.

Holding Adriel as tight as she could, she said,

"I'm so proud of you, darling. Whatever happens will happen, remember? I am what I am, and you are what you are."

Adriel discovered the answer in Leah's eyes.

Her choking and trembling made Leah pause. She began patting Adriel's back the way she'd done to console her when she was little. "Don't you see it, Adi? It's precisely because of you becoming what you are, and showing up here, that I'm already the happiest person on this earth. Where I am won't change a thing." The front of her shirt was wet with Adriel's tears. This made her pause for a second time, still holding her daughter tightly. She thought about Jacob and about what could happen next. Briefly, she looked at Richard, who still stood with his head down, avoiding her gaze. She continued,

"Look, darling, let's call Jacob in a minute, okay?" She didn't wait for Adriel to respond. "Remember that morning you got upset because he broke that toy ship of yours? The one Father got you for Christmas?" She looked at Richard one more time, sideways, and he looked at her before lowering his eyes again. "We spent the whole afternoon trying to put it together again, remember? We ended up making hot Ovaltine and watching Get Smart on the sofa. Jacob came and leaned on you and fell sleep on your legs. You pointed to him to show me he was sleeping, laughing at him, and brushed his hair with your fingers. That was so sweet, Adi…"

She kept talking; Adriel had stopped crying. They couldn't see it just yet, but Earth was already moving between the moon and the sun. The eclipse would begin as soon as the sunlight faded.

Epilogue

Nearly a quarter million children were married in the United States between 2000 and 2010. Seventy-seven percent of these marriages took place between a child—almost always a girl—and a significantly older adult. According to data retrieved from the U.S Health Department, in New Jersey alone, over a three-year period, about one hundred and fifty married children were younger than fifteen years of age; some were as young as ten.

It is impossible to know how many of these marriages were forced and how many arranged. Although the line dividing these two is thin and blurry, the biggest difference between them lies in the fact that, in arranged marriages, the choice to marry and to stay in the marriage remains with the individual, while in forced marriages, it does not.

Forced marriages take place irrespective of religion or race. Among immigrant groups, a survey published by the Tahirih Justice Center reported that while 58 percent of respondents were Muslims, 20 percent were Christians, 11 percent were Hindu, and eight percent were Buddhist. Furthermore, contrary to widespread belief, forced marriage isn't exclusive to certain immigrant groups. In The United States, forced marriages have been widely reported not just among Hindu and Muslim groups, but also among Orthodox Jews and Christians, the

Christian Patriarchy Movement, the Fundamentalists Church of Jesus Christ of Latter-Day Saints, Protestants, and Catholics, among many others. Furthermore, the reasons cited for forcing children into marriage extend beyond tradition, the most common being simple economic gain.

At the time this novel was written, child marriages are performed legally in forty eight states, either through parental consent—with a parent simply signing the marriage application—or through judicial approval. Twenty-five states set no minimum age for a child to be able to marry. Shockingly, the minimum legal ages for consent to sex and marriage do not align within most states. Thus, in many cases, children are legally married at an age at which sexual intercourse with an adult is considered statutory rape.

While the number of legally married children is well established, the number of children forced into an informal marriage is not known. There is little doubt that the number is significant. Whether or not a forced marriage is considered legal, the emotional, social, and economic consequences for victims are devastating. The U.S State Department considers the practice a violation of human rights.

This novel and especially the story of Leah were born after a change of heart. My original intention was to write about a Mexican girl being forced into marriage in the United States—a Catholic girl whose father had sold her for ten cases of beer he never received. When he went to reclaim his daughter, the marriage had already been consummated.

While I was familiar with the concept of forced marriage, it had never felt so close to me. This pivotal moment led me to understand the universality of the problem; that my story had to be one that felt immediate to as many readers as possible.

I came across the story of a woman who'd been forced into marriage as a child, and whose husband locked her in a basement for two years. She was allowed to come upstairs to care for the house and see the children for a few hours a day. When, years later, she began talking to a therapist, it became clear that she only saw the hours upstairs as reality. Only through therapy did she discover that her life in the basement wasn't a nightmare. I based Leah's story on this woman without knowing any other details of her situation. I never knew her name, her nationality or religion, or where she lived.

The rest of the novel was also the product of extensive research, although its characters, like Leah, are purely fictional.

I would like to thank Julie D. Frederick, PhD for sharing her experience with victims of forced marriage and for helping me make the emotional and psychological aspects of the characters credible. I am also grateful to Christina Morris from Unchained At Last and Casey Swegman from the Tahirih Justice Center. Both shared with me their experiences of helping victims of forced marriage. Their input was crucial to an understanding of the dynamics. Julia Alanen of the Global Justice Initiative spent tons of her valuable time speaking to me about her broad understanding of forced marriage in the United States, both as an attorney and as a strong advocate. Lastly, I would like to thank my attorney and friend Jaye Wickham Taylor for connecting me with local judges and helping me better understand the legal aspects of forced marriage.

About the Author

Alberto Ambard divides his time between writing and practicing maxillofacial prosthodontics. He co-authored High Treason, a novel Adelaide Books recently republished. His short stories have appeared in various publications.

His love of music and diverse background are often exposed in his writing. A descendant of French, American, Spanish and Venezuelan families, he grew up in Caracas, a city of immigrants Isabel Allende said to have given her a sensual vision of the world. He also lived in Capaya, a remote Afro-Caribbean village. While in the Amazon, he interacted with tribes largely unknown to civilization. He later lived in contrasting Birmingham, Alabama and Chicago.

Mr. Ambard received the José Félix Ribas Medal for his achievements in collegiate and international karate. Currently, he lives in Portland, Oregon with his wife and children. You can find him at www.albertoambard.com

www.ingramcontent.com/pod-product-compliance
Lightning Source LLC
Chambersburg PA
CBHW031342020726
47499CB00005B/1358